VOTE
VAMPIRE

Roger Bird

Matador
Unit E2 Airfield Business Park,
Harrison Road, Market Harborough,
Leicestershire. LE16 7UL
Tel: 0116 2792299
Email: books@troubador.co.uk
Web: www.troubador.co.uk/matador
Twitter: @matadorbooks

ISBN 978 1805140 436

British Library Cataloguing in Publication Data.
A catalogue record for this book is available from the British Library.

Printed and bound in Great Britain by CMP UK
Typeset in 11pt Minion Pro by Troubador Publishing Ltd, Leicester, UK

Matador is an imprint of Troubador Publishing Ltd

This book is dedicated to Julie and Oliver

Contents

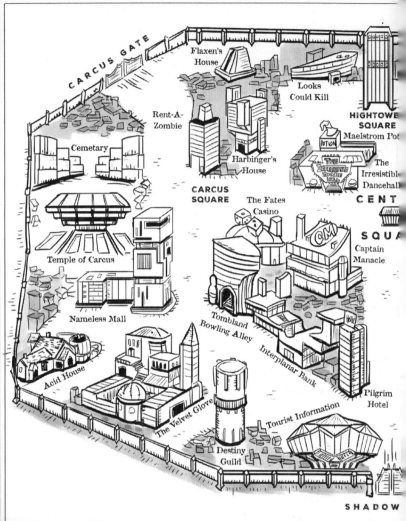

CARCUS GATE

Flaxen's House

Looks Could Kill

HIGHTOWE SQUARE

Maelstrom Pot

Rent-A-Zombie

The Irresistible Dancehall

Cemetary

Harbinger's House

CARCUS SQUARE

The Fates Casino

CENT

SQUA

Captain Manacle

Temple of Carcus

Nameless Mall

Tombland Bowling Alley

Interplanar Bank

Pilgrim Hotel

Acid House

The Velvet Glove

Tourist Information

Destiny Guild

SHADOW

C A R C

City of

Twinned wit

he Inferno

THE ABYSS

The Abyss

ns

Trident Hotel

Delirium Drive

HADES GATE

Eye to Eye

Mayor's Palace

Electrum Casino

Deck of Delusions

You Choose

RAL

RE

Astral Planar Travel

Quasicom

Demon Consulate

The Pandemonium

Court of Limbo

Play House

Seeds

Library

Botanical Gardens

Guard HQ

Hired Goons

GATE

ERON

Chaos

h the Abyss

List of Characters

From our world:

Sapphire – an intelligent and ambitious teenager, who is standing for election at school.

Henry / aka Paladin "Ferdinal" – Sapphire's boyfriend, a keen roleplaying game player.

Katherine / aka Cleric "Pumpkin" – Henry's sister, born on Halloween, friend of Sapphire.

Oliver / aka Assassin "Fredinal" – Henry and Katherine's irritating younger brother.

Amber – Sapphire's election opponent.

Leaders of Carceron, City of Chaos:

The Archmayor (recently deceased) – political figurehead in Carceron for 150 years.

The ruling "Junta" of demons – Cremorne (Leader), Babaeski (Chief Priest of Carcus, the undead deity), Luleburgaz (Head of the Guard) and Lamothe (Head of External Affairs).

Residents and traders in Carceron, City of Chaos:

Mercedes – a vampire.

Flaxen – a retired sorcerer, descended from a gold dragon.

Harbinger – runs messenger service Quasicom. Friend of Flaxen.

Marid – a genie. Proprietor of Tombland Bowling Alley. Former Chief of Staff to the Archmayor.

Souzira – runs the Maelstrom potions shop.

Mr Ottoman – owner of The Irresistible Dancehall, the popular bar and music venue.

Talisman – a wizard. Proprietor of pet shop Looks Could Kill.

Champrice – owner of the Playhouse. Former girlfriend of Cremorne.

Carina – the librarian and head of the Tourist Office.

Hijinx – friend and companion of the ruling demons.

Apollonius Crayler – manager of undead band The Horde.

Marvexio – a half-elven bard. Performer and musical promoter.

Blatherwick – ambassador from the City of Spires.

Jagglespur – proprietor of staffing agency Hired Goons. Friend of Mercedes.

Ethema – Head Druid, owner of restaurant Seeds and administrator of the election.

Gavri – a druid.

The Late Mr Melville – a spectre.

Aspreyna – an imprisoned angel.

A selection of villains in Carceron, City of Chaos:

Šapka – chief assassin of The Velvet Glove. Master of disguise. Pronounced "Shap-Ker".

Revlyn – head of the Destiny Guild of thieves.

Montrachet – a thief and apprentice wizard, who works for Revlyn.

Lamar – Montrachet's housemate.

Zarek – a swashbuckler and freelance adventurer.

Lacasso, Daysuh, Thorkell and Runsus – Demon-worshipping priests.

Gortol – an ogre.

Kuthol – bursar at the Temple of Carcus. Brother of Gortol.

Mylar – a succubus. Owner of The Inferno restaurant and bar.

Fulcrum – a negotiator and fixer in the underworld. A non-speaking crow-like birdman.

Zirca – a travelling rumourmonger and pedlar of exotica.

Captain Manacle – a slave-dealer.

Perancia – an urchin warlock, whose patron is the crafty deity Crixus Telmarine.

Azgog – a quasit, or tiny fiend, employed by Harbinger.

Familiars and pets

Redwing – Harbinger's familiar. A red micro-dragon.

Pullywuggles – Flaxen's familiar. A large tortoise, subject to a permanent Speed spell.

Charisma – Pumpkin's grey cat.

A selection of performing artists:

The Horde – famous band of four zombies, managed by Apollonius Crayler.

Tinsel – an ear-shattering solo artist at The Irresistible Dancehall.

The Deathshadows – singing thieves and assassins, caped and masked to disguise their identities.

Chapter 1

Just a Popularity Contest

"Vote for me!" Sapphire called down the school corridor. She could feel her mouth forming the unnatural grin that had become a fixture throughout the campaign. Still, it was nearly over.

A posse of the older boys, who were just shuffling into a classroom, paused and turned as she called out. Sapphire might be from a lower year, but her wavy blonde hair, bright blue eyes and confident, pert manner were always guaranteed to attract attention. She was the sort of girl who could not be ignored. And she knew it.

"This election thing is boring," grunted Phil, the tallest of the older boys. "What difference does it make? Elections are pointless anyway."

"Yeah," muttered Kev, one of his surly mates. "Why should we vote for you anyway?"

"Just remember me on election day," smiled Sapphire, throwing back her head and blowing them a kiss from a safe distance. She wasn't prepared to kiss their spotty faces to win votes; there were some sacrifices even she would not make. And for once Henry had put his foot down and insisted that would be a step too far.

The school had organised what it called a mock election, with voting on the same day as the forthcoming contest in the adult world. The teachers, in their naïve wisdom, imagined that it would motivate and inform the students about real-world issues and act as a forum to hone debating skills. The students were expected to come forward as candidates, on behalf of any party they wished and could make promises, hand out leaflets with their policies, make speeches – whatever techniques they wanted. Anything, in short, that was likely to get them widely despised by everyone else in school, or maybe get them beaten up if they became a nuisance.

Sapphire Belmont was feeling really passionate about this election. Not about the political issues at stake. Aged fifteen, she didn't care about those, or even bother to understand them. For her, this battle was personal. Her main opponent, Amber, had always been a bitter personal rival, ever since the two of them had squabbled in the sandpit at the age of two, when Amber had rubbed beloved Mr Snuggles the teddy bear in the dirt. Sapphire was not going to allow Amber to beat her; she just couldn't.

It was time to find Henry to see his latest analysis of the likely result. Henry was good at that sort of thing. He understood people well, and he was pretty bright, too. So many things he was good at. She was getting quite fond of him really. Sapphire stopped in mid-stride. No, this was no time to stop and get sentimental. There was an election to win.

Her boyfriend Henry Farnham was studying by himself in a quiet corner, but immediately looked up as Sapphire approached. His big brown eyes sparkled with delight. He knew why she'd come to find him. She really needed him at a time like this. Sapphire might appear outwardly confident and bubbly, but Henry could always tell when she was secretly nervous and jumpy. At times like that, his cool efficiency would always reassure her. Henry might be only the same age as Sapphire, but she often thought he seemed wiser.

"It's looking close," said Henry. "Katherine's been talking to the younger students. Everyone agrees it's down to just you and Amber. The other candidates don't have a chance."

Sapphire grinned again, this time in genuine amusement at the dedicated help provided by Henry's fourteen-year-old sister.

"Your sister has been very loyal. Young Pumpkin does have her uses."

Henry shrugged. "You know she hates that nickname."

"That's exactly why people call her Pumpkin – because they know she hates it. It's her fault for being born on Halloween."

"How can that be her fault? You're making even less sense than your policy promises."

"Nobody cares about the promises anyway. That's not what the election is about. I wanna know the numbers. The election's in a few days. How much am I going to beat Amber by?"

"Gotta put Katherine's data into my predictive model first before I can tell you. Then we need to talk about election day planning and get the team together. Organisation is the key to winning this." Henry was fascinated by mathematical modelling and how to analyse data. He had eagerly taken the chance to apply these techniques in Sapphire's campaign. He was confident and friendly but had no wish to be a candidate in an election. Helping someone else to win was much more relaxing.

"I don't believe it," sniffed Sapphire, in an arrogant tone. "Nobody really likes Amber. That's my big advantage. At the end of the day, it's just a popularity contest."

—

Far, far away, in another place entirely, a bald man sat at a desk in a study, reading. Dim light emanated not from an electrical source but from a glittering globe, about the size of a tennis ball, which rested by his left hand. A purring noise at his feet under the desk suggested the presence of a contented animal. The man's attention was focused on a note in his hand.

The note was made of parchment and the writing on it was a hasty scrawl. The sender had clearly been pressed for time and greatly agitated during composition. It was unsigned and addressed simply to "Harbinger".

The note read:

The Archmayor was found murdered at his palace this morning. No clues. Mercedes is in town, staying secretly at the Pilgrim Hotel. Call everyone. Must stop her.

The bald man turned slightly in his chair, towards a figure standing in the doorway. It had been watching while he read, as if expecting instructions. Standing in shadow, the figure was barely discernible, but was very short, around three feet tall, with greyish-greenish skin. It betrayed its nervousness by rubbing its left foot against its right leg and twisting its tail in its hand as it stood.

"No. No answer," said the bald man, hoarsely. The figure in the doorway nodded and left.

There was a scuffling and scratching at the man's feet. The creature on the floor was restless. The bald man reached automatically into his pocket and drew three cubes of uncooked meat out of a handkerchief. He reached down so that the creature could take them from him. A long tongue and sharp white teeth greedily snatched the cubes, one at a time, with great precision and delicacy to avoid biting its master, chewing and swallowing each in turn. Then there was quiet once more.

The bald man thought to himself, occasionally voicing his ideas as if conversing with his silent pet and seeking its opinion.

"Must be over fifty years since Mercedes was last in the city. She's always bad news. Either she did this or she knows something about it. I'll have to ask Šapka if he was involved. What do you think, my friend?"

The creature on the floor looked up at him but made no reply.

"There'll need to be a new mayor. An election. When was the last? So long ago it's hard to remember. Well over a century, anyway...

"One thing's sure. I'll need to get everyone together on this. And we'll need help."

"Oliver!" yelled Henry, his game console in his hand. "Have you been playing my game? It's not in my saved position."

A smaller boy of about ten years old put his head round the living-room door. "You weren't using it!" he countered defiantly, but from the partial cover of the doorway. "Mum said to share."

"You're too young for that game. *Defunct Trademark* has got weapons and murders and oh, you know, older boy things."

Oliver stood his ground and maintained his rebellion. "Well, you're not supposed to have Sapphire over at the house while Mum's out. Kissy-kiss-kiss," and he mouthed an imitation of what he supposed Henry and Sapphire did when alone together.

Henry leapt up and gave chase to the fleeing Oliver. "You're always interfering and messing things up. I wish I didn't have a brother!"

The commotion drew Katherine's attention and she put her homework aside. She tried to calm Henry down. She only intervened in her brothers' quarrels if they disturbed her. Not for the first time, she wished Mum was at home to shut the two boys up.

"Just ignore him. What can he do? He'll be fine when he's older."

"You don't understand," Henry snapped. "He really bugs me. Sometimes I think he's been sent specially as a personal nemesis, or an annoying goblin just messing everything up."

"Then focus on Sapphire's election," said his sister, soothingly. "Oliver's too young to vote in that at school. What's so special about playing *Defunct Trademark* anyway? I thought you liked that other game with magic and vampires? That's why you made me play it and be some stupid orc or something."

"Orc? You were a dark elf sorcerer!" Henry's fury with Oliver now switched to exasperation with Katherine. "Pumpkin, you're a hopeless case. Charisma would be better at it."

He pointed to Katherine's grey cat, who was lurking nearby and who came and rubbed herself against Katherine's legs upon realising she was being talked about.

"Oh, it's a good game," replied his sister, always on the alert to soothe down a squabble before it began. "Not sure I followed it all. Maybe if everyone was nice to that leading vampire – Count whatever-his-name-was – then he wouldn't have ruled the lands in terror for centuries. I reckon your fantasy vampires are just misunderstood."

Henry sighed. How had he ended up with the most annoying brother in the world and a sister who couldn't grasp the simplest concepts of gaming?

"Look, a vampire is always the bad guy," he explained, trying to stick to simple ideas. "They hate the living, resent their undead status and revel in the pain of mortals. They kill people, drink their blood and take control over the mindless corpses of their prey. That's evil, right? Just cos they do it all by some complex code, can't go out in sunshine, hate crosses and shun holy water, they're still mean and terrifying."

"But how did he become a vampire?" asked the ever-curious Katherine.

"Usually they're bitten – sired by someone who's already a vampire. They emerge as vampire spawn and slowly grow in power. Bet you couldn't deal with one."

"I have to deal with them every year," wailed Pumpkin. "That's what comes of having a birthday on Halloween!"

———

An unusual group of people were clustered together around a table in a long, dark room, at the house of the bald man with the strange pet. The room was furnished like a large dining room, except that it seemed to be underground, as there were no windows.

The decor suggested that this was someone's home, rather than an anonymous communal hall, or a private room at a restaurant. What little light there was flickered from silver candelabra and illuminated gloomy paintings on the wall, depicting sunsets on bleak grey desert landscapes. Whoever had chosen these must truly have a desolate view of life.

The people gathered in this room spoke a common language, but that was all that they seemed to have in common. Amongst the dozen or so present there were young and old, tall and short, dark and fair, men and women. But there were many who did not fit even these categories, who were timeless in appearance as if age did not affect them, some who did not seem human, with pointy ears or long beards. The bald man was there, with glowing red eyes, and the woman next to him had silvery hair trailing almost to her knees.

There was one other shared characteristic. They were all looking desperately worried, with an urgent look on their faces like cornered animals.

The tense atmosphere, the flickering light and the low ceiling all contributed to the mood of conspiracy – a tacit and unanimous mood that some apocalyptic decision was being incubated in the fetid air.

The red-eyed man stood up and the rest fell silent.

"Friends, we need a plan. Without the Archmayor, this city will soon descend into anarchy. Not just the chaos and freedom that we all revere; it will become a place without boundaries or safety. Above all, the tourist trade will dry up entirely."

"Harbinger, do we know what happened to the Archmayor?" asked a fat little man in a tunic.

"Not really. He'd been dead for many years, of course. So, his final demise came as no real surprise to me. But previously we'd been able to restore him to his undead limbo and the status quo was preserved. Now that he's been blasted into a million pieces, it would take the strongest magic to put him back together – and that could take years. No, this means there'll be an election."

A chorus of protest met this last statement. The bald, red-eyed man, Harbinger, put up his hands to call for silence.

"When was the last election in the city? Carina – you're the librarian."

A short, ivory-skinned woman spoke up in a quiet, precise voice which carried immediate authority, like that of a schoolteacher. The others instinctively stopped arguing in order to hear her.

"The last mayor was elected 153 years ago. There has been no election since then. He took on the title Archmayor about a hundred years ago."

"Shouldn't elections happen more often?" asked the little fat man.

Carina frowned slightly. "If you were more than just a pedlar, Zirca, you might know that there are no real rules or laws here. That's the beauty of this great city. There is no schedule for elections. They just take place when there's no alternative, to fill a vacancy when nobody else has volunteered."

"That's not all," Harbinger added softly. "Marid, you'd better come forward."

A middle-aged man emerged from the shadows at the edge of the dark room. He wore bright blue robes, decorated with silver trim. His very appearance exuded confidence and calm.

"Mercedes has returned to town," he said, in a deep, authoritative voice which made the others immediately believe him. "I don't know where she's living. But she's been seen at the Pilgrim Hotel."

He had spoken just a few short sentences, but those were enough to throw the room into turmoil. Everybody tried to speak at once. Again, Harbinger called for order.

"I think we can rule out the possibility of a new mayor seamlessly emerging. We all remember what happened the last time Mercedes came to the city. She's a vampire. Vampires will never be welcome here as masters. They have rules; they control and dictate. They try to charm people. Carceron isn't the sort of city that works by rules. Force and power are the ultimate sources of strength. Just as my magic stems from the Radiance, so the Superiors have great strength too."

"Who are the Superiors?" whispered Zirca to his neighbour at the table.

There was a hush. Harbinger smiled slightly, as if the question amused him. "It is the term we all use here, Zirca.

Perhaps you call them demons. But don't say that to their faces unless you want to be whisked off to one of their mansions to be dismembered slowly."

A very tall, beautiful woman, who had previously been silent, now spoke up. "You know I don't like hearing her name. But the point is – Mercedes will step forward to become mayor. Harbinger, we have to stop her. We need an alternative to Mercedes that all the right-thinking people of the city can support. Will you stand to be mayor?"

"No!" shouted Harbinger, raising his voice for once. "We must meet force with force. To win an election here demands a strength and stamina well beyond mine. Beyond anyone in this room."

"Who then, Champrice?" asked Carina, softly.

The tall, beautiful woman continued. "We must be practical. Who is there in Carceron who can fight a vampire as powerful as Mercedes and win, if it should come to that? What about those people at Seeds?"

"Druids!" scoffed Zirca. "And they don't even buy their own ingredients for their restaurant. Any vampire would make an easy meal of them."

"The druids will always be neutral in any contest," sniffed Carina, dismissively. "They turn indifference into an art form. Besides, they have to organise the counting of the votes."

"None of the Superiors would be mayor," continued Champrice. "It is not in their nature. The very title of mayor suggests order and method."

"What about one of the adventurers?" asked a young man, dressed entirely in black, whose face was partly obscured in the dim light. "Harbinger, send a quasit round the taverns to see who'll do it."

Harbinger pondered the idea. "It's worth checking. Perhaps Marvexio would if we asked. I will make enquiries. I suggest we meet again this time tomorrow."

His companions rose from the table, climbing a flight of stairs to a front door and heading out into the street. As if by habit, they huddled in little groups of twos and threes as they whispered goodbyes. It was dark outside and the entrance to this home was as unprepossessing as the gloomy dining room had been. The street was very narrow, with tall buildings on both sides, styled in an uncompromising and hostile way, as if challenging the right of the passer-by to gaze upon them.

"Anyone who isn't Mercedes can win," insisted Zirca, confidently, as he bade farewell for the night.

"Don't underestimate how devastating an election can be in Carceron," muttered Carina, darkly. "That's one reason we don't have them very often. And the Superiors don't want to waste their powers on such contests, when they could be fighting each other."

"Nonsense, I've seen elections in other cities on my travels," scoffed Zirca. "They're much the same everywhere. It's just a popularity contest."

Chapter 2

The Campaign Team

"What should I wear on election day? I want to look my best for the result."

Sapphire had come over to Henry and Katherine's house after school. She was full of thoughts and plans for the election – what to say in her victory speech and how she would deploy such exquisite charm and politeness in commiserating with Amber for having beaten her.

Henry was also full of plans, but he was taking nothing for granted. "Katherine, how are we doing with the younger students? Especially the girls. I can't talk to them. They just giggle."

Katherine ignored this slight. She felt important for being on the campaign team and grateful to her brother for including her. Henry was a year older and Katherine was often compared to him, or was in his shadow, but she knew he really valued her help. Sapphire was another matter: compared with her, Katherine felt very small, shy and dowdy – whereas Sapphire was confident, elegant and always seemed to know what she wanted.

She pulled herself together and focused on Henry's question. "Amber has been canvassing them heavily and making promises. She's also been handing out goodies – Belgian chocolates, mostly. Her dad brings them back from business trips."

"And what have we been doing to retaliate?" shrieked Sapphire, turning in alarm to scowl at Katherine. "Come on, Pumpkin, this was your patch. Don't let me down."

Henry almost smiled at the phrase 'Pumpkin patch' to indicate jurisdiction. But he just managed to stop himself.

"It's under control," Katherine replied, calmly as always, rather like her brother. "I got a box of cheap jewellery that Mr Evans was going to sell at his discount shop. Each piece is virtually worthless, but they look quite neat. Especially with some glitter that I added. They're even in your campaign colour scheme. I've been secretly handing the trinkets out. The younger girls love them. They'll remember those long after the taste of Amber's chocolates has gone."

Sapphire's wrath subsided as quickly as it had come. She hadn't been angry with Katherine. But her nervousness over the result had been making her edgy. At times like this she really felt reassured by the younger girl's quiet confidence and planning, which was very different from her own headstrong and instinctive nature.

"Well, never mind that," she said, turning to her boyfriend. "Henry, what about those older boys? You know what Amber's like."

"I checked with Mr Trimble. The school trip to the museum has been moved to the day of the election. If those boys haven't voted before the coach leaves – and they won't, they're too lazy – they won't have time later. Amber will find that all those boys she thinks she's charmed will be twenty miles away when she needs their votes."

Sapphire chuckled, this time a heartfelt release of tension, very different from her campaign smirk. Henry did have style in the shenanigans he planned. Her mind at once moved on to fresh priorities.

"There's going to be a debate between the candidates," she said. "I've got some ideas for that."

Katherine sat up. The details of Sapphire's policies as an election candidate had never been clear to her. "What are your main arguments?" she asked. "There are bound to be tough questions."

"Oh, yes, maybe," smiled Sapphire, pretending to yawn. "Never you mind, young Pumpkin. For my main speech I'm going to sing. Everyone knows Amber couldn't sing to save her life. They'll be so busy looking at me and enjoying the melody, they won't bother asking questions. And I've bribed Connor, the Green candidate, to tear into Amber in his speech and accuse her of all sorts of things."

"What sort of things?" asked Katherine, in horror.

"I think I asked him… to accuse her of planning to tear down the school bike sheds to enlarge the teachers' car park and to claim that she was plotting to make Chemistry compulsory through the whole school…"

"How did you bribe him?" interrupted Henry, suddenly seizing upon the aspect of Sapphire's tactics that might affect him.

For once, Sapphire seemed a little embarrassed and lost for words. "Oh… I talked to him very sweetly. I think I fluttered my eyelids a bit. You know."

Henry was having none of it. "You mean you kissed him behind the bike sheds? That's how you got the idea for the teachers' car park slur. I know how your mind works."

Sapphire's lip quivered. She knew Henry would react that way, but she couldn't lie to him. "Yes, well, what if I did?" she pouted. "Winning this election is what it's all about. I'm not interested in Connor. He's got freckles and his breath smells."

Henry frowned. There was no winning this argument with Sapphire and he wasn't going to fight with her about it in front of Katherine.

To his surprise, Katherine came to his help with a counter-suggestion. "What about the ballot boxes?" she asked, innocently. "It's not like a real election, where everything is double-checked. The ballot boxes are always supervised, but Yvonne and I have a plan. She's going to fall down as soon as she's voted or have an accident to distract attention. I'll be just behind her in the voting queue. While she's being looked after, in the confusion I'll stuff another twenty ballot papers into the boxes, all filled in as votes for Sapphire. Nobody will be able to trace the source of any discrepancy, even if they figure out there are too many votes cast."

Sapphire looked at her, genuinely impressed. "Pumpkin, I knew this was why I liked you. Behind that angelic face lurks the mind of an evil genius."

———

Shortly after dark, a heavily cloaked man and a woman walked along a dingy street towards a brightly lit doorway.

Little magical lights shimmered and danced around the door frame, under a large sign proclaiming "The Irresistible Dancehall". Either side of the entrance, at about eye level, floated a creature about the size of a football, with no arms or legs, whose countenance was dominated by a row of tiny eyes which ran around their middles. They looked almost like floating security cameras.

"The Observers ask the guests' names," one of the creatures chanted, automatically.

"Harbinger and Champrice," replied the cloaked figures.

"Pass," responded the second creature, without any indication of why the names were important, or what sort of visitors might be refused admission.

Inside the door, wide steps led down into a basement laid out as an open space, almost the size of a football pitch. The busiest part was an island in the centre, where creatures with many arms and legs were working a popular bar in a blur of moving limbs. Most of the floor was taken up with dozens upon dozens of upright barrels serving as tables, around which customers sat on stools. In each of the four corners of the room was a small, raised dais, on which musical performers struggled to make themselves heard over the din, even when using magical means to boost their output.

Harbinger and Champrice sat at a table in one of the quieter areas.

"Why does it matter who becomes mayor? The Superiors are the powerful ones in Carceron. They have power, magic, mansions, minions… everything. What does a mayor do?"

"I agree that the Superiors will always be the top dogs in the city," Harbinger agreed. "They founded the city and it was ever so. But being mayor has other benefits, especially to someone who isn't one of the Superiors. The mayors get to live for free in a big mansion, for as many years as they want, with servants, guards and various more sinister underlings. There's a huge amount of wealth and treasure in that palace and I've seen only a fraction of it over the years. That sort of patronage buys a lot of power in a city like Carceron."

"Sure – but why should that bother us? We're not Superiors."

"This is a city of freedom. People do as they please. I like that freedom. But a dictatorial mayor, who brings in heaps of rules and restrictions, now that's a problem. And it would drive the tourists away. Without the tourists we have nothing." Harbinger scowled as he sipped the bubbling drink before him. His careworn face became even more crinkled, like a parchment being crumpled by an invisible hand.

Marid and Carina joined them at the table, with some information to share.

"We cannot let a vampire run the city. Mercedes must not become mayor. But she already has allies. She's been planning this thing and is well organised. Jagglespur is running her campaign. He came to my bowling alley with a group yesterday evening and I listened to their idle chatter as they rolled the skulls. Right now, we have no candidate and no campaign team. Hardly anyone in the city was here when the last election was held."

"What about our candidate?" interrupted Carina.

"Marvexio won't do it," said Harbinger, gruffly. "He will support us, though. Anyway, I don't think he's powerful enough to beat Mercedes. I think there's only one person in the city other than the Superiors that would make Mercedes stop and think. It's true he hasn't been out much lately, so we'd have to get him known. What about Flaxen?"

Champrice laughed, a high-pitched, hysterical trill that set the crystal glasses quivering on the table. "Perfect! A vampire challenged by a lich. The ultimate undead head-to-head. At least Flaxen is too old to have ambitions of devastating the city and changing its ways or making us his minions."

Several people at the table who had been about to interject paused and looked at each other. The idea of a lich, a spellcaster who had preserved their body and life force after death through the use of strange rituals, was not everybody's idea of a saviour.

"What makes you think he would do it?" asked Carina. "I don't think he's been seen in public for about a decade, except when he sits on his own at a table here at the Dancehall."

Everyone looked at Harbinger who, for once, fell quiet, wrapping one arm around the top of his bald head in contemplation. After a minute, he spoke.

"He wasn't always like that," said Harbinger, eventually. "He used to be a highly successful sorcerer and he retired here to Carceron. To continue his work, he performed the rituals necessary to become a lich, maintaining his body and soul so that even after his mortal life ended, he could continue in much the same form, even though he was now undead. It didn't involve evil rituals, such as some spellcasters use. Only in Carceron could such a creature be tolerated, even revered. But he changed when he split up with his girlfriend."

"Girlfriend?" Champrice's voice expressed her disbelief. "Undead spellcasters have girlfriends?"

"Yes, the elf Souzira. She lives in the city – you must have met her? Copper-coloured hair, very easy-going, pleasant lady."

"Why did they split up?" asked Marid.

"Not sure," answered Harbinger. "Flaxen never talks about it. But my guess is that Souzira felt the relationship wasn't going anywhere. You see, Flaxen is going to live indefinitely and Souzira will only live for about another six hundred years. There was no pressure to move in together, get married, have children – all the things that mortal couples do. So, they just drifted along and I think she got bored. And I think her father wanted her to marry someone who wasn't undead."

"We're getting off the point," interrupted Champrice. "The point is: Flaxen is certainly powerful enough. But can he be *persuaded* to be our candidate? I don't mean a Suggestion or a Quest spell; can he be *talked* into it?"

"It is the best solution," agreed Harbinger. "I will go and see him. Champrice, come with me. But persuading him will be tricky. He never really got over breaking up with Souzira. But when he hears it's to stop Mercedes – he might just do it!"

"What's he got against Mercedes?" asked Champrice, sensing gossip.

Harbinger's expression turned stony. "Flaxen and Mercedes used to be in a relationship together. About five centuries ago. I don't know the details. It ended badly."

—

Later that same night, Harbinger and Champrice were walking along Eternal Road, in the north-west corner of the City of Carceron. Hallucinatory magic made the rows of forbidding-looking townhouses seem infinitely long, stretching far into the distance, which is how the road was named. The houses were all identical, built from a concrete-like material, with very small windows. There were no house names or numbers.

Harbinger knew which house was Flaxen's without the need of names and numbers. Champrice struggled in the blackness; unlike Harbinger, she did not have extravision. Then she gave a sudden gasp as a high-pitched voice spoke loudly, just in front of them. It came from the door knocker, which had been shaped like a stone gargoyle.

"Hey! Who are you?" screeched the voice.

"Harbinger and Champrice," they answered, for the second time that evening.

There was a long pause. Then the voice spoke again. "The Master says you get lost!"

Harbinger was in no mood to argue with a minor enchantment. "Either you open up now, or I'll blast down the door and banish you to the Glooms of Hades," he said, in a tone of steely calm that was more intimidating than any shout.

The door opened at once and the voice did not speak again.

The door led straight into a front room, dimly lit with artificial light similar to that in Harbinger's home. Reclining on a sofa was a man dressed entirely in gold clothing. Although the man looked as though he were in late middle age, his hair and beard were still fair, and he had a mature, handsome expression. He did not look up as his visitors entered but motioned them in silence to be seated. Champrice noticed that the furnishings were expensive, with gold leaf fittings, gold-framed mirrors and a thick, honey-coloured carpet.

"You know why we have come," said Harbinger, simply, as he sat down. "Flaxen, I think you have met Champrice."

"Knowledge is a boon, certainty a burden, omniscience a curse," said Flaxen. His voice sounded quiet and depressed. Champrice wondered how long it had been since he last spoke to anyone – weeks or months, perhaps. "Yes, I have heard the news. The Archmayor is dead – finally dead. And *she* is back."

He managed to drop his voice and hiss the word "she" so that the echoes of it slithered around the room for several seconds. There could be no doubt that Mercedes was on his mind.

Champrice's heightened senses told her that there was something else moving around the floor. She could not see or hear it, but she could detect the slow footsteps of some creature, small and low down. Flaxen seemed to recognise her unease.

"Don't tread on Pullywuggles. He's always interested in visitors. Now you've been here once, he will recognise you in the future."

Champrice was not reassured by this. What was Pullywuggles? Was he dangerous; might he attack? Maybe he was invisible? Flaxen gave no further information, however.

"And what is it you really want?" cried Flaxen. "How do *you* hope to defeat *her*?" He was suddenly energetic and sitting up to face Harbinger.

"There will be an election," said Harbinger. "We need a candidate to beat Mercedes, someone who knows what elections are like, can withstand the pressure and who knows what Mercedes is really capable of. You knew I would come. You know that you are the only person in Carceron who can do it."

There was silence for a minute. Flaxen rose and began to pace the room. Champrice wondered if he ever trod on Pullywuggles by mistake while pacing – whoever Pullywuggles might be.

"Come out of retirement and live at the palace, eh?" said the old sorcerer-lich. Perhaps he was taken with the trappings of office. "I certainly don't want to decay into some splintery boneclaw."

"We need you to preserve the city as a tourist attraction. The demons can't dictate to you. Please?" Champrice gazed at Flaxen imploringly. It was worth a try.

"Champrice, we haven't met before." Flaxen's tone was suddenly businesslike. "If we are going to fight a campaign against Mercedes, we don't just need a candidate, such as my poor self. We need a campaign team and the best one available. People with a novel approach. Campaigners who can be imaginative and unscrupulous. Who have immediate experience, not just memories from campaigns centuries ago. There's nobody in Carceron – I think – Harbinger?"

Harbinger scowled. "I know what you're asking me to do. And you're right. We need to perform a Summoning. The ritual will search for the ideal campaign team and bring them all instantly to the city. You're right, it's essential. If I can arrange it, then will you be our candidate?"

Flaxen smiled for the first time and Champrice realised how charismatic and charming the old sorcerer-lich could be when he chose, however many centuries old he might be.

"I will," said Flaxen fervently, and bowed low. "But I want the best campaign team, or it's no deal."

Chapter 3
The Summoning

"Are you *quite* sure you know how to do this?" Harbinger tried not to let his anxiety show in his words.

He was standing with Marid in the back room of Looks Could Kill in Hightower Square, one of the more dangerous emporia in Carceron. All sorts of creatures were kept on the premises that had the power to petrify or paralyse their prey. Basilisks were always in demand and there was an occasional gorgon in stock. At the lower end of the scale, Creeping Omnivores were kept in a hutch and could be offered for sale to tourists who couldn't afford or be trusted with anything more deadly. There was even a medusa in a holding pen – a very rare creature to capture – who would command a premium price once tamed. The shop also did a thriving spin-off trade in stone statues.

Talisman, the proprietor of the shop, seemed surprised and offended by Harbinger's question. "It's very similar to a teleportation circle, but it works in reverse," he explained. Talisman was an accomplished wizard, retired from adventuring. "You describe in detail what you want to summon. It's not like conjuring or enslaving a specific creature. You have no real control over where the spell summons your desired creature or creatures *from*. I've found it wise to impose a limit within the ritual on how many creatures are summoned. I once let an unknown quantity of Invisible Servants loose at a funeral…"

Talisman shuddered at the memory, and the medallions around his neck clinked and rattled in sympathy. He continued, "The spell opens a gate. It might be to another location on this plane of existence, or any other plane. It happens immediately. If it has not summoned the specified creatures within, say, a minute, then no such persons exist for you to obtain. When they do appear, they would normally teleport straight into the middle of the summoning circle."

"Ah, but Carina says that humans don't teleport into the city anymore," Marid pointed out. "Too many tourists got kidnapped that way. They now appear just outside the Shadow Gate to the south, so that they can be checked in at Tourist Information. Carina will look out for them for us."

"True," admitted Talisman. He didn't think it would be safe for strangers to teleport into the back room of his shop, certainly.

"How soon can you perform the ritual?" asked Harbinger impatiently.

"Oh, it's not complex. Takes about ten minutes to cast. But I'll need supplies. Harbinger, send some quasits to collect them, will you? The Megastore has most items and Pentagram Supplies can fill in the more unusual items like a bottle of air elemental farts. Oh, and see if Dragonhire will let me have a few scales from a metallic dragon. Any dragon will do, but metallic ones make better conductors."

"I'll go," interrupted Marid. "I don't think a quasit can be trusted to bring back the right things. No offence, Harbinger, but I think your creatures make better messengers than component suppliers."

Harbinger shrugged. "Maybe you're right. I never really trust my quasits. You know how it is."

Talisman brightened up. "Well, if you can get the components here this morning, I'll also need the exact wording for the creatures you're trying to summon. Then I can summon them here by lunchtime."

"I remember what happened last time we sent your quasits to buy spell components," smiled Marid. "You know how you specified only the best items? According to the shopkeeper at Pentagram Supplies, the quasits were testing components in the store, discarding anything they thought wasn't of any use. There is a notice up saying, 'You cast it, you bought it', but quasits always ignore rules anyway."

Talisman shuddered. "I certainly remember how much gold we had to pay him to settle up and persuade him not to set the beldark guards on us."

"We're looking for a campaign team that knows how to win elections," explained Harbinger. "People who understand it all, marketing and dirty tricks, who have recent experience and lots of imagination. If they understand about demons and vampires, all the better. Doesn't matter where they come from, but obviously we don't want solars or angels being summoned!"

Talisman was making notes, quickly jotting down shorthand onto blank parchment.

"I assume you'll want them speaking Common? I

can work that into the ritual. Don't want any language difficulties slowing us down."

"That's right," agreed Marid. "But don't worry. I think we'll get on well with these experts. They'll probably be professionals who've been doing these campaigns all their lives."

———

In another part of the same city, a very different meeting was taking place. Rather than being held in the back room of a shop, this one reeked of privilege and wealth. In one of the mansions in Delirium Drive, four figures sat in elegant chairs at a polished dining table which could have accommodated a dozen or more. The room was plainly furnished and in the strangest of taste. It had no windows. Instead of a fireplace there were two iron braziers on one side of the room. Light also fell from red candles set in silver candelabra on the table. There seemed to be no papers, agenda or formality about the meeting. It merely proceeded as needed.

The four creatures in the room varied in size and appearance, but they all shared certain features. They had red scales or fur in place of skin; all had tails and three had horns. The smallest of them constantly fidgeted with his claws during the meeting, as a nervous habit. The largest, sitting at one end of the table, was a huge figure with an expressionless face. His impassive eyes, square jaw and clenched fists told their own tale of a creature at once strong, overbearing and utterly ruthless.

Any human present would not have understood a word

of their guttural speech, but their conversation was also focused, like that of Harbinger and his friends, on Mercedes and the need for an election.

The leading figure spoke first and set the tone. "An election is of no interest to us," he said, firmly but unemotionally. "There will always be a mayor in this city. Carcus expects it."

"We are already getting a lot of enquiries from other planes, Cremorne," said the nervous demon. "Many others will come to the city just to see and take part in the election. It will be good for business—"

The female demon, who had no horns, interrupted him. "You are weak, Lamothe," she said, in a voice that hissed like escaping steam. "Why should we care about business?"

Cremorne raised a hand. There was immediate silence. "Mercedes has asked to see us," he declared. "I have asked her to join this meeting."

As if triggered by his words, the door opened and a tall, dark-haired woman entered. She was finely dressed, all in black with silver jewellery. She walked with poise and determination, in a way that caught the eye. The four creatures present were either immune to her charms or already knew her well enough to avoid bothering with her appearance.

The woman stood near one of the braziers and smiled in greeting. "Thank you for inviting me to your meeting," she said politely and demurely, by way of greeting.

"What do you have to offer us, Mercedes?" snarled the female demon.

"You already know me," smiled Mercedes. "I can give you everything you want. Carnage, wreckage, pain and suffering to the weak. There will always be a City of Carceron. I can make it more fun."

Her tone was that of an eager agent showing a prospective buyer around a house, but to anyone other than demons her words were chilling and horrific.

"You will need support?" asked Lamothe, vaguely.

Mercedes beamed at him. "Many will come to the city," she explained, equally vaguely. "I have Jagglespur to run my campaign."

"We are not interested in mere mortals," scoffed the female demon, hissing at her.

"Many will come. Babaeski, make arrangements," declared Cremorne, as if announcing a decision.

The demon who had not yet spoken turned his scaly head but said nothing.

Cremorne took this as indicating acquiescence. He looked like someone who always managed to engender obedience and servitude, willingly or otherwise. Willing obedience saved time. But clearly he found forced obedience more fun.

Mercedes smiled inwardly. This election was the culmination of her long-held desire. Some people seek elected office because they want to achieve something, perhaps through a burning sense of injustice, or through a humanitarian desire to improve the lives of their fellow creatures. Others are driven by a more selfish desire simply to *be* someone, to hold office, further their careers, be feted at banquets and acknowledged by the populace at large. But there is a third sort, much rarer than the other two, which seeks power for its own sake. Not power to achieve great outcomes and save worlds, but power to dominate and control, to persuade or subjugate others to their will. Mercedes enjoyed power in this way; she admitted it to herself and cared not whether others saw it too. She squirmed with excitement merely at the prospect. She knew that she was capable of wielding great power, if only the voters of Carceron could be coaxed, tricked or forced, just once, to vote her into office.

"Your campaign needs appeal," continued Cremorne. Later he could decide whether Mercedes was a worthy candidate. "How will you persuade those in the city who still have minds that they should vote for *you*?"

"I have a slogan which both disguises my purpose and appeals to voters," grinned Mercedes. She had evidently foreseen such a question and her preparedness added to the impression she gave of effortless power.

She paused briefly for effect.

"Vote Vampire."

***

Henry, Katherine and Sapphire were taking a day off from Sapphire's campaign. It was a Saturday and they were all exhausted from a combination of schoolwork and soliciting votes from classmates whom they barely knew or didn't like.

Henry had insisted on a complete rest from politics. He had persuaded the reluctant Katherine to give roleplaying games another go and had even coaxed Sapphire into trying it as a way to chill out and vent her frustration on imaginary foes. Oliver had wanted to play too but had fled when Henry threw a well-aimed cricket ball at him and called him a "meddling little goblin". The only intruder who had been allowed to stay in the room was Charisma, who sat at Katherine's feet.

Katherine was playing a cleric called Pumpkin this time, having tired of her previous dark elf sorcerer. She had liked the idea of dark elves having silver hair but found the rest of the character dull. The idea of a cleric who could heal and help people was much more appealing. As well as being the Games Master running the adventure, Henry had added one of his own former characters to the group, Ferdinal the Paladin. The paladin was supposed to protect any weaker characters and rescue them if they got into trouble. Sapphire had been unsure what character to play. Henry had suggested a warlock, a spellcaster bound to an arcane patron, a sorcerer with innate magical power, or a wizard who learned magic from spellbooks. Katherine, in a stroke of genius, had pointed out that if Sapphire were a bard, she was entitled to sing whatever songs her character chose to perform. So equipped, the party started out, rejoining an adventure that Henry and Katherine had previously begun, trying to outwit a powerful vampire noble. Sapphire kept her own name for the character, immodestly insisting that Sapphire was the best name imaginable.

Choosing equipment and clothing for the adventurers had delayed things. Henry had been careful to select suitable armour and weapons for his paladin. Katherine had been guided by Henry in suitable gear to pick for Pumpkin the Cleric. But Sapphire had been fussy. She had eventually selected a wardrobe for her fictitious bard that would have satisfied the most selective of peacocks and had added an assortment of accoutrements, from perfumes and a disguise kit to manacles and a blowpipe, which made her character seem dangerously overburdened.

The scenario was going badly for the characters. They soon found themselves stuck for leads on where to strike next. Having wiped out a band of marauding goblins ("I bet Oliver was with them," muttered Henry), Pumpkin the Cleric had cast Speak with the Slain to interrogate their late foes about the whereabouts of the vampires.

The spell worked, but the goblins had refused to divulge any information, being understandably resentful towards the adventurers who had slain them only a few minutes earlier.

"We need to kill someone more *co-operative*," snapped Sapphire the Bard, which Henry said showed she must be of an evil mindset or ethos.

"Charisma thinks you're evil anyway," said Henry, with a knowing nod of the head, as the grey cat stalked across the room.

"That cat's a demon!" sneered Sapphire, tossing her blonde hair in anger. "It's vicious and deadly. Can't you keep it out of the room while we're playing?"

"Try keeping a cat out of anywhere," thought Henry, but he already knew better than to say that aloud.

Pumpkin the Cleric then suggested a powerful ritual to help to scry for information. "It exposes our position, so they will know where we are, but it may help draw the eye of our foes and tempt them into a mistake," she explained rather lamely.

Sapphire was unimpressed and her bard then expressed strong views on the general uselessness of clerics, rituals, scrying and Pumpkin especially. "How will a spell help us if it exposes us to vampires?" she asked.

For once, Pumpkin was not to be squashed so easily. "I'm going to cast it anyway," she retorted, "at a high level for maximum range and effect. So, stay out of the way!"

Katherine was no actress and she never attempted to portray her cleric, Pumpkin, performing spells and rituals. But as she spoke, the living room in which they sat began to shake. A glass of water in front of Katherine quivered and toppled over onto the carpet. A noise like the roar of distant traffic began, rapidly increasing in volume. The room became darker and strangely misty, so that the three players could hardly see one another.

At this critical moment, the door of the room opened and Oliver looked in. "What are you guys doing?" he complained, peevishly. "Mum will kill you when she gets home…"

But at this point his words were drowned out by the increasing roar. Sapphire gave a little shriek. Katherine sat wide-eyed, gripping the arms of her chair as if worried she would be swept away. Henry grabbed at his dice, which were tumbling onto the floor. Oliver, still in the doorway, screamed loudly and shut his eyes.

And then, suddenly, there was silence. Slowly the mist began to clear.

Harbinger was back at his shop. Despite all the turmoil with the Archmayor's death, he still had to earn a living. His office was sparsely furnished, just his own desk and chair and numerous wooden chairs around the other walls, facing the centre. On several of the wooden chairs sat the creatures with grey-green skin, like the one that had delivered the portentous message to him so recently. The creatures mostly sat in silence, but they seemed jealous of each other or competitive by nature, since from time to time one would taunt or jeer at another, provoking a short exchange of petty insults. None of the creatures seemed prone to violence, however, for the altercations always took place at a safe distance. Harbinger ignored his quarrelsome cronies and brooded.

The door opened and the creatures looked up, expectantly. The man in black leather clothes, who had attended the secret meeting at Harbinger's house, entered the shop and approached the patron.

"Ah, Šapka," said the distracted Harbinger. "Any messages to send today?"

"No, actually I have a message for you from Talisman," answered Šapka, softly. His voice was smooth and honeyed, and although he spoke barely above a whisper, the warm tones of his voice offered immediate reassurance and comfort. But Harbinger knew Šapka well and his anxiety did not abate.

"Talisman says that the ritual has worked," continued Šapka. "And three adventurers will soon appear at the Shadow Gate. He has already sent one of your quasits to Carina, who will be expecting them at the Tourist Information Office."

At this, Harbinger's hopes began to rise. "Really? Three adventurers? What are their names?"

"Talisman says the spell identified Ferdinal the Paladin, Pumpkin the Cleric and Sapphire the Bard. They work as a team. But… he says there was a complication with the spell.

He wouldn't tell me what. Said it wouldn't affect delivery of the three campaigners and we should expect them in the normal place."

"We can attend to Talisman later," said Harbinger, grimly. "Redwing can watch the shop. I'm off to Tourist Information immediately to meet the newcomers and greet them accordingly. You coming too?"

Šapka looked shocked. "Certainly *not*," he said, emphatically. In a calmer tone he added, "I haven't decided which side I'm on yet."

———

Slowly the mist began to clear. Henry, or Ferdinal, as he now was, Pumpkin and Sapphire were standing next to each other. Nobody was injured, although all three had a slight ringing in their ears.

They were standing outdoors, facing a twenty-foot-tall featureless wall made out of concrete, or some similar material. There was a huge double gate set into the wall, which opened outwards judging by the marks in the grey, dusty ground. But there was no sign of any doorbell or system of requesting admittance. Ferdinal glanced up at the top of the wall, but that too was bare, devoid of any crenellations or guard posts. There were no windows to be seen anywhere.

It wasn't bright daylight, but a murky partial light like late afternoon on a winter's day. The sky was grey and the ground in all directions was equally grey and bland. Only a faint breeze, whipping up small clouds of dust and tiny pebbles, suggested activity. Pumpkin thought that the strangest thing was the absence of sound coming from the fortification in front of them. There was only the sound of the breeze and their own rapid breathing.

Sapphire was the first to notice an even bigger change. All the peacock-coloured clothes, expensive accessories and exotic perfumes she had demanded for her bard in the game had miraculously appeared. She was actually wearing and carrying them! Talk about a wish coming true. She looked at the others. They too were decked out in the apparel and weaponry of the characters that only a moment ago they had been portraying in a game.

Pumpkin looked round, startled. There was no sign of the living room at home. It, and all other civilisation, had vanished. Wherever it was they now were, there was no way back.

All three of them no longer looked like teenagers. Somehow they had retained the same features, but had become taller, stronger, more mature versions of themselves. It was as if they had grown up in an instant, so that the clothes and weapons of their characters fitted them perfectly.

They were no longer three teenagers who went to school each day. They had matured in an instant into young adults. Henry was now a real-life version of Ferdinal the Paladin, Sapphire was a bard and Pumpkin a sorcerer.

They had become the very same characters that they had designed.

Chapter 4

Welcome to Carceron, City of Chaos

Ferdinal the Paladin looked at his two companions. They did not seem terrified by the change. He was relieved that he wouldn't have to waste time reassuring them. Sapphire had a lot of pluck; it was one of the things he admired in her. And Pumpkin, well, maybe she had inherited some of the faith that her cleric character possessed.

Perhaps the fact that they had been absorbed in playing such a game just at the moment that they were transported into it had lessened the impact. It almost felt as if their encapsulation of the characters they portrayed had been so realistic that they had altered reality to become those characters. But that did not explain why they were all in such a strange place.

No-one had spoken yet. They were all still shocked and slowly absorbing their new surroundings.

Sapphire turned to Ferdinal and glowered at him. "You're the Games Master, Henry," she snapped. "You're not supposed to make it this realistic. Put us back in the living room, right now."

"I don't think it's that simple," said her boyfriend, rubbing his chin and looking up at the wall. "This isn't something I've done, nor Pumpkin either. It's not part of any game. I don't know where we are, but something or somebody has brought us here."

At this moment, a door opened within the huge concrete gate. Pumpkin jumped as a well-dressed lady with perfect ivory-coloured skin beckoned to them to approach.

"Good afternoon," beamed the newcomer. "My name is Carina and I am in charge of the Visitor Experience at the Tourist Information centre. I am also the city librarian. Welcome to Carceron, City of Chaos!"

Henry felt that some introduction was called for. "I'm Henr... er... Ferdinal," he said. Somehow his character name felt more relevant to these surroundings. "This is Sapphire – and Pumpkin."

"Do please come this way," smiled Carina, ushering the three Heroes through the door. "Up these steps, please, and you will have your first view of the city. This is your first visit, I think?"

"Er... yes," said Sapphire, who was not often shy. "Where are we, exactly? You said Carceron. Isn't that in Nevada?"

"That's Carser City, idiot!" said Ferdinal, scornfully.

"Don't worry," grinned the ever-beaming Carina. "You must all be quite surprised. But I know why you are here and we can sort everything out as soon as Harbinger gets here. It was his idea."

The three Heroes were slightly reassured by her words. This woman seemed to know what had happened and it seemed to be part of some deliberate plan. She seemed open and friendly, not remotely creepy or sinister.

As she spoke, Carina led the Heroes up a long flight of steps. These also seemed to be made of the same bland, grey concrete.

"The city is named after the great undead deity Carcus," explained Carina, still climbing the stairs, in answer to Sapphire's question. "There is a large temple dedicated to him here. You don't *have* to worship him here, of course. There are no rules. But it's probably wise. Lots of people do."

This explanation sufficed to put an end to the Heroes' thirst for further knowledge on the subject.

At the top of the steps was a large room, about forty feet square. Now at last there were windows.

Pumpkin gasped. They had climbed to a great height while Carina was talking. All of a sudden there were the sights and sounds of a walled city, not very big, but incredibly busy. Windows on three sides of the room looked down upon it.

What she saw amazed her. Pumpkin had always imagined a fantasy city to resemble something from the English Middle Ages, with narrow streets, timbered Tudor buildings, and horses and carts. But the city of Carceron conformed to no such ideas. The city was forbidding in its architecture, cold, grey and hostile. The buildings were in a variety of styles, but all were built in different shades of grey, from a similar concrete to the outer walls.

The Tourist Information tower was in the middle of the south wall, virtually above the gateway through which they had entered. Almost immediately to the east was a forbidding-looking guard tower. To the north-east was some sort of palace, and to the north-west a temple. There were squares and shopping areas, and the city's wide streets were busy with all manner of people – and creatures. There were not only humans, but also elves, dwarves, misshapen-looking beasts and several flying creatures, zooming above rooftop level.

Only on Pumpkin's far right, in the south-east corner of the city, was there anything that looked green and growing. She could just catch a glimpse beyond the guard tower of what looked like a large walled garden.

Sapphire was examining a shape in the middle of the large room. It seemed to be a statue of someone about her own size but covered by a dark sheet so that the sculpture could not be seen.

"That's the Archmayor," explained Carina. She added casually, "He was murdered two days ago, blasted into a million pieces while he was on his own at his palace. We covered up the statue until it can be taken away and smashed."

Sapphire shuddered at the innocent callousness of their guide and wondered if everyone in the city was similarly blasé about murder.

Ferdinal was examining the windowless south wall of the room. Fixed to it were four large images, each depicting very ugly people. They had angry, evil-looking eyes and horns; some had fur, one held a forked trident and one clutched some sort of religious symbol. Carina stood beside him and beamed again.

"I see you're admiring the portraits of the Superiors," she said, helpfully. "On the left is Cremorne, the most powerful. He's now the leader of the Junta, the group that runs the city. Then Babaeski, with the symbol of Carcus, runs the temple. He's the most evil," she said fondly. "Lamothe, he's the quiet one, runs the Demon Consulate. Any demons from the outer planes who visit the city or need assistance will go to him. And Luleburgaz runs the city guard. You need to steer clear of her; she can get vicious."

"Um… are they demons?" asked Ferdinal. He recognised the baleful expressions from illustrations of fantasy monsters.

"Of course." Carina seemed surprised. "What would you expect? But they prefer to be called Superiors. Travellers come from all planes and dimensions to see them. Speaking of that – which plane have you come from?"

"I don't really know," said Ferdinal. He looked helplessly at Pumpkin.

"That's right, you're the paladin," said Carina, realising that the idiot iron-wielder wouldn't have any answers.

Pumpkin realised that this was a chance to find out what had happened. "We're not tourists," she said, clenching her fist slightly. Didn't Carina realise they didn't want to be here? "We did not come on some holiday; we've never even heard of Carceron until you said the word just now. We just want to get out of here as soon as possible, see?"

"Well… it may not be that easy," said Carina, rather taken aback. "You see, we need you."

Now the three Heroes were even more confused. How could a city that they had never heard of somehow need them?

Carina sensed their bewilderment "Harbinger will explain," she said, in a voice intended to be reassuring. "I've had a quasit to say he's on his way. In fact, this is the man himself!"

Harbinger came into the room and stopped suddenly in mid-stride.

Sapphire examined him with interest. Apart from his odd-coloured azure robes and blazing red eyes, he could be mistaken for a middle-aged man anywhere. At least it suggested there might be a few more normal people in the city.

"Carina, are these the… experts?" Harbinger's voice shook with emotion. "They're children!"

"Hey!" exclaimed Ferdinal. If there was one thing he hated, it was some pompous grandpa making out that younger people knew nothing. Besides, he realised that in transforming from Henry into Ferdinal he had matured and grown in an instant. Perhaps Harbinger meant it figuratively?

"How come we understand you? You're from some other place. We're all speaking English!" Pumpkin, interrupting, had found yet another puzzling complexity.

Harbinger looked impatient. "We took care of that in the summoning. You're actually speaking Common, which is the main form of communication in most planes. The demons speak Demonic as well. You'll also hear some Elvish in the city and dialects of Primordial for dealing with elementals. Other languages aren't spoken much. And speaking Celestial counts as heresy – I hope you don't know any Celestial?"

"Didn't even realise we knew Common," shrugged Sapphire. She'd never enjoyed learning foreign languages.

"Carina said you needed us for something," added Pumpkin, truculently. She had no desire to linger in this place. "Just tell us what you want and then you can send us home the same way you brought us here, I suppose."

"Very well," said Harbinger, seeming to reach some

conclusion and taking control. "Then come with me. We need to talk somewhere more private."

Harbinger led the Heroes down the steps and into the street through another door, inside the city walls. He set off northwards, with Pumpkin following behind.

Ferdinal and Sapphire walked side by side. Sapphire's hand instinctively sought out Ferdinal's, although she never ever held hands in the street at home. This time, she sought reassurance and comfort.

"This is all your fault, Henry, for making me play that stupid game," she said, jokingly rather than in anger. "Just let's go home as soon as possible, okay?"

———

Harbinger led the Heroes outside but hesitated briefly. He decided to take the group directly to his own home and explained as much to Pumpkin. She caught a glimpse of large buildings to her right – a guard tower, some sort of theatre and an official-looking building, and a broad street straight ahead which looked as though it led to the main shopping area.

Harbinger led them off to the left, along a slightly narrower street. As he walked, he gave Pumpkin a fold-out tourist map of the city and began to explain the landmarks they were passing, as if introducing old friends to a new neighbourhood. Pumpkin couldn't help thinking that the way this bald man treated all this as though it was perfectly normal and natural was one of the strangest elements of all.

"The city has been here for thousands of years," said Harbinger, as they walked. He seemed to feel the need to act as guide and was making conversation. "Originally, creatures from other planes would hide out here if they were wanted for crimes, or in fear of more powerful enemies. Gradually it became a permanent settlement. People would sometimes visit in order to see those who were on the run. Then it developed its own momentum as a place of pilgrimage. The outcast nature of the residents became the very thing that attracted visitors. So of course, they played on that and made a living out of it!"

As they walked along, Ferdinal thought he saw a short creature in dark clothes watching them from a doorway. He had bright eyes and – surely – that was a long beak? Ferdinal thought where he had seen a picture of such a creature before. Of course – it was from the game. This crow-like thing was a wily, dextrous, flightless bird that couldn't speak but communicated through mimicking noises. The crow seemed to eye up the little group keenly, smile slightly and vanish into one of the shopfronts on the left. "I suppose to these people, *we're* the ones who look different," he thought.

"Off to the left," said Harbinger, pointing as they walked, "is the Southwest District. That's where all the real lowlifes of the city hang out. The Assassins' and Thieves' Guilds are both based there, plus succubi… and other creatures." As if to prove his point, a very dirty-looking beggar thrust a bowl towards Sapphire as she passed. The sudden movement made her quicken her pace and shudder.

They passed an austere, solid-looking building on their right. "That's the Interplanar Bank," said Harbinger. "We don't risk depositing money there for long, but it's a good place to arrange transactions or transmit money over long distances."

Sitting on the steps outside the bank was a poorly dressed girl of about Pumpkin's size. Her bright eyes followed Pumpkin, and, as she walked past, the girl stuck out her tongue and threw a stone, which missed.

Harbinger turned round at her in fury. "Get lost, Perancia. Don't try my patience."

At this the urchin made a defiant noise, leapt up and ran off down a side alley.

Pumpkin loved art and often amused herself by sketching. She found the architecture of Carceron quite astounding. The buildings seemed to have been built at different times, but all were made from the variants of the same drab, grey material. Evidently there had been a unity of purpose behind the architecture, unfettered by history or tradition. Somehow the hostile buildings symbolised the grim, unfriendly feel of the city, which seemed to challenge visitors to even try to fall in love with it.

The road widened out into a square, dominated by a large temple on the left. The temple's forecourt consisted of a large rectangular moat. It occurred to Pumpkin that this was the first time she had seen a water source in the city. Harbinger seemed to anticipate her question.

"It's salt water," he said, grimly. "It's a cruel mockery of thirst. That's the Temple of Carcus, demon lord of the undead. Babaeski, one of the Superiors, is usually there with lots of priests of Carcus helping him make and enact evil plans." Harbinger said this as if pointing out a feature, with no suggestion that this bothered him at all. "On the right of Carcus Square is Tombland Bowling Alley, run by my friend Marid the Genie. You'll meet him later."

Throughout the last ten minutes of the walk, the

variety of passers-by in the street seemed to contrast so strongly with the uniformity of the buildings. Most people seemed to be humans, either trades people or tourists. But Pumpkin had to admit that her brother was right and there was a significant number who could only be demons. The demons did not seem to attack at random; they generally ignored anyone who wasn't a fellow fiend. But the tourists were clearly fascinated by them.

Harbinger led the way along a small alley in the corner of the square and into a narrow town house. There was no hallway, the door opening directly into a comfortable front room. As they sat down, Sapphire said with sudden realisation, "I'm simply starving!"

Harbinger nodded and left the room. They heard him giving instructions to somebody in a back room. Ferdinal then realised something that should have occurred to him earlier. The light in this room was artificial, but it wasn't from electric light. It occurred to him that he hadn't seen anything electric-, or gas-, or solar-powered. Nobody had a phone. No shops were brands or chains that he recognised. This city was a complete technological and social enclave. Magic seemed to fill in all the roles that technology filled at home – and many more besides.

Pumpkin became aware of a hissing noise at her feet. Looking down she had yet another shock. There was a creature the size of a domestic cat only a few feet away, looking up at her. But it was no cat. It looked like – and could only be – a miniature dragon, with red scales, little wings and a tail that ended in a triangular spike. It didn't look dangerous, but it was clearly upset about something.

Hearing the noise, Harbinger returned. "Redwing,

you're supposed to be at the shop!" he said, in a mildly reproving tone. The little red creature looked at him and then back at Pumpkin.

"Ah, I see," said Harbinger. "Redwing says you're sitting in his spot. I'm afraid he's very particular. Could you move along the sofa slightly?"

"You're sure he doesn't bite?" asked Sapphire, suspiciously.

Pumpkin shifted position and at once the creature leapt with the agility of a cat onto the spot she had vacated. Ferdinal was fascinated by Redwing.

"Is he a micro-dragon?" he asked, with interest.

Harbinger smiled, as if pleased at the chance to explain arcana to eager new followers. "Some lore masters contend that a familiar is an actual animal; others claim that it is a fey representation of the beast form. Personally, I believe that the familiar is an extension of the wizard's own personality. When a familiar is injured or killed, it is a sure sign that some harm will shortly befall its master, so strong is the bond between the two."

"Does a wizard choose the familiar or is it just chance what sort they get?"

"If a familiar is bestowed as a boon by a deity or supernatural patron, there may well be real choice. Of course, you must be devout or loyal to the patron for that to work."

"I've heard that birdmen get crows as familiars," said Ferdinal.

"They do. But then most birdmen are pretty stupid. They may not know what else to ask for."

"Then there are special familiars," continued

Harbinger. "Redwing is a micro-dragon, a wonderful companion. Some spellcasters will tell you that an imp or a sprite suits them better. By far the easiest special familiar to find is a quasit, as they're often sent out by masters to seek wizards who can be corrupted and turned to evil. So, the quasit serves them, trying all the time to bring them under fiendish control. Best avoided unless you know how to control them. I've worked with quasits for years, without any trouble."

"How come Redwing doesn't speak?" asked Sapphire. "You still understand him?"

"We have a telepathic bond," said Harbinger. "He understands Common, but he can't speak. I think he understands Draconic as well, but I don't."

At that point two of the short greyish-greenish quasits came into the room, carrying trays.

"Is the food vegan?" whispered Sapphire to Ferdinal.

Harbinger heard and seemed to find the question odd. "It is conjured food," he explained. "It's not from animals, or plants, or fish. There are restaurants in Carceron that serve all those things – high-class dining is a speciality of the city. But conjured food adapts itself to the diner. You will eat whatever it is that you desire when you put the food into your mouth. That is what it then becomes. It was originally developed by a spellcaster with a nut allergy, who was scared of eating out."

Pumpkin was looking at the drink the quasits were pouring into silver goblets. The liquid was bright in colour, bubbling and steaming.

"May I offer you a beaker of Pink?" asked Harbinger, politely, offering Pumpkin a foaming goblet.

"What's Pink?" asked Pumpkin, although the liquid did smell good.

"Well – it's made from aquaberries in the Botanical Gardens. Fruity, plus lots of sugar and water. Some variants are alcoholic. The Dancehall serves a fantastic intoxicating blend of it. Famous for it."

Pumpkin meekly accepted the goblet and took a swig to be polite. The liquid felt alive inside her, as if seeking out and activating all the corpuscles in the body and setting them tingling. It felt warm and soothing, but on a hot summer's day it might have the converse effect and be cooling and refreshing. She wondered if this was what happened when a character in her brother's silly game drank a magic potion. But there was no obvious magical transformation from the draught – it was just a fabulous and tasty beverage. Perhaps the sugar in it made it addictive.

"I think I'm going to like it here," she said, beaming like Carina.

"Yes, but *why* are we here?" demanded Sapphire. She glared at Harbinger.

Chapter 5
Can't Stay, Can't Leave

"I must admit, I thought you'd be older," said Harbinger, his red eyes sparkling. "I'll explain. My friends and I are powerful in various sorts of magic and we brought you here because you have a particular talent and knowledge. Only with your help can we save the city."

Ferdinal looked at him closely. There was a compelling honesty about Harbinger. He really did seem to be pleading for help and did seem to believe that he, his sister and his girlfriend had some sort of superpower of their own. It was really quite flattering. But it was odd that Harbinger had thought the three of them would be older. In transforming into Ferdinal the Paladin, he felt older already.

"The Mayor of Carceron was found murdered two days ago," explained Harbinger. "We all called him the Archmayor because he'd been in charge for 153 years. He was already dead and lived on in an undead state, simply serving the city he loved. For him, undeath was not a transition of hatred into an evil creature of malice; he was simply extending the duration of the role at which he was so good. You see, the mayor is not the most powerful figure. The Junta of four demons runs the city, its guard force, its temple and so on.

"The mayor provides balance and protects the tourist trade, which is key to businesspeople such as me. His influence resolved disputes, stopped any one figure becoming too powerful and maintained the delicate equilibrium of chaos that has been the lifeblood of Carceron since it was founded. The Archmayor was a great figure and his death puts us in immediate peril.

"Not all undead are so benign – in fact, very few are. There is an ancient vampire called Mercedes who has reappeared in town after staying away for decades. I am certain that she is behind the murder. The reason is equally obvious. She wants to be the new mayor. For her, it's not about preserving the city and its traditions. She will bring skeletal hordes here to capture, rob and enslave tourists, and then, having driven away all trade, do the same to those of us who live here. In short, it means ruin for Carceron.

"The tourist trade here is huge. People, mostly humans, come from all other habitable planes because they worship chaos, evil and demons. If they went to any of the Outer Planes, they would probably be stuck there and devoured by whatever evil lord happened to reign supreme at the time. Here in Carceron they can see demons close up. It's not without danger, but that is part of its appeal.

"Tourists are safe within the walls of the two hotels, the Trident Hotel, near Hightower Square and the Pilgrim Hotel near the Shadow Gate."

Here Pumpkin ventured to interrupt him. "If it's such a big tourist trade," she asked, "how come there are only two hotels?"

"There used to be others," admitted Harbinger, "but they closed because they could not guarantee the safety of their guests. Their wards and glyphs were overcome by spellcasters and then the assassins or demons got in. But the Pilgrim and the Trident are very well guarded. A few tourists stay at the casinos as well – Electrum, The Deck of Delusions and The Fates – but that's risky because there are no real protective measures there.

"Carceron is not the capital city of this plane. The City of Spires is the capital, ruled over by King Perihelion. But Carceron is entirely self-governing. The King does not interfere in its running; he is far too wise even to try. So, we cannot expect any outside help with what must be done.

"And this is where you come in. We have to have an election now to replace the Archmayor. Mercedes is already a declared candidate and most people are too scared to oppose her. Elections here in Carceron follow few rules and are perilous to the candidates. You are here because we summoned the best political campaign team we could find, with recent experience of the tricks of the trade, imagination, who have some understanding of vampires and demons and what they might do. The spell sought you out and summoned you because you are the best. That is indisputable. The magic does not lie."

There was a pause.

"Why don't you just resurrect the old Archmayor and let him carry on?" asked Ferdinal, who was familiar with the application of spells in such situations.

"Resurrect him? He'd been undead for over a century! If we'd resurrected him, we would have destroyed the undead entity we hoped to bring back. Talk sense, fighter, or stick to swordplay!"

Ferdinal scowled. It was quite an insult to a paladin to address him as a fighter.

Pumpkin had a different concern. "But how do we get home afterwards? You've talked about us helping you. But when do we get to go home? Mum will be worried sick!"

"The election is in a week's time," said Harbinger. "The way a summoning works from a far-off plane, any time that elapses here will be just a pocket dimension for you back home. No time will pass on your home plane; you will reappear in an instant and in the same place you left. The gap is a mere flicker of existence."

"And you can do this, right? You've done it before?"

Again, Harbinger hesitated. "It was actually Talisman who summoned you. He's a wizard who retired from adventuring and runs a shop in Carceron. He said there was a complication with the spell. I don't know what it is yet. Once we know what happened we will know how to reverse it and send you back."

"You mean – you don't know how we'll get back?" Sapphire's lips quivered, and she reached out instinctively for Ferdinal's hand and clasped it hard.

Harbinger was about to reply when there was a knock at the door.

━━

"Unglyphed," called out Harbinger without getting up from his chair. The door opened and two figures hurried in. Pumpkin thought the tall man dressed in scarlet and silver must have come straight from a theatre rehearsal, while his companion was about human-sized, but with pointy ears and had a lute strapped to his back.

"Marid and Marvexio, let me introduce Sapphire, Pumpkin and Ferdinal," said Harbinger, coolly. "You look as though you bring news?"

"There's bad news and worse news," said Marid, grimly. "I've just seen Šapka. He says that he's had a full description of our new campaign experts, from Fulcrum of all people, and Šapka says he isn't going to back us. He doesn't think we can beat Mercedes."

"Mercedes is making an announcement in Central Square in a few minutes," added his companion. "Probably to launch her campaign. It all looks carefully planned." Marvexio was more laid-back. He looked as though nothing would flurry him much.

"Who's Fulcrum?" asked Sapphire, insulted that some complete stranger had decided that she and her friends were utter dolts.

"Underworld fixer," explained Harbinger, briefly. "He acts as a go-between for Šapka, head of the Velvet Glove, a fancy name for assassins, Revlyn, head of the Destiny Guild of thieves and various demons. He brokers deals and stops feuds breaking out. He hardly says anything – he's a birdman. But he's wily and never misses anything. Not like most birdmen. Demons don't trust each other, but somehow, they trust Fulcrum."

Ferdinal remembered the beady-eyed creature he had seen in a shop doorway. That must have been Fulcrum. He'd reported straight to Šapka. Evidently news travelled fast in Carceron.

But Sapphire felt a rising anger, both at being summoned without warning to some ugly city and then being judged lacking in ability by a crow in a shopfront. All the while, Harbinger and these so-called friends of his were automatically assuming that she, Henry and Katherine would give them some unspecified help in an election? Why should they? Sapphire had her own election to worry about back at school. Surely this was more important.

"Why the hell should we help you?" she yelled out. "You've done nothing for us, just dragged us here. I want to go home *right now*!"

As she raised her voice, Marvexio whipped the lute off his back and played a couple of high chords on it, whose notes resonated and merged and hung in the air in Harbinger's front room. "Just give us a chance," he said, softly. "Come and hear what Mercedes has to say. Then meet our candidate – he's quite something. Then you can decide."

Sapphire felt her wrath instantly subside with Marvexio's soothing words and chords. She felt suddenly at ease. What this bard said made perfect sense. Of course, she must find out more. Perhaps she would learn some tricks for her own election. And who was this Mercedes anyway? She was probably some dimwit like Amber, back at school.

"Er… there's something else you should know," said Harbinger to Marid, confidentially. "There was a complication with the summoning spell. I need to see Talisman to find out what."

"Then we'd all better go to Central Square right now," said Marid, with determination. "Everyone will be there."

So saying, Marid and Marvexio got up and opened the front door. Ferdinal, Pumpkin and Sapphire followed them out. Harbinger came last, with Redwing sitting on his shoulder, purring like a cat.

As Harbinger shut the door, Ferdinal asked him, "Don't you have to glyph the door again as you leave? To lock it, I mean?"

Harbinger smiled again. "The glyph is a magical device, not a lock. Redwing and I can pass in and out freely. Any guest can leave freely. But to gain entry to the house, a guest must be invited in by me, by unglyphing the alarm. Otherwise, it would explode. It wouldn't damage the house, but it's powerful enough to obliterate most casual intruders."

The little group headed eastwards along the alley, which opened almost at once into a large square. There were shops all around the edge and what looked like space for market stalls in the southern half. To the left, on the north side of the square, was a large bar, with the sign "The Irresistible Dancehall" above it. On the far side of the square, just visible, were various suppliers who seemed to stock magical ingredients, braziers, occult items and potions. There was a shop in the far corner which seemed to be offering winged creatures (were they dragons?). Harbinger's shop with its quasit messengers was here and a sort of travel agent with the sign "Astral Planar Travel" invitingly above the door. And there was a shop whose entrance was boarded up, with a tall guard at the door, beside the sign "Captain Manacle's Slave Emporium". Sapphire shuddered at the sight. Other streets entered the square from the north and south.

The square was full of people: creatures of all sorts, tourists, messengers, demons, all bustling about and jostling one another aside. The centre of the square contained a wooden stage – perfect, thought Pumpkin, for outdoor plays or concerts.

But then she gasped as she realised what was in the centre of the stage. There was a strange sort of cage there, about ten feet on each side and equally tall. The sides of the cage were not solid bars but arcing bands of golden light, all constantly moving and evidently dangerous to touch. Inside the cage was a long-haired, tall but terrified-looking creature, shimmering white in colour, with large, feathered wings which it had furled up around its body, either from abject fear or to prevent them touching the sides of the cage. It gazed out forlornly at the crowd, who in turn were ignoring it or jeering insults at it.

"How horrible! What's that?" she demanded of Marid, who was next to her.

"That's the Arcane Cage," said Marid, proudly. "That's been there for centuries. It was put there by Erith Edelwald, the first Mayor of Carceron. Each month we put a fresh victim in it and dismember the current occupant. We've got an angel this month. It's a famous one, a noble celestial called Aspreyna."

Before Pumpkin could reply, there was an ear-splitting noise, like air horns being sounded from all corners of the square. A procession entered from the southern end of the square, marching up towards the stage and up its steps. Ferdinal, Pumpkin and Sapphire were too far away to see them clearly until the newcomers were on the stage, about a hundred feet away. They could not get closer owing to the densely packed crowd that had now gathered.

The first two people onto the stage were tough-looking fighters wearing metal armour. The first was short and stocky, possibly a professional warrior, the second looked human. Behind him followed a truly horrifying figure dressed in black clothes and studded leather armour, who Pumpkin thought looked like a jailer or a torturer. Then came an amazingly beautiful woman. She was tall, with elegant shoulder-length dark hair. She wore a black gown, low-cut at the front, which accentuated her trim figure. As she turned to face the crowd, her diamond necklace and earrings glinted in the half-light that seemed to pervade the city. As she smiled and waved to the crowd, her perfect white teeth gleamed and shimmered and seemed to have diamonds set into them. Her large yellowish eyes sought out individuals in the crowd, playing and toying with each in turn before moving swiftly and effortlessly along to another Observer and repeating the trick. Almost unnoticed behind her came two more figures: an ogre with a club and a young man in leather armour who was partly obscured by the others now packed onto the stage.

The woman in the black gown raised her arms and there was immediate silence from the hundreds of people in the square.

"Many of you know me and all realise the reason why I am here," she said in a crystal-clear voice that carried perfectly, trilling each letter "r", which echoed around the edges of the square. "I am Mercedes. I have returned to my home city in its hour of need. You, the people of this great city, are crying out for leadership. You need someone who knows and understands the very heartbeat of this mighty metropolis. You need a leader who will defend and protect your interests. Who looks into your eyes and reaches deep into your soul…"

At this she paused and scanned the crowd. Her eyes picked out a handsome and streetwise-looking warrior in black armour.

"Zarek. My freelance friend! Come, swashbuckle your way over. Join me! Be the hero of the day."

Mercedes slowly beckoned with one arm. Zarek, who had been leaning nonchalantly against a shopfront, chatting with other Observers, suddenly stiffened and stood up straight as he caught Mercedes' eye. Without a word, he strode up to the stage and up the steps, turning at the top to wave and smirk back to the crowd behind. Cheers came to him from those around the foot of the steps.

Ferdinal wondered how Mercedes, as a vampire, could go out freely in the light of day. "Perhaps the light in Carceron isn't bright enough to be real daylight," he thought.

"And now I make my first campaign promise," cried Mercedes, her voice rising. "To support the traders and businesspeople of this city. To show I am on your side I will open a branch of my own franchise, Transfusion, here in this square as soon as I'm elected!"

"We need to get away from here right now, before she tries to charm us!" Marvexio's voice was insistent.

He hustled Sapphire and Pumpkin away, back towards Harbinger's house. Harbinger and Marid were close behind. Ferdinal's gaze was fixed on the beautiful Mercedes on the stage; he could hardly tear himself away. Just as Harbinger pulled him away, the ogre on the stage shifted position in order to yell some insult at the crowd beneath him. For the first time, the young man in leather armour, who had been the last to mount the stage, could clearly be seen. There was no doubt who it was.

"*Oliver!*" yelled Ferdinal. As he rounded the corner of the square and the stage vanished from view, he thought he could just see the man in leather armour tilt his head in recognition and wave a hand dismissively towards him.

Then he realised. Oliver had once tried to play the roleplaying game with them. He had played an assassin character. Trying to copy his elder brother, he had named the character Fredinal. He must have been in the room just as the Summoning brought him to Carceron, along with Sapphire and Pumpkin. Now Oliver was trapped in Carceron too. He wouldn't know where he was or how to get out. Ferdinal decided he'd have to tell the others. Pumpkin would be desperately worried.

This must have been the complication with the summoning that Harbinger had been whispering about to Marid. And Oliver had materialised in a different part of the city; he hadn't appeared outside the gates with the three of them whom the summoning had targeted.

Well, there was no doubt about what to do. Ferdinal realised he'd have to rescue his little brother, too. Now it was personal.

Chapter 6

The Candidate

Harbinger led the group quickly back into Carcus Square and on to Flaxen's house in the Eternal Road. It was not far – everything in Carceron seemed to be close by. This time he did not pause to knock at the door but muttered some invocation and the door flew open at once.

Flaxen was still lying on the sofa in the front room, where he had been the previous day. His hand covered his forehead, as if he had a severe headache.

A large group swarmed into his front room, Harbinger first, for he had forced the door to open. Ferdinal entered last, still trying to work out if it really was Oliver and why on earth he would be on Mercedes' campaign team in this bizarre city.

Flaxen sat up, instantly alert. "Don't tread on Pullywuggles," he said urgently. "He's too slow to get out of the way."

Sapphire looked all round her feet but could see nothing. She looked at Flaxen. How handsome he must have been when younger. Even now, in what looked like middle age, he still had youthful looks and a smile that made her blush and look away. Flaxen seemed timeless in appearance; he could have passed himself off for almost any age. His eyes briefly met Sapphire's and she realised how unhappy he looked. She knew at once that, like her, he was a fellow candidate in an election, and he felt alone and vulnerable in facing the gruelling days ahead. In that instant, Sapphire understood some of his pressure and she knew that she in particular could help him.

Ferdinal turned to his sister and his girlfriend. "We need to talk, urgently," he whispered.

"Flaxen," said Sapphire, sweetly. "Do you have a back room? We won't be long. Need to talk."

Flaxen smiled and waved an arm past his desk towards a corridor. The three Heroes left the front room and walked along a short corridor, past some stairs and into a small, bare room at the back which might once have been a kitchen but now seemed disused.

Ferdinal sat on an empty beer barrel. "There's no easy way to say this." He hesitated. "We have to stay. I saw Oliver in the crowd. He was on that stage with Mercedes' supporters."

Pumpkin too had come to a decision. "We have to stay," she repeated, "in order to free that poor caged angel, Aspreyna. It broke my heart seeing the terrified thing in that electrified prison, with demons taunting it. I'm not leaving until we've set it free."

Sapphire ignored the obvious question about how this could be done, given that the Arcane Cage was almost as old as the city. "Flaxen needs our help," she said simply. "He's desperately unhappy. Harbinger's right, we're the only ones who can help him. I'll still be home in time for my own election, if what they say is true and time sort of folds up so everything we do here is just a blink of an eye back home."

The three Heroes looked at each other, with determination on their faces. They all had come to the same conclusion, by different means and for different reasons. But their resolve was unshakeable.

Marid put his head round the door. "Have you seen Pullywuggles?"

Pumpkin resented the interruption. "What's a pullywuggle?"

"He's a tortoise. Flaxen's familiar. He tends to hibernate for years at a time. Flaxen puts him away in a pocket dimension when he does that. He's quite old. When he started slowing down, Flaxen cast a Speed spell on him and made it permanent."

The three Heroes quickly looked around, but there was no sign of a tortoise in the back room.

Marid continued, "Now, Flaxen's tortoise is very interesting. I don't know any other spellcaster that has had one. The tortoise exemplifies wisdom and patience, but I don't think the creatures are well understood by most people. That's Flaxen all right."

"How would you get a tortoise as a familiar?" Ferdinal's curiosity was aroused.

"It depends how and where you summon them. To obtain a hawk, you might stand under a known flight path during a migration. Cats are plentiful in towns. If you really wanted a toad you could lurk near a pond. But in theory you could get any small creature if you knew where to look and could form a bond with it. There is a story that it's possible for people to turn into familiars or be turned back. It's said that some shape-changers spend their existences changing like that, through a series of painful transformations…"

The Heroes ceased conferring and went to explore the house, looking for the tortoise. When they returned to the front room, Flaxen was sitting at his desk. In the middle of the desk was a creature about the size of a cat. It was hard to spot at first, despite its size, as its brown and gold markings matched the decor of the study. Flaxen and the creature had been deep in conversation but turned as the Heroes entered the room, and Pumpkin gasped when she saw it was a large tortoise, very similar to the African Sulcata that her friend Gillian kept.

Flaxen and the tortoise continued their conversation, conversing in a strange and alarming language that was quite unintelligible. Ferdinal thought Flaxen's rendition sounded like someone trying to belch in Morse code. Pumpkin, of a more poetic turn of mind, wondered if the tortoise's speech sounded like a bittern booming in a reedbed.

The sorcerer waved to the others to sit down. "Allow me to introduce you to Pullywuggles," he said, with a gracious wave of his hand. The tortoise gazed at the newcomers steadily but made no motion of greeting.

Ferdinal's curiosity was bursting. "What were you two saying?"

Flaxen smiled his wry, lopsided smile. "When a spellcaster summons a familiar, he chooses one language he knows, which the familiar can also speak automatically. I wanted to pick one nobody else in Carceron would know. The obvious choice would be Celestial, the tongue of solars, pegasi and unicorns, but that would be considered heresy in this town. The language you heard is known as Deep Dialect, known to earth-dwelling creatures like Burrowers – very rare indeed. As to what we were saying, that's no concern of yours. The reason I chose an obscure dialect is especially so as not to reveal my ideas to other people."

"Why don't you communicate with him telepathically?" challenged Pumpkin.

"I find it tiring," admitted Flaxen. "When I started out as a sorcerer, I had boundless energy. But in recent centuries I have had to conserve my powers, to channel them into the most powerful magics in the known world." As he spoke, his brows furrowed and his relaxed manner took on sudden purpose and focus.

Harbinger rose. "I have to get back to my shop," he announced. "I can't trust those quasits for long. Flaxen will take care of you." Marid and Marvexio also rose and followed Harbinger out of the door. From the front room, the Heroes and Flaxen could hear arguing in the street. Harbinger was deep in heated debate with the door knocker again and the two of them were trading insults.

Flaxen waved his arm in a gentle arc and the noise of the street died away.

"Marid has given me the details of Mercedes' campaign launch," he said. "We've identified several of her supporters. It sounds as though Jagglespur, who runs the agency Hired Goons, is her campaign manager. From Marvexio's description it sounds as though Gortol the Ogre is involved and Captain Manacle the slave-dealer – never liked him. None of them are really first-rank people, though. Perhaps she has others behind the scenes. And there was one young man – sounded like an assassin from the description – who was on the stage today, whom we haven't identified."

"Ah, yes – about him," said Ferdinal. "That's my brother Oliver."

Flaxen seemed delighted. "Ah, well, that gives us something to go on." He didn't sound surprised. "All the same, Oliver is a strange name. He may be using another name in the city. I will find out."

Sapphire noticed how Flaxen had already changed in the hour or so that they had been at his house. When they arrived, he had been drained of energy, seemingly too weak to move, uninterested in anything other than finding his beloved tortoise. Now, he was all alert and active, eager for news and quick on the uptake. She had an idea.

"You need a makeover," she said to Flaxen. "Those gold robes and bracelets are all very well, but you need your hair tidied, your wrinkles seen to and those bags under your eyes taken out…"

Flaxen seemed amused and his eyes twinkled. "Perhaps some potions from Maelstrom would help? And I can ask Hijinx or Champrice for help. They're professionals at that sort of thing."

"Why do you want to be mayor?" asked Pumpkin, suddenly. She knew very little about this handsome ex-sorcerer. What had made him perk up like this?

Flaxen sighed and leant forward in his chair. "There's something you should know about my motivation. Mercedes and I used to be in a relationship. Hundreds of years ago. We fell out. I don't like talking about it. But I am determined not to let her become mayor."

━━

There was a long silence. Somehow Flaxen's simple words and honest emotion made him seem more human. He wasn't just the ancient undead lich that they had been led to expect. For all his age, his magic and his strange house, he seemed to be a real person after all.

Pumpkin broke the silence in her practical, businesslike way. "We want to help you, Flaxen. And we want to get out of this city as soon as your election is over. But we need some more details. You've told us who is backing Mercedes. Who do you have on your side? And what about the demons – will they be involved in the campaign? Who runs the election, you know, counts the votes?"

Ferdinal smiled to himself. His little sister seemed to be taking charge. She didn't seem to be bothered about Oliver at all and she didn't seem to be panicking about being stuck here anymore. She had grasped the job that needed doing and was evidently preparing to enjoy herself.

"The druids run the election," explained Flaxen. "You see, they were here even before Carceron became a city. The Botanical Gardens, where the druids hang out, was the original part of the city before the buildings you see today were built. That's why the demons haven't driven the druids away. They figure that somehow the druidic power, being older than the city, helps its survival. We do come under attack, you know, from paladins, solars and other obnoxious do-gooders, so anything that protects the city is valued. The druids don't care in the least about good or evil. The head druid, Ethema the half elf, will announce the result. You'd have to ask her for further details. She and her colleague Gavri run the vegetarian restaurant Seeds, next to the Botanical Gardens.

"As for who is on our side – there are the four of us in this room, plus Pullywuggles, of course. Harbinger, Marid and Marvexio the Bard can be counted on. Also, any other shopkeepers will be terrified of Mercedes because she'll drive away the tourist trade. So, Talisman the wizard who runs Looks Could Kill, Carina the librarian and Champrice, who owns the Playhouse. Some of the assassins might help – they'd be very valuable – but I'm not sure about Šapka. We'll try, anyway. Marvexio might be able to get Tinsel the singer to support me, she's very popular. And Zirca the pedlar, although he doesn't live in the city."

"If he doesn't live here, I suppose he won't be able to vote?" asked Ferdinal.

"Why not?" asked Flaxen, surprised.

"But… if he lives somewhere else, surely he votes there instead?"

"What a strange idea," laughed Flaxen. "Here in Carceron, anyone can vote in the election. Doesn't matter if they live on another plane, provided they can travel here to vote. The hotels will all be full. And you can vote as many times as you please. There are no rules here in Carceron. We like chaos. You must have noticed that?"

Pumpkin was finding this too much to take in. An election in which there were no rules! That really did open up possibilities.

"Do you have to be human to vote?" she asked.

"No, any creature can vote. Including undead, animated corpses, golems and constructs. I can even remember illusions trying to vote, but they usually can't be made to pick up a ballot paper or record their vote in any way. Of course, the ballot papers are uncontrolled too. You can stuff the ballot boxes, conjure up extra ballot boxes and stuff those. No rules." Flaxen seemed to be reminiscing about other elections he could remember from centuries earlier.

"Now, the demons. It's hard to say. Mercedes must have done some sort of deal with at least some of the Superiors. I can't believe she would have murdered the Archmayor and just left the demons' reaction to chance. Again, Šapka may be able to find out more."

"Flaxen, if there are no rules in the election, are there any laws at all in the city? Do people get arrested – are there things you can't do?" Sapphire was curious to know her rights.

"Well, don't go near the Hades Gate, it's always shut to protect the demon lords' mansions nearby in Delirium Drive," said Flaxen. "And there's officially a curfew in Carceron, you're not allowed on the streets after midnight, but that isn't really enforced. But this is a city of randomness and chaos – the law is whatever the strongest demons say it is. And Luleburgaz is the Superior in charge of that. If her guards arrest anyone, they're taken to the Court of Limbo. You can go and watch the proceedings, they're quite fun. A prisoner is brought in and all demons present in the court decide the punishment based on whim. There's no trial. Everyone who's arrested is presumed to be guilty."

"But are there no laws at all? Isn't there a parliament, a law-making body?"

"Of course there is. We're very proud of it. It's a big tourist attraction."

"Well, what does it do?" demanded Sapphire.

"It's called the Pandemonium," said Flaxen, proudly. "The word is the same in Common as it is in Demonic. As the name suggests, any demon can be a member of it. They turn up if they can be bothered to debate issues and pass laws, really strong, evil ones. But we're also chaotic, so nobody can be bothered to obey or enforce them. It's simply a matter of whoever is most powerful sets the laws."

Pumpkin felt that they were back where they had started with this bit of the conversation. Perhaps she would go and watch a session at the Pandemonium to see if it really did look like a proper parliament.

"The Festival of Pandemonium is being held in a couple of days' time," added Flaxen. "It's held, well, as often as the demons want, but about once every year. The Pandemonium building is likely to be the centre of events, as usual."

Ferdinal tried to pull together some sort of plan. "So, we want to see the druids to understand how they conduct the election," he said. "And we'll want to see all your key supporters, give them targets for how many voters they have to bring out to vote for you. Then there's the thieves and assassins, they could be crucial as they already have networks of people they can use."

"All the entertainers could be useful," suggested Pumpkin. "Marvexio, Champrice, Tinsel and others. It will add some razzmatazz to the campaign. They can help campaign in restaurants and bars and casinos. We can get all the tourists to vote! And we'll need campaign merchandise – banners, clothing, etc. I suppose gold is your colour, Flaxen? Where's best to buy apparel in Carceron?"

"There's a big arcade of clothing shops at Nameless in the Southwest District," said Flaxen. "They sell all sorts of brands. Browse around. And yes, definitely a gold colour scheme."

"We'll need to keep an eye on the demons," added Sapphire. "See what they're up to. And Mercedes, try and find out what sneaky schemes she's pulling."

"All that – and more," put in Pumpkin. "Above all, we need a plan for how we're going to mobilise large numbers of votes. And what magic is needed to do it. What's the population of Carceron, Flaxen? Demons and people, all combined."

Flaxen pondered. "Perhaps as much as fifty thousand in all," he said. "It's not a large city, but densely populated."

"And how many votes get cast at an election?" asked Pumpkin, thinking that even with a high turnout it should be straightforward to mobilise a majority.

Flaxen smiled. "For an election like this where both sides are really motivated? I should think – several million votes. As I said, you vote as often as you can at election time."

———

Pumpkin was shocked to realise the scale of the task ahead of them. But it could only be tackled one step at a time. She took out the map of Carceron that Harbinger had given her. Sure enough, there was Nameless, down a narrow street near the Destiny Guild of thieves. That would be a good place to start. She looked at the back of the map, and there was a guide to the restaurants and bars. The perky tone of the guide was in stark contrast to the grisly descriptions. It listed the following establishments:

The Abyss (Hightower Square) – A bar run by demons, for demons, with fun for everyone. The bar has many tiers going down into the ground, but nobody knows how many levels there are in all. Renowned for its monthly Beldark Baiting nights. Customers are advised not to sit at tables reserved for Demon Princes.

Acid House (Southwest District) – The oldest inn in the city, with tall-backed wooden snugs and an intimate atmosphere. Can get rough, and strangers are not always welcome. Serves strong ales and its own-brand whisky, known as Acid. A five-drink minimum is the rule on most nights.

Eye to Eye (Hades Gate) – A cosy and small gourmet hangout where diners pick body parts off a moving conveyor. The latest idea in nouveau cuisine. The management has a policy of serving 100% recycled food, but despite this it is not considered good etiquette to cast a Purify spell here.

The Inferno (Hightower Square) – Hand-cooked steaks flame-grilled before your eyes. The proprietor, Mylar, has made a reputation for only picking the freshest and plumpest ingredients from the slave markets. Advance booking recommended via Quasicom.

The Irresistible Dancehall (Central Square) – The place to be in town on a Saturday – everyone goes here. No food served, but top-quality music with a magic mouth singing the latest songs from The Horde. Tables are set around the edges, with the dance floor in the centre. Floorshows and wandplay can be seen on four small, raised stages near the corners of the hall.

Seeds (Botanical Gardens) – It's strange to find a top-class vegetarian restaurant run by druids in such a carnivorous city. But Seeds is famous for the variety of its cooking and its finest-quality ingredients, many of which are stolen from the neighbouring Botanical Gardens.

YouChoose (Hades Gate) – The demons' favourite. Diners select their living victims from the aquarium or from the cages in one corner of the restaurant. Other produce is supplied by leading caterers Tentacle and you can interrogate your meal before eating using Speak with Animals or Speak with the Slain. In terms of drink, the restaurant is famed for its list of reds, ranging from vintage "O" to premier cru "AB negative".

There was even an ominous postscript: "While in town, be sure to make time to visit one of our fantastic casinos: The Deck of Delusions, The Fates and Electrum. You won't want to leave!".

While Pumpkin was reading the guide with mounting horror, Sapphire asked a practical question. "Flaxen, what currency do you use here? We'll need a lot of money for campaign expenses."

The old sorcerer smiled again. "It's dangerous to carry too much money in a city like this," he said. "But here is a purse of gold and silver pieces. This will be enough for any minor tips and bribes. For bigger costs like hotels, gambling, drinking and buying gear at Nameless, I'll lend you this."

Flaxen reached into a drawer of his desk and brought out a gold medallion on a chain. It was glowing brightly. He gave this and the little purse to Pumpkin.

"It's a Medallion of Credit," he explained. "It draws on a reserve of gold deposited in my name at the Interplanar Bank. Everyone in Carceron uses these for larger transactions. Normally only I can use my own medallion, but as I am lending it to you three, you will be able to use it too. Right now, it is glowing because it's fully charged. As you use it to make purchases, its glow will diminish until it goes dull in hue and has to be topped up by the cashier at the bank. Only I can do that. I have other medallions I can use, too. Each one holds only a finite amount of credit."

"There's no time to lose," cried Sapphire. "We need flags, banners, hats, anything gold in colour. It doesn't need Flaxen's name on it. If it's big, bright and the right colour, we can use it. Let's go, team!"

She leapt to her feet. The idea of a shopping trip in a strange city using something akin to a stranger's credit card was simply too good to be true.

Ferdinal and Pumpkin grinned and got up too. They had to begin somewhere and they could see that the impulsive Sapphire had a retail itch to scratch.

"We'd better be going," said Ferdinal to Flaxen. "Thanks for the money. Shall we meet you back here?"

"I'll meet you this evening at The Irresistible Dancehall," said Flaxen. "Everyone goes there. You can't avoid it. No choice, no save, as they say."

Chapter 7
Shopping Spree

The three Heroes left Flaxen's house, being careful not to tread on Pullywuggles. As they walked along the Eternal Road back towards Carcus Square, Ferdinal became aware of someone following them. Looking back, he saw about fifty feet behind them the same urchin who had thrown a stone at them earlier, when Harbinger had first led them through the streets.

"You're Perancia!" he shouted. "You're following us. Why? Who sent you?"

The ragged street girl stopped. Sapphire and Pumpkin turned round to face her too. Perancia hesitated. The Eternal Road was a dead end; you could only get out at the western end by the Carcus Gate, and the Heroes she was following were between her and an escape route. She knew she couldn't fight three of them, either. She could try to run, but she thought Ferdinal could probably catch her.

Perancia decided to confess. "All right, I was following you," she said, with a belligerent flick of her head. "Well, what about it?"

"Who sent you?" demanded Ferdinal, advancing towards her.

Again, Perancia considered trying to flee, but thought better of it. These three didn't look dangerous.

"I was paid to," she said, in a quieter voice. "Montrachet paid me. I often work for him and Lamar. They gave me… five silver pieces," she added, exaggerating the amount to try to start a bidding war.

"How would you like to work with us? You know, join the winning team. We pay in gold, not silver," coaxed Sapphire. As Perancia still hesitated, she added with a stroke of genius, "We're just going to buy clothes at Nameless. If you show us the best places to go, we'll get you something there as a present."

Sapphire had found the way to Perancia's loyalties. Anything valuable and shiny, and so what if it meant ditching her current employer? Relaxing at last, Perancia walked along with the Heroes towards Carcus Square.

"There are some top shops at Nameless," she said, with the confident air of a tour guide. "How much are you looking to spend? Each brand is in a different store at Nameless. Dark Celestial is the most exclusive. You want that?"

"We're looking for anything gold in colour," said Pumpkin. "So Dark Celestial doesn't sound right. We want clothing plus banners and flags and so on. What are the other shops?"

"Druids all shop at Natural One," said Perancia, knowledgably. "But that stuff all looks scruffy and ragged. You don't want that. There's an underwear shop that sells naughty things – that's called Planar Shift. And a new store is about to open selling demonic apparel, that's Junta Wears Angel."

"We want more general clothing, not underwear," said Sapphire sternly. "Don't you have clothes stores there with a wider range?"

"Oh, yes," said Perancia. "There's Divinity by Fabric8. That's a sweatshop in the Southwest District that supplies direct to Nameless."

"I don't want to buy clothes from a sweatshop," said Sapphire angrily. "That's unfair to the workers – it only encourages exploitation."

Perancia looked at her uncomprehendingly. "They don't have *workers*," she said, amazed. "Workers have to be paid. They use zombies. Those don't wear out, and they can work all day and all night without getting tired. Fabric8 only ever use zombies – they say it's more ethical, whatever that means."

Sapphire was temporarily lost for words. Pumpkin, never a fan of shopping, had been thinking about Perancia's earlier information. "If it was Montrachet who was paying you, Perancia," she said, "I'd like to go and see him and demand to know what he's up to. Where would I find him?"

"Nearby – probably at the Destiny Guild," said Perancia, listlessly. Her mind was still on shopping. Perhaps Sapphire would let her buy something for herself at Necrotic Splurge. Their slogan ("Pure Indigence") appealed to Perancia's wayward mind.

Then Perancia stopped in mid-stride. "Yes, what is it now?" she asked impatiently. The remark was addressed to nobody in particular. She seemed to be having a conversation with herself in the street. "No, CT, I won't do it. That's a stupid idea."

Perancia carried on walking again. That conversation seemed to be over. Ferdinal, Pumpkin and Sapphire hurried after her. "What just happened there?" asked Ferdinal.

"Oh, that was my stupid patron, CT. Crixus Telmarine. He makes such wacky suggestions sometimes," said Perancia, crossly.

"What do you mean patron, is he your boss?" asked Sapphire. "We didn't hear anyone talking."

"He speaks to me in my head," explained Perancia. "He's supposed to guide me. I'm learning to be a warlock and he's my patron. But we don't like each other very much."

Ferdinal found it extraordinary that some powerful spellcaster or other-worldly being took the trouble to coach a reluctant urchin who didn't even like him. "What did he ask you to do?"

"He said I should murder all three of you and turn the bodies over to Rent-a-Zombie." For once, Perancia looked sheepish. She felt the idea needed justification: "They do pay good money for corpses, providing there's nothing missing. But it's a stupid idea. Why would I kill you when you're about to buy me an expensive present?"

Now it was Ferdinal's turn to be left speechless by the urchin warlock. Pumpkin had had enough of this dirty little would-be assassin. "I'm off to the Destiny Guild to find this Montrachet," she said, with determination. "I'll catch up with you later."

"Is it safe to go alone?" began Ferdinal, as Pumpkin strode away. But the question was redundant, as his sister was clearly determined to go her own way.

———

The shopfront of the Destiny Guild was not at all encouraging. It looked like a very basic takeaway food outlet. The customer area had a couple of hard wooden chairs for those waiting for appointments. A potted plant stood in a corner, although Pumpkin thought it looked artificial. There was a counter, barred off from the customer section by a metal grille, more like the security arrangements one might see at a bank that felt at risk from robberies. Instead of a food menu on display, painted on the wall was a list of services available and the fees in gold pieces. Some services were vague ("Information gathering"), others alarmingly specific ("Corpse disposal" and a range of prices according to body size and number of limbs). At the foot of the list was the single word "Murder" and a note that the fee for this was subject to negotiation. As if to put any fears to rest that the establishment feared reprisal from the authorities, the small print below the price list explained, "For your comfort and safety, the Destiny Guild enjoys Demonic Immunity."

So that was okay, then.

Behind the grille was a thin, nervous-looking boy of about her own age reading a scroll. He was dressed in leather armour but was wearing a pointy wizard hat. He looked up at Pumpkin with large eyes, with the depth and rich colour of garnets.

"Welcome to the Destiny Guild, professional problem eliminators. How may we help you?" he smiled, eyeing up the potential customer as he spoke.

"Er… are you a wizard?" blurted out Pumpkin. She hadn't meant to say that. Somehow, the young man was not what she expected. The surroundings also seemed incongruous. Was this really a famous guild of thieves? And this young man with the large eyes and the well-trimmed goatee beard seemed too, well, *nice* to be a professional villain.

The young man twitched and seemed deeply hurt by the question. He took a moment to compose himself and did not immediately reply. Pumpkin could not help feeling that, for a city so dominated by evil, a lot of people seemed to have over-sensitive feelings.

Pumpkin returned to her original purpose. "I'm looking for Montrachet," she said, aggressively.

"That's me!" cried the boy, sounding even more surprised. "Nobody ever asks for me. What's the matter?" he asked, instantly on his guard.

Pumpkin had approached the guild headquarters angry and determined to find out who was following her and had expected to find a den of unshaven lowlifes playing cards in some dingy back room as their lair. But the guild was laid out much more like an ordinary shop and this Montrachet seemed like a pleasant, rather shy young man – not at all like a villain who instructed urchins to follow victims around. Her wrath lost its impetus. She felt a little foolish.

"Er… I've got some information for you," she said, racking her brains for some way out of this absurd situation. "I can't talk now. Perancia sent me. Is there somewhere nearby we can meet late this evening?"

Montrachet remained suspicious. In Carceron, strangers who turned up at the Thieves' Guild without appointments were never to be trusted.

"Nearest bar is Acid House," he replied, eyeing Pumpkin carefully. His hand stole to the eggshell grenade of dust the guild kept under the counter, in case he needed cover in which to flee.

"See you there later today," said Pumpkin vaguely, desperate to get out of the shop, away from this extraordinary situation. To prevent further discussion, she opened the door and stepped briskly back into the alley, heading for the shopping complex, Nameless.

———

When Pumpkin reached Nameless, she was amazed by the variety of different stores. It was like going to a huge out-of-town shopping mall at home, except that here in Carceron the merchandise was more exotic and the people simply bizarre. Were they even people?

Most of the shoppers were certainly humanoids of some sort, of human size or similar. Pumpkin saw creatures that resembled illustrations of goblins from children's books. Some lumbering tough folks must be orcs, she decided, from the way their teeth stuck out and they seemed to be quarrelling with each other over the clothes for sale at a primitive shop called Hide Me, which sold animal skins. There were plenty of humans, certainly, rich and poor alike. A few seemed to be stumbling like automatons, staring ahead of them and moving with purpose, yet only partly aware of their surroundings. Pumpkin gasped. These were zombies. And it looked as though they were being sent about the place delivering messages or refilling shelves with new stock!

Pumpkin found Ferdinal, Sapphire and Perancia at a general store that sold a wide variety of products. The shop was optimistically called Wish, with signs on the wall explaining that all goods on sale were sourced and displayed instantaneously by the proprietor using a bespoke spell tailored to each customer.

"Oh, hi, Pumpkin," said Ferdinal, trying to disguise in his voice the relief he felt at seeing his sister. "Look, this city isn't exactly safe. I think we should stick together as a group as much as possible."

"Nervous, are you, Henry?" teased Sapphire. "Worried that some goblin will run off with you?"

Perancia giggled, enjoying as always watching an argument unfold without having had to go to the trouble of starting it herself.

"Call me Ferdinal," snapped her boyfriend. "While we're in this weird place I'm going to stay in character. And as a paladin, *I'm* the one who's supposed to see that *you're* all okay!"

Pumpkin noticed that the others were all carrying bags from various stores. For a moment, she regretted not joining them on the shopping trip. No, she told herself. She must be firm in her purpose. There was a job to get on with and then they could all go safely home.

The Heroes felt a rush of wind next to them as they stood outside the storefront of Wish. Perancia took a step back, as if by instinct. "That'll be one of the Invisible Servants," she said confidently, as if showing off her streetwise knowledge. "You mustn't get in their way. They're always in a hurry on some errand. Of course, it's hard to avoid them if you can't see them."

"So, how come *you* can see them, if they're invisible?" sneered Sapphire.

"Extravision," said Perancia, smugly. "CT gave it to me. It only works for invisible things that are very close."

Ferdinal wondered whether darling CT would equally capriciously take that power away if Perancia continued to be so rude and offhanded to her patron. But he kept the thought to himself.

"What have you bought?" asked Pumpkin, twitching at the bags Sapphire was carrying.

"Wait 'til we get back to Flaxen's!" grinned Sapphire. "When he gets this makeover, it will give him his biggest shock for centuries."

"Most of the items for sale in shops in Carceron are cursed," warned Perancia, suddenly jealous of all the purchases.

"Why's that?" asked Ferdinal, scornfully. "Who wants to pay money for cursed items?"

"The tourists generally pay anyway," retorted Perancia, indignantly. She felt that her expertise was being challenged. "But the people who live in Carceron, whether they're human, or demons, or whatever, are chaotic, or evil, or both, right? They're not going to pay for goods unless they're forced to. So, the shopkeepers put curses on most items in the stores. When the customer pays, they remove the curse and the item can safely be taken away. If an item's only worth a few iron drabs, they might not bother with a curse."

"Have you ever had one of these curses?" asked Pumpkin, full of curiosity.

"Just once," said Perancia, in a serious tone. She lowered her voice to a confidential whisper. "I took a velvet cloak once. As soon as I was outside the shop, the cloak vanished back onto its display shelf and I was enveloped in slimy tentacles, which tickled me for ten minutes. I was writhing around on the floor, quite helpless with laughing. Everyone saw me."

Perancia scowled as the others burst out laughing themselves at the thought of it. She desperately sought to turn the laughter against other people.

"The chests at the Interplanar Bank are trapped, too," she confided. "One of Šapka's wizard cronies tried to dispel the magic to get the real chest back so she could open it. What happened was that the real chest reappeared in the bank, but the wizard was immediately teleported to where the chest had been, in the Ethereal Plane. That was about six months ago. I think she's still there."

As if on cue, the party came upon a booth at Nameless that seemed to be a small bank, or currency converter. A sign below the counter showed various standard rates of exchange:

Electrum Exchange		
1 Platinum Piece	*=*	*10 Gold Pieces*
1 Gold Piece	*=*	*10 Silver Pieces*
1 Silver Piece	*=*	*10 Copper Pieces*
1 Copper Piece	*=*	*10 Iron Drabs*
The Superiors are pleased to inform visitors that Electrum Pieces are not legal tender in Carceron		

"What are iron drabs?" asked Ferdinal. "I've never heard of those. They can't be worth much."

"You can buy simple necessities with them," said Perancia dismissively. "A handful of iron drabs will buy some powdered soup or a scrap of torn vellum that's been scrawled on one side. But mostly iron drabs are used to taunt people. Because they're so worthless, they are promised as wages for some low-grade tasks, or as a paltry reward for an unwanted service. That's demons for you."

Pumpkin did not have long to find out what had been bought. Everyone was in a hurry to dash back to Flaxen's house in the Eternal Road. When they arrived, they found Harbinger and Carina there. Perancia, hearing Harbinger's voice from inside the house, fled down the street and could not be coaxed back. "Catch ya later," she called, and was gone.

Harbinger's face was solemn. "We have to start with a very unusual ritual," he said. "It doesn't even have a formal arcane name, but it's known as a De-Liching Ceremony. It brings back a sliver of Flaxen's former life force from centuries ago, so that he is no longer wholly undead. He will become recognisably human once more in his mind, but his body will remain in the state of indefinite suspended animation that is common to the undead."

Carina's face was also serious. She was present to help Harbinger with the ceremony, but dreaded to think of the consequences if it went wrong. Would Flaxen turn into a chaotic monster who would unleash his powerful magic on all present? The Heroes sensed her unease and stood watching. Were they to help?

"In case you're wondering," said Harbinger grimly, "no, I have not done this ceremony before. I don't know anyone who has. By the way, the rituals that Flaxen used to become an undead lich weren't the soul-devouring, evil ones that some spellcasters use. That's why Flaxen is still recognisably human and amiable, not some skeletal fiend. He prolonged his life but didn't take on extra powers. Even so, we are trying to reverse a major metamorphosis of the soul. That might not be pretty."

Flaxen was the only one present who looked completely unconcerned. He sat in an upright chair in the middle of the living room, reading a leather-bound book. Sapphire thought he had the air of someone waiting to have his hair cut, rather than an all-powerful undead sorcerer waiting for some amateur to tamper with his life force.

"Can we stay?" asked Ferdinal. "I'd like to see how it works."

"You can watch if you like," said Harbinger, still in the same tone of voice. "But sit well back at the end of the room, and whatever happens, don't say anything. I've already had to shut Pullywuggles outside to stop him interfering."

Sapphire thought to herself that any arcane ritual that could be thrown off course by a pet tortoise did not stand much chance of success, but she did not say it aloud.

"We can do the candidate's makeover using your goods from Nameless as soon as the De-Liching is done," suggested Carina.

Flaxen looked up from his book and spoke for the first time. "Oh yes, that reminds me," he said placidly, as if his mind was on other things. "I'll need my Medallion of Credit back, if you've finished with it."

Ferdinal handed it back, then hastily took his seat with Pumpkin and Sapphire at the end of the room.

Harbinger had arranged a row of components along a side table. Carina brought a small brazier into the room and set it beside the table. The brazier was already alight and giving off smoke, but the smell was sweet and heavy, as if it were burning fresh flowers rather than coals. Carina did not seem to find the metal brazier either heavy or hot. She lifted it with the casual air of one rearranging the furniture prior to a big social gathering.

Harbinger began to chant. It sounded like a speech of some kind, but the Heroes did not understand a word of what was said. At first the chant was low and continuous. Occasionally Harbinger would break into some sort of catechism, throwing questions at Carina, who would answer them in the same low voice, in the same incomprehensible tongue, while performing other tasks with the utensils on the table. She was breaking up cubes of some sort of combustible material at intervals, throwing the dust onto the brazier, which produced momentary fragments of brilliant rainbow colours when she did so.

Flaxen continued reading his book, looking bored and oblivious to what was going on around him.

After about fifteen minutes of this, Harbinger also focused on the items on the table. His chanting continued, but it sounded more like a peroration, building up in tempo and urgency. Suddenly, Harbinger picked up a bowl from a row of four on the table and upturned its contents over Flaxen's head, still chanting as he did so. A shower of tiny golden particles rained down on Flaxen's head. At this point the Heroes noticed that he was no longer intent upon his book but was gazing fixedly ahead, as if in a trance.

Carina took up the chant, as if adding a verse of her own, while Harbinger was silent for a moment. Then she, too, emptied a bowl over Flaxen's head, enveloping him in a fine red mist, as if the bowl had contained powder paint.

Then Harbinger and Carina both chanted in unison, each saying the same words and the Heroes could make out the name "Flaxen" in the chant. The man himself still sat motionless in the chair, oblivious to all around him.

Harbinger and Carina each took one of the remaining bowls and emptied its contents over Flaxen, abruptly ceasing their chanting at the same moment. There was a brief flash of light, as if a firework had been ignited in the room. The brazier at once stopped smouldering and the light from its coals vanished. Then Harbinger and Carina stepped back.

Flaxen's book fell to the floor. Pumpkin, in her mind, counted the seconds as a strange silence fell on the room. She felt desperate for someone to say or do something, anything, to break the terrible hush, which seemed to hang heavy over everyone, stifling them all.

After about twenty seconds, Flaxen rose slowly from the chair. His limbs seemed stiff and unfamiliar, as if he had woken from a long sleep. He turned and looked at Harbinger. The Heroes could see his expression clearly. Flaxen was actually smiling. His book lay forgotten on the floor.

"Where's Souzira?" he asked.

Harbinger gaped at him. For once he seemed at a loss for words. Carina gave a little sob and put her hand to her mouth.

Sapphire was watching Flaxen's face. His voice had sounded more human, less artificial. It was as if his mind had previously been working on some other problem and only partially devoted to his current conversation, but now it was back to normal, how a voice should be.

Harbinger collected his wits and made an effort to reply. "She runs the Maelstrom Potions shop now. In Hightower Square, Flaxen. I'm sure you must know it?"

"I do indeed." Flaxen's voice was stronger, authoritative, but soft and friendly at the same time. Pumpkin was looking into his eyes. Previously colourless and languid, like those of his old tortoise, they were now bright and dancing. The pupils of his eyes briefly flickered gold in colour.

"You remember your campaign managers, Flaxen?" Harbinger seemed to be probing the old sorcerer, testing that his memory still worked. "They have bought some material for your campaign. Would you like to try it?"

"Of course."

Harbinger nodded to the Heroes. The ceremony seemed to be over. Nobody seemed to know if it had been a success and there was no summing-up or discussion. Perhaps, thought Ferdinal, it was rude to do so while the subject of the ritual, Flaxen, was there in the room in front of them.

"Who's Souzira?" blurted out Pumpkin. She had not heard the name before and yet it seemed so important.

"Souzira is my girlfriend." Flaxen seemed surprised at the question. "She ought to be here."

Harbinger and Carina exchanged glances.

"But, Flaxen," said Carina quietly, "she broke up with you. You haven't spoken to her for nearly three hundred years. Don't you remember?"

Chapter 8

Working the Streets

It took some time to establish that Flaxen's memory was essentially unimpaired but that he had certain blind spots about personal matters. He seemed very quick to grasp the idea that Mercedes was in Carceron once more and must be stopped in her plans. The Heroes all noticed a rising level of energy and determination in the sorcerer, as if the ceremony had stripped away decades if not centuries of inaction and restored to him at least some of the vigour of his younger days. Flaxen responded with eagerness and surety when questions were raised. He was very keen on the idea of standing for election as Mayor of Carceron in order to thwart Mercedes.

"I shall look forward to seeing her again," he said, narrowing his eyes and speaking very quietly. "There is unfinished business to settle. And we must protect the city."

This turned out to be the cue to begin Flaxen's makeover. The old sorcerer took to the process with great glee, proving at times to be as vain as a peacock and as insecure and skittish as a young kitten. Sapphire produced hair products and make-up from the shopping at Nameless. Flaxen needed no help applying gels, powders and unguents. He seemed very proficient in the use of every kind of make-up. Flaxen even conjured up a disembodied but withered hand in midair, to pass him products or apply them in hard-to-reach places, while he talked. He addressed the hand as "Claw", but it made no remark in reply, silently carrying out his requests.

"We need as many of the traders on side as possible," he mused. "They all talk to their customers and it doesn't matter if the customers are local or not – they should vote anyway. Claw, I need more Yellow Mold Paste, my teeth are still far too dull. Do we have anyone on Mercedes' team that might talk to us? Claw, bigger tassels on my slippers; there are some in the drawer, there. No point trying to corrupt the druids, they've seen it all before and we don't have anything they want."

Sapphire wondered if Claw would obey telepathic instructions and the old sorcerer was simply showing off by talking to it aloud. And Flaxen did seem very vain. "Probably due to his dragon ancestry," she thought to herself.

———

That evening, Pumpkin found herself back in the Southwest District. Harbinger had lent her Redwing for the evening. The micro-dragon, smaller and lighter than a cat, lay across her shoulders, with his head close to her right ear and his tail hanging down on the other side of her head. Pumpkin found his silent presence reassuring. She could sense that the little creature was immensely watchful and alert, and she felt she could rely on him to warn her of any impending danger.

Redwing also proved to be an excellent guide and navigator. Pumpkin had no need for a map or directions to Acid House. The little dragon would occasionally advise her to "turn right here" or "watch out for the guards coming round that corner". Redwing never spoke actual words. Pumpkin could simply hear each sentence appear in her mind as a thought or instruction – exactly as if the dragon had spoken aloud. She found that it would accept her responses in the same way: she only had to think her answer and the dragon understood it. Slowly, Pumpkin began to realise how strong the bond was between a spellcaster and their familiar. There was an invisible mental link, with each sensing the others' thoughts and needs.

Pumpkin was angry with herself. She should have been firmer with Montrachet earlier. He just hadn't been what she expected as the frontman of a Thieves' Guild. That little pointy beard, the slightly lost look in his deep, dark eyes and those bewitching dimples that he had... No. She must not allow herself to be distracted like this. Montrachet was young but he was yet another of the villains in Carceron, just like all the others.

Acid House was different from most of the buildings in Carceron. It was in a street much more in keeping with a medieval city, with old wooden buildings overhanging a narrow alley. Acid House had no windows but a black metal sign hung over the alley to show customers where to head.

Pumpkin entered through a narrow door. Inside, the inn was a large single room and it was very full. The atmosphere was dense and cloudy, so it was hard to see more than ten or fifteen feet. There were tall, wooden-backed snugs all around the edges of the inn, at which groups of dark-cloaked figures were clearly plotting conspiracies or dividing the spoils following their plots. The middle of the room was full of drinkers standing up, chatting furtively in groups, and Pumpkin found that many of the customers were much taller than she was, blocking her view yet further.

Redwing was never at fault. He guided Pumpkin by instinct to a snug on the left side of the inn. Here, Montrachet was seated, with a pitcher of murky liquid and two empty glasses in front of him on the table. The nervous wizard still had the bewildered look about him, but Pumpkin saw that, like most residents of Carceron, he was very aware of everything going on around him.

She sat down opposite him in the snug, with Redwing still coiled around her neck like a colourful scarf.

"I see you've brought a friend." Montrachet did not seem entirely pleased.

Pumpkin wondered if he had some fear of tiny dragons, or perhaps Montrachet was worried that the dragon would pass secrets back to its master. She decided to brush the matter off.

"It's thanks to Redwing that I found you," she said. "It's so dank and misty in here, I don't know how anyone can find their companions."

Montrachet allowed himself a slight smile and his dimples appeared fleetingly on his cheeks. "All the regulars in the inn develop an immunity to the haze. That's one way we keep outsiders away."

"What are the other ways – or shouldn't I ask?" Pumpkin couldn't help saying.

"Don't you know? We slit their throats and sell the bodies to Rent-a-Zombie."

Pumpkin felt that this was not really helping her cause. "I've been talking to Perancia," she said directly. "She said you paid her to follow us. Why?"

Montrachet seemed neither surprised nor embarrassed by the question. "It's just routine," he said. "New visitors to town, we often have to find out if they're rich or famous, then report to Šapka. He likes to know about anyone who hasn't visited the city before. Perancia often does work like that for us."

"How did you come to do a job like this, anyway? I thought you seemed more like a wizard?"

Montrachet ignored the question and squared his lip. All of a sudden, he looked purposeful and businesslike. "You said you had some information for me," he said. "You said Perancia sent you. We pay for information if it's valuable."

Redwing shifted position on Pumpkin's shoulders and hissed softly as a warning.

"Let me pour you a drink," said Montrachet, more diplomatically.

"Ooh, is it Pink? Yes, please!"

"No, you can't have Pink at Acid House. Their most popular drink is Ochre, but I prefer Vermillion, the taste is smoother. Try some."

Pumpkin sampled the dark, swirling liquid that Montrachet poured into her goblet. It was indeed smooth, but in an insinuating, probing way, which seemed to root out secrets as it suffused her body. The sort of refreshment that you would give to a suspect or informer, to prompt them to confess all their knowledge without prompting.

"Hey! Don't think I'm going to betray friends and work for you just cos you give me some watered-down poison!" Pumpkin hiccoughed loudly.

Montrachet paused, looking hurt rather than furtive. Once again, Pumpkin reflected that Carceron people, despite their murderous lifestyles and casual disregard for good and evil, often seemed quite sensitive souls. She wondered how someone like Montrachet had got caught up with thieves in the first place.

"I don't know what you're so angry about," he said, his garnet-coloured eyes opening even wider. "Haven't you realised, this is the way things are in Carceron? It's our equilibrium and it works. You have loyalties and bosses, yes, but when you have a task to do, you do it by any means necessary. Friend or foe, you treat both the same. Vermillion doesn't betray your secrets. It just helps you be yourself."

Dimly, through her Vermillion haze, Pumpkin began to understand the city. Montrachet wasn't an evil spirit as such. He was just conditioned by a city that was so far removed from normal social behaviour that he saw nothing wrong with treating someone so shabbily. Even someone he cared about… or did he?

At this moment, two strangers approached their table through the haze. The elder one was wearing elaborate, fine clothes, with large rings on his fingers. The other, a young man about Montrachet's age, had untidy, raven-black hair and scornful, piercing eyes which made you think they could sense your every weakness and would profit from the knowledge.

"He's here, Lamar," said the older.

"Clearly a man of few words," thought Pumpkin, as the man slipped away again through the crowd.

"Didn't know you had a girlfriend, Monty," grinned Lamar. He cast an inspecting gaze at Pumpkin, who sat straight up and ignored his look.

"This is Lamar," said Montrachet, wincing at the unwelcome nickname. "We share a flat. Er… I don't know your name," he added lamely.

Pumpkin felt an immediate desire to help him and back him up. "Names aren't important," she said, with brisk determination. She turned to Lamar. "Who was your bejewelled pal?"

"You haven't met Revlyn, then," said Lamar, scornfully. He seemed to be evaluating whether to believe her. "If you really didn't know, he's the Head of the Thieves' Guild. Monty – Šapka's been looking for you."

With that, Lamar ambled off. Redwing settled down again, resting his head on Pumpkin's shoulder blades, as if to nap. He knew she would be safe now until it was time for him to lead her back to Flaxen's house.

Montrachet finished his drink. "I really ought to go," he said, apologetically. Šapka might be head of a different guild, but if he had requested Montrachet's presence, it was akin to a royal summons.

"Me too," said Pumpkin, getting up to go. But she left her Vermillion unfinished on the table.

As they went their separate ways outside Acid House, Pumpkin wondered again why Montrachet had joined the Thieves' Guild. She decided to ask him. But this was not the moment, standing in the alleyway.

"Er… can we meet up again?" she asked, feeling slightly

foolish as the words came out. "Somewhere more neutral this time, like The Irresistible Dancehall? There's lots I want to ask you."

Montrachet gave his faint half smile, once again showing the hint of dimples on his cheeks. "Of course," he said. "I'd like that. But in Carceron hardly anywhere is neutral!"

———

While Pumpkin had been out at Acid House, back at Harbinger's house Sapphire had been sorting through the various colourful merchandise from Nameless. Ferdinal and Harbinger had been coaching Flaxen on how to behave on the campaign trail and what to say to people he met.

"It's no good incinerating Mercedes' supporters," Ferdinal explained patiently. "She'll only retaliate, and before we know it, half the city's residents will be dead. That won't do the traders any good."

Flaxen was sitting in a chair opposite, his head bowed, listening intently. Harbinger tried not to smile as the young paladin trained the old sorcerer.

"You have to identify your voters and prepare to mobilise them on election day," Ferdinal went on. "Only occasionally do you meet someone who is genuinely undecided that you need to persuade."

"I doubt we'll meet many of those in Carceron," put in Harbinger.

"Won't it be obvious that Mercedes is unsuitable?" asked Flaxen quietly.

"We can't rely on that. A lot of people here probably don't remember her," said Harbinger. "She hasn't been in the city for about fifty years and a lot of her evil work was a lot longer ago. People here may be chaotic, but many of them aren't evil."

"Vote for chaos, not evil," announced Sapphire brightly, looking up from her piles of gold tinsel. "That's not a bad slogan. We can use that."

Flaxen looked up. He seemed captivated by Sapphire's suggestion. "It's true. People in this city don't like vampires, not because they do bad things but because they live by rules and hierarchy. Everyone here lives for themselves, they like freedom, they take what they can get. But they don't like to be bossed about. Even the demons let people do their own thing; they just destroy a few now and again for pleasure. Vampires are evil, but they're not chaotic."

"I see, a sort of live and let live," mused Ferdinal. "But turned into a die and let die philosophy."

"It's our equilibrium," said Flaxen simply. "And it works. It's a way of life and we have to protect it."

Pumpkin returned, escorted by Redwing. Harbinger was relieved to see her but didn't want to embarrass her by saying so.

"I'm exhausted," sighed Pumpkin, flopping down onto a chair. She would explain to the others later what had happened. Redwing swooped nimbly down onto the floor and hid under her chair.

"I've made up a sort of bedroom for you all," said Harbinger, taking charge as usual and indicating a side room. "It's not very comfortable, but we can sort out a more permanent thing tomorrow."

Sapphire shuddered. She didn't like the idea that she might be in this awful city for any extended period.

"Get some sleep," said Flaxen kindly. "You're probably tired anyway after all this. I can put you to sleep magically if you like—"

"No, Flaxen," interrupted Harbinger. The old sorcerer's eyes were flashing and he was just beginning to wave his hands. "You'll have plenty of chances to do that on election day."

———

A strange procession made its way into Hightower Square the following morning. The square was already busy, as the shops did not seem to have regular opening hours, so there were plenty of passers-by and traders whose attention was diverted by the newcomers.

At the head of the group strolled Flaxen. He was dressed in gold clothing that seemed to shimmer and catch the light, so that it hurt the eyes to watch him for long. He was smiling and waving to well-wishers that he recognised in the crowd.

Behind him walked Harbinger, who had arranged for a number of key supporters to place themselves along the route, to take it in turns to cheer and wave. Harbinger was more than usually alert, his eyes constantly sweeping the crowd for dangers, enemy spellcasters, low-flying demons or hired heavies. His vigilance was nothing compared to Redwing, who sat on his shoulder, silent as ever, but with eyes expanding and contracting, glowing and darkening as he raked the horizon for hostiles.

Marvexio and Zirca were on either side of Harbinger. The bard was playing a tune on his flute, attempting to copy a popular song by The Horde, called "Cold Flush". Zirca the pedlar maintained a steady banter with everyone he recognised, playfully teasing them, pretending to threaten them, smiling and laughing, or telling witty one-line jokes that were part of his normal patter. Harbinger had paid him to campaign, so he would give it his best.

Ferdinal, Sapphire and Pumpkin formed a third row. Ferdinal in the middle held a large banner, with Flaxen's name in large gold capitals. Underneath was Sapphire's slogan, "Vote for chaos, not evil". Much more compelling than Mercedes' catchphrase, "Vote Vampire". Sapphire and Pumpkin on either side were handing out items bought at Nameless: gold buttons and badges, cords of tinsel wound round to look like scarves, and strings of bunting for any supportive traders to decorate their shops. It occurred to Pumpkin that nobody had given any thought to campaign promises: what Flaxen would do if elected, why he was a good choice or even why he wanted the job. No written material was being given out. People were just told to support him for the simple reason that he wasn't Mercedes the vampire. It didn't seem like much of a pitch.

Perancia appeared out of nowhere, an annoying habit she had developed. "Give me some of the buttons," she whispered to Sapphire.

"You can have a box of fifty," replied Sapphire, without pausing her routine of smiling at the crowds. "Are you joining the campaign, then?"

"CT said I should give it a go," said Perancia sulkily. "He wants me to be more active. He says, 'The chaos you get is the chaos you make.' He's always saying stupid stuff like that to make me do things. He says it's motivational."

Perancia took the box and stalked along behind Ferdinal. She handed the buttons out mainly to tourists, whom the other Heroes had tended to ignore, doubting that such visitors would bother to vote. Perancia had other ideas. As she pinned each button to a visitor's robes, she deftly managed in most cases to slip her questing fingers inside to lighten their purses without anyone noticing. Gold goes on, gold comes out, she reasoned. Nobody had said the buttons were free.

"If we're promoting chaos, does that mean we're now chaotic?" whispered Pumpkin to her brother.

Ferdinal considered the point. "I don't think so," he said. "We're just the campaign managers. We don't have to believe it all. And at least we're not evil."

An angry-looking voter waylaid Flaxen as he strolled along. "What are you going to do about my house?" he demanded, belligerently. "Every time there's a dust storm, my bedroom fills with grey sand. I've tried sealing spells, but I think the cavity insulation has magic resistance. And the landlord is a holding company on the Elemental Plane of Air. They're no good. If you're mayor, what are you going to do about it?"

Several others in the crowd fell silent and turned expectantly to Flaxen, awaiting his answer.

Flaxen had been listening with an expression of benevolent concern. Sapphire realised that she had adopted the same look herself when seeking support in the election at school, prior to making some outlandish and barely credible promise.

"My friend," smiled Flaxen, facing the angry man and putting a hand on his shoulder, "I solemnly pledge that I will do absolutely nothing. I will do as little as it takes. I am the candidate for chaos. No way will I help you!"

Sapphire gasped. It was not the response she had expected. Why had Flaxen gone out of his way to antagonise the voter, in front of a crowd of people? To her surprise, the angry man's face broke into a warm smile.

"That's more like it!" cried the man. "I put the same problem to Mercedes and she made all sorts of promises. We don't need that Lawful stuff here in Carceron. We don't want promises here!"

"Yeah, vote for chaos, not evil!" shouted someone from the back of the crowd. A cheer went up.

Flaxen beamed and passed along towards another cluster of potential voters.

Sapphire glanced at Harbinger. "I think he's a natural," she said, impressed.

As the procession moved into Central Square, Pumpkin spotted Montrachet in the crowd. She suddenly heard a voice in her head as the young wizard sent her a telepathic message. "See you later. I've got something for you," said Montrachet's voice. Pumpkin could sense that a reply was expected, but she didn't know what to say so just nodded and smiled in Montrachet's direction.

Harbinger spotted a rival crowd forming in Central Square. Captain Manacle and Zarek seemed to be gathering a group from the shop Hired Goons and were giving them rapid orders on what to do. Quick as a flash, Harbinger directed Flaxen to change direction and head off towards the Trident Hotel. If necessary, he would use an invisible Arcane Wall to block off the rival gang from attacking Flaxen's party.

Flaxen came to a halt. He was face to face with a very beautiful auburn-haired woman who seemed from her delicate eyes and pointy ears to have some elven blood, thought Sapphire.

"Souzira," said Flaxen simply, exhaling the name so that it sounded more like a sigh.

"I *am* going to vote for you, Flaxen," said the woman. Her voice was unsteady, as if choking on pent-up emotion. Pumpkin felt very sorry for her, without really knowing why she felt it. It couldn't be much fun, being in love with a decaying, centuries-old sorcerer, could it?

Flaxen smiled and took one of Souzira's hands in both of his. "Demons curse you," he said softly, and Pumpkin thought the tone of voice was exactly the one she normally heard used when someone said, "God bless you."

The procession moved on and Harbinger moved them inside the lobby of the Trident Hotel for safety. "I don't think Zarek's hirelings will attack us," he said, "but it will do no harm to wait here for a minute. The hotel has various protective spells to ward off attacks. Otherwise, there wouldn't be a single tourist alive in the city."

The hotel was very grand inside and the Heroes gazed about them for a moment. It looked a lot like an upmarket hotel of the sort used by top businesspeople and movie stars. The main difference was the colour scheme. In addition to gold leaf and white marble, the dominant colour was a lurid blood red. The carpet in the lobby was not a uniform red, as if manufactured to a standard design. It had contrasting splashes of different red shades, as if paint had been spilled or dribbled across at multiple different points. It had been made to look, thought Sapphire, as though a host of assorted creatures had bled to death on this very floor, the bones and gore being swept away to leave only the two-dimensional splatter on the fabric. From what she'd learned of this city, that was probably exactly what had happened here.

Harbinger was again taking charge of the formalities, asking the zombie at reception for a room for the three Heroes. He seemed to take it for granted that they would want to share one large room together.

"Here's your token," he said, giving a red disk to Sapphire. "Your room is at the back. You should be safe in here and it will be much more comfortable than my back room. Anyway, I need to fill that with boxes of gold buttons."

"How will we stay in touch with you?" asked Ferdinal.

"I'll leave one of my quasits in the room," said Harbinger, as if that was the most natural thing in the world. "They're lazy creatures, but they know not to disobey me. I'll lend you Azgog, he's one of the more reliable ones."

Flaxen approached them. "I've been talking to Souzira," he smirked. "She gave me these tickets." He handed out small paper tickets to Harbinger and the Heroes. Each one was labelled "The Playhouse, Carceron. *Wyrmfeast*". But there was no indication of the date of the performance, nor any indication that each ticket gave exclusive rights to a specific seat.

"Why are we going to see a play, Flaxen?" asked Sapphire. "You need to be campaigning."

"Mercedes is there," said Flaxen. He wasn't smiling now. "I want to keep an eye on her."

Chapter 9

The Irresistible Dancehall

Flaxen had got good tickets for the Playhouse. As he had explained on the way there, the best seats were those at the back, as far from the stage as possible. Most performances involved live slaughter on stage and since many of the creatures in the productions were impossible to tame, it was safest to sit at a distance. If it were necessary to see any close-up action, or to see past Observers in the lower rows who had levitated themselves up to block the view, you could use the Playhouse's own Goggles of Viewing which you could peer through to gain a close-up angle on the stage, with free extravision – all for one gold piece. The extravision would wear off after each performance, but it would be enough to stop anyone picking your pocket in the darkness.

The proprietor of the Playhouse, Champrice, had welcomed Flaxen and his group and escorted them to their seats, being careful to avoid encountering either Mercedes or any peckish-looking demons on the way. Champrice seemed to have an air of flawless efficiency, as if she had expected and forestalled all such trifling difficulties. It was easy to see why she was able to keep order at such a crowded theatre with its eccentric clientele. Pumpkin could not help wondering if Champrice had other hidden talents which were less obvious.

This particular play, *Wyrmfeast*, was all about a vicious dragon. As far as the Heroes could make out, this dragon would eat anything as if for a bet. Its friends were constantly goading it on to ever more bizarre feats of gastronomic zeal, using its appetite to deplete the ranks of their foes in the process. This enabled them to gain key advantages in the commercial and political worlds, by the simple expedient of deploying their friendly dragon to devour anyone who stood in their path. In a grand finale, the dragon is finally slain when a poisonous plant is disguised to look like a tasty innkeeper. Too late the dragon realises its mistake and falls prey to this simple ploy, collapsing on the stage but being animated again by the backstage hands in time to take its bow at the final curtain.

"Don't they get through a lot of actors like this?" whispered Pumpkin.

"No," said Montrachet reassuringly. "All the famous actors have been polymorphed, resurrected or animated hundreds of times. That's how they keep track of their seniority at the Playhouse. Of course, some of the new ones learning the trade get killed in each performance."

Pumpkin did not feel very reassured.

Sapphire had her eye on Mercedes, sitting with her entourage in the front row. Mercedes seemed to have no fear of being splattered by blood or hit by flying corpses from the stage. In fact, all the stage gore seemed to run harmlessly off the vampire's spotless clothing. Mercedes seemed supremely relaxed, as if she were effortlessly in control of everything.

Ferdinal held Goggles of Viewing, scanning the ranks of Mercedes' henchmen. They were easy to identify, each sporting a large "Vote Vampire" badge. There, in the seats next to her, sat several of her known backers: Captain Manacle, Zarek and Jagglespur. From Pumpkin's description, the man in the garish robes and jewellery might be Revlyn of the Thieves' Guild. And – there could be no mistake – there was Oliver! His own brother Oliver, albeit now looking very grown-up as Fredinal the Assassin, dressed all in black. How could Oliver have got so closely involved with the Vampire Party?

Demons seemed to be enjoying the performance enormously. At each new violent death on stage, they would cheer or salivate, according to their appetites.

"At least we know what we're up against," whispered Sapphire to Ferdinal. "None of Mercedes' heavies look as though they know anything. She's the only impressive one in the Vampire Party."

"Yes, that's true," pondered Ferdinal. "But vampires are still pretty deadly. So is everyone in this city. I guess we'll just have to try to look more powerful than we really are, to scare them off!"

Pumpkin, overhearing this, thought that was one of the stupidest things her brother had said in months.

―

That evening, Flaxen and Harbinger took the Heroes to Mr Ottoman's establishment, The Irresistible Dancehall. There they met up with Marid, who was still mourning the loss of the Archmayor.

Pumpkin found Marid a fascinating character. She couldn't help asking him questions about the dead Archmayor, as Marid seemed best able to satisfy her curiosity.

Marid leant back in his chair and sighed. Pumpkin realised that Marid was emotionally affected by the Archmayor's death. Marid might be a genie, a callous trader who dealt with demons and a former Chief of Staff to an undead wight. But there was a surprisingly human element to his reaction to the Archmayor's demise. Marid had lost a real friend, and he seemed subdued and diminished by the loss – even though the Archmayor was a weak figure who had met his mortal death centuries earlier. Pumpkin felt a sudden urge to reach out to Marid and help him through his grief, providing him with an oasis of sympathy and understanding in a city that was cruel and heartless.

"Tell us about the Archmayor," she said, putting her hand gently on the genie's arm. "What was he like – as a person?"

Marid's demeanour changed at once. "The Archmayor was such a wicked man," he chuckled. "I was his Chief of Staff at the palace for decades. He never had magical powers, never stood up to the demon lords. He was ugly and his flesh was decaying, however much balm we used to buy from Maelstrom to slow the process."

Ferdinal thought it made the Archmayor sound like a toxic and pathetic leader. Why would anyone want someone like that in charge? But he said nothing. Slowly he realised that those very qualities of non-intervention, consensus-building and never being a threat to the more powerful figures were exactly why the Archmayor had remained so long in office.

"But people liked him," continued Marid, still reminiscing. "He helped the city grow its tourist trade. He provided balance, always managed to stop feuds escalating into Armageddon. Even the demons knew that he stabilised the place and they fought each other instead of bothering with toppling him. Being mayor isn't about power; it's more subtle than that. Demons only care about the exercise of raw power and direct dominance."

Sapphire too began dimly to draw lessons from Marid's conversation. She was interested in the Archmayor only in as far as he offered lessons and ideas for her own campaign. For the first time, she began to wonder why she wanted to win the school election? Was it really just about beating Amber? That didn't seem to matter right now. Somehow, she cared more right now about helping Flaxen than about herself, and she realised what a magnetic and forceful personality Flaxen must have, even in his weakened state, to be able to harness the assistance of complete strangers.

At this moment, the sinister, cadaverous figure of Mr Ottoman approached and loomed over their table. "Pumpkin?" he asked, looking around.

"Yes, that's me." Pumpkin was suddenly startled. What did the restaurant owner want with her? Was she about to be ejected for some secret breach of demonic etiquette?

"Someone at the door for you," said Mr Ottoman, dismissively. "The Observers won't let him in. His name's Montrachet and he says he's got something for you."

Pumpkin leapt up, almost upsetting her drink. In no time she was at the door, where the two Observers were glaring suspiciously at Montrachet, who seemed nervous and embarrassed by the attention. He was holding a small sack, which seemed to have something alive inside it.

"It's okay, he's with me," she said, leading the young wizard in.

"Erm, look, this is a bit awkward," said Montrachet, shuffling his feet. "I've got something for you, only it's not really a present. I think it's yours already."

He held the small sack towards Pumpkin, keeping his grasp over the top to keep it closed. Again, the contents of the sack squirmed as he extended his arm.

Pumpkin was nonplussed. "It's not something horrid, is it? You shouldn't keep living things in sacks."

"I think it's yours," insisted Montrachet, keeping his eyes on the sack. "Šapka wasn't sure, so he had it magically identified. I don't think it's dangerous."

Pumpkin grabbed hold of the wriggly sack. Screwing up her courage, she relaxed her grip on the top slightly, to peep inside. At first, all she could see was a pair of small, unblinking green eyes with black pupils gazing back at her. The squirming ceased. As her eyes penetrated the dark interior of the sack, Pumpkin heard a muffled purr. The creature in the sack was her grey cat, Charisma! She hadn't even realised that the cat had found its way to Carceron. Of course! Charisma must have been in the room when the Summoning happened and Charisma had been swept to the new city, just as Oliver had.

A wave of relief and joy swept over Pumpkin. She knew she would have been inconsolable if anything had happened to the cat. But Charisma appeared none the worse for the experience.

"We fed it some meat," said Montrachet nervously. "Stewed goblin. She seemed to like that best."

Pumpkin fought back a sob. She was simply so overwhelmed to find her cat safe in this dangerous place and surprised that anyone in the city would be so thoughtful as to keep the creature safe and return her. Without even thinking about it, she flung her arms round Montrachet's neck and hugged him tightly. She was still holding the sack containing the cat, which swung round as she hugged and hit Montrachet squarely on the back. The cat, sensing an antagonist within range, lashed out with her claws from the inside of the sack and the young wizard winced in pain. He made a mental note never to get a cat as a familiar.

"Hope that's all right," he said, disengaging from Pumpkin's embrace and shuffling his feet again.

"It was sweet of you," said Pumpkin earnestly. "Now come and join us at Flaxen's table. I'll get Flaxen to put Charisma safely away in a pocket dimension, like he does with Pullywuggles. We've been hearing all about the Archmayor from Marid. And you must make sure to vote for Flaxen, you know. Promise me?"

She turned her blue eyes to gaze searchingly at Montrachet. He crumpled under the assault.

"Oh, er, yes, I suppose so," he stammered. "I mean, if it's important."

Pumpkin wanted to stamp her foot. Here was an intelligent wizard who could not have failed to spot the upheavals in the city and he was not even sure if it was worth his time to vote!

"Of course it's important!" she scolded. "Now, come and meet the candidate."

She led him over to Flaxen's table. A group of half-orc tourists were crowding round and Pumpkin noticed that Claw, Flaxen's magical, disembodied hand, was signing autographs for them. Flaxen was at his most relaxed and was well and truly holding court over the assembled group.

"And then I thought," Flaxen was saying, "why should I spend my time working on an autobiography? I'll just cast Invoke Simulacrum and get my duplicate to ghost-write it for me! I call him SimuFlaxen. Then there was the time Souzira persuaded me to cast Instant Clone and we…"

He broke off. Harbinger was shaking his head and mouthing the word "No!" very clearly.

Flaxen would probably not have been able to finish that story anyway. A shadow fell across the table and the Heroes became aware of a muscular figure, about eight or nine feet tall, standing behind Flaxen. On either side of the newcomer were swarthy-looking beldarks, whose tanned skin looked more like a red scaly hide in the dim light. Ferdinal realised that he was gawping at one of the Superiors, one of the top-ranking demon lords, probably one of the four of the Junta who controlled the city.

Flaxen rose, turning to face the demon. Each gazed unperturbably at the other. The half-orc tourists backed away, whispering to each other. Across the rest of the Dancehall, Sapphire noticed, everything went on as normal: the singing, dancing, drinking and gossiping were unaffected. The looming demonic presence only seemed to cast a gloom over the immediate area.

The demon spoke. He seemed to be a creature of few words.

"This election. You got any problems with the Junta? We're going to run the city anyway."

"No problem," said Flaxen, nonchalantly. He seemed totally relaxed.

"Mercedes says she'll let us do anything."

"I'm not one to interfere either. That's not the mayor's job."

"Do you trust Mercedes?" blurted out Sapphire. She couldn't help showing that she wasn't afraid of this thing – even if she was.

The demon turned its head towards Sapphire and gazed at her for a few seconds. Then it laughed, a coarse unsettling bellow that set the glasses rattling on the table.

"Trust? That's a human thing. I don't even trust my scales not to fall off. Power. Control. That's what counts. I trust myself to be strong. I trust others to be weak. I win. They lose."

"Not a bad summary of an average tyrant's manifesto," thought Sapphire. But she didn't say it aloud.

"This is my campaign team," said Flaxen, still in the same bland tone of voice. "Sapphire, Pumpkin, Ferdinal – this is Cremorne of the Superiors, leader of the Junta. And his, er, assistants," he added, pointing to the hulking demons flanking the leader.

He spoke as if making introductions at a cocktail party and Ferdinal could not help reflecting on the incongruity. But then, how should one be introduced to a demon leader? No established protocol seemed suitable.

They were interrupted by a voice from behind Cremorne.

"There you are you naughty thing!" came a high-pitched voice. It was Hijinx.

Cremorne turned and gazed at her. Then, accompanied by his flanking henchmen, he strode off, with Hijinx leading the way, to a table on the far side of the bar.

"Don't let that slow manner fool you," hissed Harbinger after the demon had moved away. "He's actually very quick and highly intelligent. He just does those pauses to make people sweat. It's a power and control thing. It's true that the Superiors don't usually care too much about elections. The mayor doesn't have any real power, you see. That's why they don't mind who gets the job, so long as it doesn't affect them."

Cremorne's departure had left a vacuum next to the table. Shyly, Montrachet pulled up a chair and Pumpkin introduced him to Ferdinal and Sapphire. "He's a wizard," she said proudly.

"Still with the Thieves' Guild, Montrachet?" asked Flaxen, sipping his frothing golden drink.

The young wizard looked down and blushed.

"He's a rogue?" asked Ferdinal scornfully.

"No, he really is a wizard," said Pumpkin, feeling compelled to defend him.

"There's something I need to tell you," said Montrachet. He was still looking down at the table as he spoke. Flaxen, Harbinger, Marid and the Heroes looked at him, and Marid took a sip of Vermillion.

Montrachet stood up, grasped Pumpkin's hand and led her away from the table to a slightly quieter corner of the noisy bar.

"I'm not really a wizard," said Montrachet, speaking slowly and suppressing evident emotion with each word.

"I came to Carceron five years ago. I grew up in a village, miles away, on another plane of existence. It was near a forest and was home to humans, elves and half elves. My best friend was the son of a minor noble who owned the town. He was ever so clever and was going to go to some wizard city to train as a spellcaster. He had all the books and everything. I wished I could do that. One day he and I were walking through the woods when we were attacked by goblins. We killed three or four and the rest fled, but my friend was pierced by many arrows and died a few minutes later. I had been in trouble with the Town Watch before and was terrified of being accused of my friend's murder."

He paused and gulped. "This is turning out to be quite a confession," thought Pumpkin. She said nothing but squeezed his hand in support.

"There and then," continued Montrachet, "I took a sudden decision. My friend was noble, intelligent, was going to be a wizard. I yearned to do all that. So, I buried his body in the woods, took his clothes and his spellbook and his noble medallion – and I set out on the career for which he had been destined and I had craved. I became the noble wizard that I had always wanted to be."

He paused again. This time Pumpkin waited, watching his face earnestly.

"I trained among the wizards for a few months," said Montrachet. "I learned some magic and I had all my friend's spellbooks. But they must have known that I was not suited to an arcane career. They set me tests and written exams which I was quite unable to pass. So, one day, I was brought before the Wizarding Council – a bunch of the oldest and most decrepit-looking people. They didn't ask any questions.

They told me outright that I shouldn't be here. Then one of them started casting a spell – it took him several minutes. It was clearly pre-arranged, for the others just watched him. I was fascinated; it was the most intricate magic that I've ever seen. The next thing I knew, I was standing outside the Carceron city gates, with all my possessions and books and Carina standing there smiling at me, just as she welcomed you and your friends. I ended up working for Revlyn because he really likes using a little low-level magic in the course of his work. I think he knows I'm not a true wizard, but I work hard for him and he likes me."

Montrachet's voice trailed off. Pumpkin felt desperately sorry for the young man. He was clearly very muddled and had made some very bad choices. Time after time he had been in situations he was totally unable to handle if his account was to be believed.

Pumpkin went with her instinct. "Come with me," she said, firmly, grabbing Montrachet's wrist. "We'll go back to the table and join the others. If it makes you feel any better, I'm not really a cleric, either."

"Really?" Montrachet gazed at her in astonishment.

"Well, I was a dark elf sorcerer for a while. But I got bored with that, so my brother said I could be something else."

The Irresistible Dancehall was packed full of people. Ferdinal noticed that, with the bar so busy, it was very hard for people to move about to order drinks. If the bar's ceiling were higher, he thought, it would make sense to employ some sort of flying creatures to ferry orders to and from the tables. He was fascinated to see bar staff flitting about on the ground, actually passing through the customers, while holding trays of drinks high above their heads. One of them approached Flaxen's table, carrying a large circular tray.

"Another jug of Vermillion for you," said the waiter, in a deep voice, placing a decanter of steaming red liquid on the table.

"Oh, Melville, is that you?" asked Flaxen, in a tone of mild interest.

"The Late Mr Melville, if you please," said the waiter, in the same sepulchral tone, but with a hint of faint rebuke. "Show some respect for the dead."

With that, the waiter dashed off, again passing through the throng of revellers to collect further orders.

"How is that possible?" asked Sapphire, wide-eyed.

"When the bar is this crowded, Mr Ottoman employs spectres as temporary staff," explained Harbinger in a low voice. "They're incorporeal, so they can pass straight through other bodies. But they don't like to be reminded of it. They're undead, but they don't really want to be. Sometimes they can be quite huffy about it."

Ferdinal thought that was probably something of an understatement.

Pumpkin and Montrachet were just sitting back down and rejoining the group. Once again, Pumpkin managed to astonish Montrachet.

"We've been talking about magic," Pumpkin announced. "Montrachet's going to teach me how to be a wizard. We may not be in town for very long, but I want to learn something useful while I'm here."

This remark brought forth approving nods from Flaxen

and Harbinger, while Sapphire was predictably scornful. But another surprise soon trumped that announcement.

The Heroes became aware that a figure was standing overlooking their table. She was tall, with dark hair, dressed in a glittering azure tailcoat. It was Mercedes. Gortol the ogre was standing next to her, his head almost brushing the ceiling of the dancehall.

Mercedes was eyeing Flaxen. Sapphire could not help staring at Mercedes' large, deep lustrous eyes. With an effort, Sapphire turned away. Fortunately, the vampire had not been staring at her.

Flaxen rose from his seat and stared unblinkingly back at Mercedes. Nobody else moved. Eventually Mercedes spoke, in a voice scarcely louder than a whisper and yet everyone at the table could hear her clearly. She addressed Flaxen, as if nobody else were present.

"Why are you doing this?" she whispered. "You don't even want it. Being mayor means nothing to you. An idle diversion, a moment of fun, then you will be bored and shut yourself away again. You don't deal with people. You don't like people. Leave this work to those who were fashioned for such a calling. Put aside your jealousy, relax. You don't have to do it. Don't stand in the election."

Harbinger and the Heroes watched intently as Flaxen gazed back.

Finally, he spoke. "Have you learned nothing?" asked Flaxen softly, with his usual faint smile. "Your voice has no power over me and your eyes cannot bend my will. I *have* to stand. You know that. Only I can stop you. Oh, and one more thing. It isn't really a calling if you stand for election having murdered the last incumbent. That doesn't count."

He sat down and turned his back on Mercedes. She glared at him for an instant, then slipped away effortlessly through the crowd of revellers. Gortol grunted and turned away, knocking drinkers and dancers aside as he made for the exit.

Ferdinal shuddered as Mercedes left. He realised he had been gazing into her eyes and had for a moment been captivated by her beauty and power. Mercedes' beguiling powers must be even deeper than he had realised. She had the ability to select and enthral someone nearby without even looking at them or paying them any attention. Flaxen might be a powerful sorcerer, but Mercedes' abilities were more subtle and well concealed.

"That's one of the great things about old friends," smiled Flaxen. "You can go your separate ways for five hundred years, then resume the conversation with them right where you left off."

Chapter 10
Never Split the Group

After the encounter with Mercedes, Harbinger gathered Flaxen and the Heroes and escorted them back to his house. By now it was late at night and the Heroes were feeling exhausted.

"Never mind the Trident Hotel," said Harbinger tersely. "You can sleep here again tonight. Pumpkin, I don't think your cat is safe in the city. I'm going to perform a short ritual to dismiss her to a pocket dimension until the election is over. You can be reunited with her then. Flaxen, I need to talk to you."

So saying, he abruptly left the Heroes in their room. They could hear Harbinger and the old sorcerer talking in low voices well into the night. Occasionally they heard a door open and another voice would speak. "Probably one of Harbinger's quasits coming in to report," thought Ferdinal as he drifted off to sleep.

In the morning, Harbinger and Flaxen had serious faces. It did not look as though either had slept, although in Flaxen's case, he had probably not slept for hundreds of years. Pumpkin wondered whether the De-Liching ceremony had turned him fully human again, or whether he was permanently freed from the need to sleep. She vowed to ask him at a suitable moment.

"We've been discussing everything," said Harbinger, as the Heroes joined them in his sitting room. "Flaxen and I are disturbed by Mercedes' confidence. We both think that the Superiors, the ruling demon lords in the Junta, may be secretly backing her. Or at least some of them are. We need to find out. If so, it makes our task much harder."

"It would explain why the demons are so utterly unconcerned by the death of the Archmayor," added Flaxen.

"In short, we need to double-check who our friends are," said Harbinger.

"Ooh, good, a proper election canvass," said Sapphire in a businesslike tone. "We know all about that."

Before they could get going, a quasit came into the room. Usually the creatures ambled slowly, as if each step was an unwelcome effort. This one was dashing, although it gave no clue in its face as to the nature of its message. It whispered in Harbinger's ear. Harbinger snapped a quick question back, in a language the Heroes did not understand. The quasit whispered further news, then dashed out again.

Harbinger looked even more grave than before. "It's worse than I thought," he said. "Azgog is dead. There's been an attack on the Trident Hotel overnight. The room in which you were all going to stay has been ransacked and all the furniture torn to pieces. The hotel staff found Azgog's body in the debris."

There was a pause. The Heroes felt they should say something sympathetic, as if Harbinger's friend or relative had died, but ordinary condolences didn't seem to fit the situation.

"I'm sorry about Azgog," said Pumpkin, softly. "Were you very fond of him?"

"Nobody likes quasits!" snapped Flaxen, as Harbinger winced. "Nasty things! No, the hotel attack is serious. I can't remember the last time the hotel was attacked. Someone must have used very powerful magic to turn off its warding glyphs. I'll tell you what, Harbinger. I bet this gets discussed at the Pandemonium."

Pumpkin remembered the demon parliament building. It was going to be the centre of events at the Festival of Pandemonium. Now it seemed as if it was going to have a real debate of some kind.

"Can we watch?" she asked. "I'd like to see a debate there."

Harbinger and Flaxen exchanged glances.

"Well," said Harbinger, cautiously, "it's like this. You can go if you like and watch from the gallery. But don't let them see you. Spectators at the debates have sometimes been, well, eaten. The demons get bored quickly, see?"

Sapphire wondered at Harbinger's calmness. He had just had news of a savage attack in which one of his creatures had been killed. Yet in an instant his mind had moved on to the future, to practical next steps.

"Never mind the Pandemonium," she said dismissively. "What about the canvassing, to find out which way everyone plans to vote? You said we need to find out what the demons are up to. How?"

"Tell us more about the four demons in the Junta," said Ferdinal. "Then we can make some plans."

Flaxen nodded. "You've met Cremorne already," he said.

"Carina showed us pictures of all four at the tourist centre when we arrived," said Sapphire.

"If the demons are involved in the election," explained Harbinger, "it's bound to involve the Temple of Carcus. That's overseen by Babaeski, but really, it's his priests who run it. If they're animating corpses and all that, the temple clerics must know about it."

"The weakest one of the Junta is Lamothe," added Flaxen, thoughtfully. "He's the only one who I think could be bullied or persuaded into giving away information. Whatever you do, avoid Luleburgaz. With all those guards she has, she'd be too deadly. And Cremorne is even worse."

"Let's split up then and learn what we can about the temple and about Lamothe," said Sapphire briskly. She felt it was time they did some more campaign managing, rather than being swept along by the tide of events. "Henry, that is, Ferdinal and I can go to the temple. Pumpkin, you can spy on Lamothe."

"I don't want to go on my own," interrupted Pumpkin indignantly. Hadn't Azgog the quasit just been slaughtered on his own in the supposedly safe hotel room?

"Oh, don't worry," said Harbinger. "I've already paid Perancia to join you. And you can take Redwing again, just in case. He'll do whatever you ask."

"Perancia doesn't seem like a very reliable ally," thought Pumpkin. But she had ideas of her own, which she kept quiet for now.

Ferdinal and Sapphire set off for the Temple of Carcus. They knew where it was, for it was a huge building, not far from where Flaxen and Harbinger each lived. Sapphire was glad to be alone with her boyfriend for a while and quietly slipped her hand into his as they walked towards Carcus Square.

Ferdinal was glad too. He didn't feel self-conscious about holding hands at a time like this; Sapphire gave him a silent reassurance, which was just what he needed. They didn't really have a plan of what to do. Harbinger had explained that the temple was always full of tourists, so there would be no trouble getting in and looking around. It's not as if most places in Carceron had rules about keeping out, except for Delirium Drive, where the top demons lived, and the Mayor's Palace, which had been shut up since the Archmayor's demise.

As they came into Carcus Square there was no mistaking the temple, which loomed large on the far side. Sapphire couldn't help thinking what a large graveyard it had just to one side. For a city of this size it did seem big, with the marked plots very close together. There must be room for hundreds of thousands of burials… No, she wouldn't think about that.

Walking through the crowded streets, Ferdinal's mind was not entirely on the task ahead. He was worried about how the three of them were ever going to get back home – very little had been said about that and probably wouldn't be until after the election was completed. And he was worried about his brother Oliver.

Pumpkin set off from Harbinger's house with Redwing on her shoulder again. She liked the feeling of the little creature perched there, giving occasional telepathic hints of where to go. Just outside the house she spotted Perancia lurking on her own. The urchin warlock immediately ran over and stalked along at Pumpkin's side.

"Harbinger said you'd need me again," she declared proudly. "Where to this time?"

Pumpkin felt Redwing trying to give her a stream of directions telepathically about the Demon Consulate and Lamothe.

"No, we're not going there yet," she said cryptically. "First, I want to go to the Southwest District. If there's any reconnaissance to be done, we'll want a professional. I want Montrachet to come along."

She hadn't told Ferdinal and Sapphire in case they mocked her. But Perancia was able to redress any deficit when it came to mocking.

"Ooh, is he your *boyfriend* now?" she gurgled, puckering her lips and making what she considered to be affectionate noises.

Pumpkin sighed. She knew this would happen. "He's not," she snapped. "He's a professional rogue and I want his help. You're only here cos Harbinger paid you. What's to stop some demon from buying you out and turning us in?"

"I thought of that," said Perancia, with her usual disarming frankness. "Actually, CT says I'm to help you. He says he'd like to know more about what the demons are up to and I'm to tell him later. So really Harbinger needn't have paid me at all."

"Well, that will have to do," thought Pumpkin, as they trudged together in the direction of the Destiny Guild of thieves.

"Why is Crixus Telmarine your patron anyway, if you two don't get on?" asked Pumpkin. "Why does he bother with you?"

Perancia did not seem at all offended by the question. Pumpkin wondered if the urchin had already asked herself the same thing.

"He says I have a lot of potential," said Perancia smugly, as they walked. "Untapped genius. Raw power. That sort of thing. He wants to help me unleash it. I think he likes the whole unplanned devastation thing that it causes."

For once Perancia had found a subject that interested her, and she became talkative.

"CT is fun, too," she said. "He has all these crafty suggestions, ways to get ahead. That's what drew us together. But he knows he doesn't control me and sometimes I just ignore him."

Montrachet was once more on duty behind the Enquiries window at the Destiny Guild's headquarters. He seemed only too happy to desert his post to accompany Pumpkin and Perancia on some undisclosed quest.

"I'm supposed to stay on duty," he confided, "but you know what it's like in Carceron. It's not as if there are any real rules. If you feel like going off to do something else, you do it."

"What's your plan, then?" asked Perancia, as they walked through the streets. She didn't really fancy tagging along behind Montrachet and Pumpkin. She thought about running off but remembered that she had to obey CT's instructions and spy on the demons, too.

"We can't just chat about it in the street," snapped Pumpkin, nervously eyeing a swooping Shadow Demon patroller. "Is there anywhere near here we can chat privately?"

They were standing not far from the Shadow gate, where Pumpkin and the others had entered the city a few days earlier.

"There's the library," said Montrachet uncertainly. "That's normally pretty empty."

"Idiot," snorted Perancia derisively. "It's quiet in the library. Anyone else there would hear everything we say."

At this point Pumpkin heard a voice in her mind again. It was Redwing giving directions. He had been listening as always and had a novel idea.

"Redwing suggests sitting in the Botanical Gardens," she said decisively. "He says it's very near. We'll go there. At least the druids don't sound dangerous."

The group headed east from the Shadow Gate, towards a part of the city Pumpkin had not seen before. There seemed to be a greater concentration of demons here, she thought, spotting two hefty guards with scales and horns, beldarks, in the distance. To the north-east she could see a large, open space. Beyond it was the side of a formal building like a small temple, surrounded by iron railings. Between the building and the railings were thousands of grey metal chips or pebbles, which added to the drab uniformity of the scene.

The entrance to the Botanical Gardens was next to the library. Instead of being a pleasant arboreal gateway to an oasis of greenery, for which Pumpkin secretly longed, the entrance was another restaurant. You could only get to the gardens by going through Seeds, the vegetarian establishment run by druids. "Another minor example of the commercialism in the city," thought Pumpkin. "Even access to a green space was somehow restricted."

The gardens themselves were unexpectedly pretty. Pumpkin thought that it was the first truly beautiful place she had seen in the city. The back door of Seeds restaurant seemed to be the only way into the gardens, which were surrounded by a high wall of the same concrete-like material of which most of Carceron seemed to be built. All structures in the garden were of the same grey construction: benches, trellises, even the bandstand in the centre.

It was the luxuriant foliage that was so eye-catching. Any other botanical garden would be dominated by multiple shades of green, with grass, bushes and trees forming a subtle spectrum of verdant delight. Not this garden. The grass varied in colour from one section to another – light blue near the entrance, orange in some places and a startling cerise near the bandstand. All other growing things showed similar spirit, with azure bark and scarlet branches competing for attention. There were even different colours of leaf growing on individual trees and bushes. "The druids must have sought out and nurtured floral exotica for centuries to achieve this effect," thought Pumpkin.

"I wonder how old these plants are?" she said aloud.

"I've heard you can tell the age of a tree by the rings in its trunk," put in Perancia, helpfully. "If you want to know their age, we could cut one down and count the rings?"

Pumpkin stared at her for a moment. Apparently the young warlock was quite serious and genuinely trying to help. Pumpkin ignored the remark and walked on.

Redwing was telepathically directing Pumpkin towards a small summerhouse, tucked away in a quiet grove. Perancia was already scampering ahead towards it, but she stopped suddenly at the entrance. As she approached, Pumpkin could see why. There were three people already there, deep in conversation. One of them she recognised as Fulcrum, the crow-like negotiator or fixer. The other two were human, one dressed all in black and one in very fine, expensive-looking clothing, rather like a courtier from Elizabethan times.

Pumpkin, Perancia and Montrachet stood at the entrance to the summerhouse. Redwing sat silently on Pumpkin's shoulder. The man dressed in black rose from his seat and smiled.

"Good morning," he said, in a more friendly tone than Pumpkin was used to hearing from strangers in the city. "You must be Pumpkin. My name is Šapka. Allow me to present Apollonius Crayler, the leading showman of our day, and Fulcrum, who knows everyone and everything."

Crayler beamed, extended an enormous hand and squeezed Pumpkin's own. Fulcrum merely stared with beady black eyes but said nothing.

"What are you doing at the meeting spot?" asked Perancia aggressively. She did not seem pleased to see them.

Šapka smiled a wintry grin, but his eyes sparkled. "I don't think Revlyn pays you to ask questions, young warlock. This was our meeting spot long before it was yours."

Pumpkin turned and scowled at Perancia. Why would Revlyn, the head of the Thieves' Guild, be paying Perancia, and why had she not admitted it sooner? Šapka was still smiling. His remark had been intended to sow discord amongst the intruders and it had clearly hit home.

"Everyone seems to be paying that warlock," thought Pumpkin. Perancia seemed to be getting gold from her patron for training, from the demons for spying and from Revlyn for double treachery. Also, Harbinger had paid Perancia to guide her today and Perancia had just had free clothes from Nameless at Flaxen's expense. "I'll deal with her later," thought Pumpkin, and tried to put Perancia's treachery out of her mind for a moment as she turned to Šapka and Crayler.

"You're all leading people in this city," she began, trying to be brave but amazed that she could speak to key underworld figures so casually. "You know we're helping Flaxen win this election. You all know that if Mercedes won it would be disastrous for the city's tourist trade. Where do you stand? Are you backing Mercedes?"

She took a step back, almost afraid of her own audacity.

Fulcrum looked at Šapka and Crayler and made some mysterious clicking noises with his beak. This seemed to be his normal way of talking, but no words were audible. Crayler continued beaming, but his eyes were darting around the group, watching everyone closely.

"Actually, you're quite right," said Šapka, sitting down and stretching out his legs. "And that is the focus of our discussion. Now, Crayler and I have to work with whichever candidate wins. We couldn't do otherwise. Fulcrum here can fix a lot of things, but even he can't fix the result of an election. There are just too many people involved. So, if you are proposing some sort of deal?" His voice trailed off and the wintry grin returned to his face.

Crayler beamed again. "I assume you are authorised to speak on behalf of the Flaxen campaign?"

Pumpkin's heart beat faster. She hadn't thought of herself in that capacity at all. But, hadn't Harbinger summoned her and Ferdinal and Sapphire precisely so that they could take decisions in the campaign? Pumpkin glanced at her companions. Montrachet was watching her in awe. He seemed amazed that she could face up to leading figures in the Carceron underworld without any apparent nerves. Perancia was lurking at the back, scowling. Redwing had fallen silent. "There's no time to confer," thought Pumpkin. She had to take the lead.

"I think we can do a deal," she announced, with a haughty decisiveness that belied her true thoughts. "You may not want to be openly associated with the campaign. But there's a lot you could do to assist a Flaxen victory. And I'm sure he would be a very laid-back mayor once elected. He'd let you—"

"Get away with murder?" smiled Šapka the Assassin. "Thanks. We already do that. But Crayler here has ambitious plans to rebuild the city's reputation for live music and attract a wide variety of bands to perform at the Decahedron, once it reopens. There is a lot of gold at stake here."

"And in return?" Montrachet spoke at last.

"Oh, we can certainly help with the election," grinned Crayler. As he smiled, it looked as though all his teeth had been shaded gold, a very vulgar display, thought Pumpkin. "Getting bodies to the right place on the night is my speciality as a promoter. Don't worry about that. Actually, there's something you could do to help me right now!"

He reached into a pocket in his robes and drew out a number of rolled-up posters.

"They're to advertise the next performance by The Horde," explained Crayler. "You need to post them up on walls. The beldarks, the patrolling demons, take them down after a while, though."

"Each poster has a picture of The Horde, with a magic mouth singing a few lines from their songs," whispered Perancia. "They're really annoying, which is why they're always being taken down."

"We'll put up your posters," said Montrachet quietly, as he accepted the bundle. "A small price to pay for their co-operation," he thought.

Crayler grinned his gilded smile again. Fulcrum made a clicking and crunching noise. He didn't seem to speak any intelligible words, but the noises made some sort of repertoire of stock phrases, which close associates seemed to recognise. Pumpkin was intrigued.

"He says he'll stay in touch with Perancia to co-ordinate our activities," said Šapka, getting up. "It's time we were going."

The Heroes did not follow Šapka and his friends but stayed in the summerhouse for a minute or two. Pumpkin was still wondering what to do about Perancia's seemingly constant treachery, when Redwing's eyes suddenly started flickering. Pumpkin heard his voice in her mind again. He was fixated on a figure some distance away in the heart of the gardens, who seemed to be deep in conversation with someone just out of sight.

The creature that Redwing had spotted could only be a

demon. He was even clutching his tail in one hand, twisting it and touching the pointed end, just as a nervous human might bite their nails. Pumpkin stayed in the cover of the summerhouse and cautiously pointed him out to the others.

"That's Lamothe," said Perancia, in surprise. "He must be talking to one of the Invisible Servants. It's really odd for him to be in a place like this, with no guards around. Let's startle him."

Montrachet looked shocked at the idea of creeping up and startling a leading demon, but Perancia had already begun sneaking through crimson undergrowth towards the creature. "Better make the best of it," he thought, and Montrachet and Pumpkin slowly followed Perancia through the bushes, while Redwing stayed in the summerhouse, his eyes getting even larger.

"Boo! Caught you!" yelled Perancia, tugging the demon's tail and skipping round to face him. Montrachet and Pumpkin hurried up, expecting to have to apologise profusely to avoid instant violence.

To their amazement, the demon got down on his knees, his face in his scaly hands, and actually cowered before them. "Could this really be a leading member of the ruling demon Junta?" wondered Pumpkin. She changed her plan at once.

"Who were you talking to?" she challenged, in an aggressive tone.

The demon looked up. Even on his knees, his face was almost at Pumpkin's level. Once more he took his tail in his hand and began to twist it anxiously. "I know who you are," he responded, a bit shakily. "I could have you arrested, you know."

"I know who you are too," shot back Perancia scornfully. "You're Lamothe. Of course you could arrest us. But we'd tell everyone you were in the Botanical Gardens conspiring to betray everyone!"

"That sounds more like a playground taunt," thought Pumpkin. But the demon quivered, as if struck.

"Can't talk," he said. "The others in the Junta are backing Mercedes. Not me. But we have to find the Archmayor's will. It's the only way we can find the Book of Misdeeds."

With those few words, he unfurled large red wings and soared off, over the wall and out of the gardens.

The Heroes watched, amazed. Things had just got a lot more complicated.

Chapter 11

Count Your Friends

Just as Ferdinal was walking with Sapphire to the Temple of Carcus, thinking about his brother Oliver, suddenly he found himself face to face with him in Carcus Square. The bustling crowds of demons, zombies, quasits and a few humans made it impossible to spot people at a distance; bumping into someone was the only way of meeting them.

"Oh! Oliver! I've found you," said Ferdinal, grasping his brother's arm. He noticed that Oliver had changed, too, just as he, Sapphire and Pumpkin had. For a start, Oliver was now his own height. And he was dressed not in casual clothes, but in black leather armour, reinforced with metal studs, with shortswords strapped to his waist.

"Not Oliver anymore!" snapped his brother. "You must call me Fredinal now. What do you want, Ferdy, stopping me in the street like this? I'm on an errand for Mercedes. It's bad enough you being here at all. I don't want people realising I know you."

For a moment Ferdinal was too shocked to reply. Here

was he, the loyal paladin, trying to save his little brother, and this was the thanks he got.

But Sapphire was quicker. "Listen, you ungrateful little wretch," she yelled. "We're here looking after you! You're in all sorts of danger and we all need to get home."

Oliver, or Fredinal as he was known in Carceron, shrugged his shoulders. "Can't go now. Busy with the election. Mercedes is gonna win. And she won't have much use for you when she's rounding up all the unbelievers in this city."

He pulled himself roughly away from Ferdinal's grip. "On your way to the temple, are you?" he sneered. "Well, it's not too late to repent. Just remember not to ask for mercy. The undead, ever-living god isn't big on mercy."

As he strode away, Ferdinal and Sapphire looked at each other uneasily. The conversation had not attracted any attention from passers-by. Clearly, grabbing people in the street and yelling at them was sufficiently commonplace in Carceron that nobody even paused to look.

"I don't know what Mercedes has done to him," said Ferdinal, with determination. "But this makes it even more important that we beat her. I'm not having my little brother trotting round a demon city dressed in a leather onesie running messages for some crazy vampire."

Before they reached the temple, they passed Marvexio the Bard. When he realised where they were headed, he was surprised.

"It's much more dangerous in there than you think," he said, with the same sly, inscrutable expression he always wore. "What do you think happens to all the bodies in this city? Where do you think the zombies are made? They don't rate human life very highly in this city unless you can protect yourself, and right now, with demand for bodies rising as election day gets closer, it's worse than ever."

"We've got to get in," said Ferdinal simply, clenching his fists in readiness.

"Do you want to come too?" asked Sapphire.

Marvexio shook his head. "No way. But I can make you both invisible. Most of the acolytes and priests won't spot you then. Just look out for the higher-ranking clerics."

The bard led the two Heroes over to the side of the square and cast a quick incantation. Ferdinal and Sapphire both vanished. Immediately they realised that the hardest task would be not to lose track of each other. They held hands again, this time without any sense of self-consciousness.

"That lasts for an hour," hissed Marvexio. "Use it well."

As Marvexio moved away through the crowd, Ferdinal and Sapphire turned towards the entrance to the temple.

"What shall we do if we lose each other?" whispered Sapphire.

"Whistle a tune," said Ferdinal, after thinking for a moment. "Something the people here won't know – maybe 'Pop Goes the Weasel.'"

Sapphire smiled to herself. A few days ago, she would never have believed she could be running invisibly round an undead temple whistling "Pop Goes the Weasel" to locate her boyfriend. And yet, it was a sensible suggestion.

The vast iron doors of the Temple of Carcus were wide open. Although there were shadow demons standing guard, Ferdinal realised that they didn't seem to be stopping anyone behaving as they pleased. Despite the constant reminders, it was hard to keep in mind that there were no laws in Carceron. People did as they pleased, until someone more powerful chose to intervene.

The interior of the temple was made of black and white marble, very different from the materials used elsewhere in the city. The harsh, imposing effect was much the same, however, as all the fittings were made of black iron – doors, seats, statues, even the altar. The only relief from this effect was that two huge red candles burned on the altar, drawing the eye in that direction. Behind the altar was a mural of swirling red and black colours, which seemed to move as you gazed at it. About a dozen humans, all evidently tourists from the clothes, were watching the mural in silence.

"Don't look at it," hissed Sapphire, gripping Ferdinal's hand even more closely as he started to move towards the altar. "It's designed to trap you. Once you look at it, you probably never leave the temple."

At once Ferdinal realised the danger he had been in and drew in his breath sharply. Fortunately, nobody seemed to hear.

The temple was almost as busy as the square outside. Clerics in black and white robes hurried about, all clearly on urgent ecclesiastical business. Occasionally there would be a group of humans trudging slowly through the temple, led by two clerics. That bunch must be zombies, Sapphire realised. It occurred to her that there might be many thousands of zombies in the city if you knew where to look.

On one side of the temple there was a tour group, being led round by a cleric in red robes, whose name appeared to be Thorkell from the questions put to him by the group. Ferdinal wondered if the red-robed figures would be able to see through their invisibility. Instinctively he pulled Sapphire away from the tour group.

Sapphire giggled quietly. "You see those tourists? One of them is wearing a souvenir hat."

Ferdinal looked. There was no doubt about it. It was a broad-brimmed straw hat, with lettering on both sides that said, "I visited Carceron and I survived".

"I wonder if they will survive their visit," he whispered back.

"I expect the guide counts them. You should always count your friends here."

Sapphire's eye caught sight of some sort of noticeboard on one side of the temple. There was a whole side chapel reserved for it. She pulled Ferdinal across to come and examine it.

The side chapel was about the size of their living room at home. It was empty of people, but the board was fascinating. It was divided into sections, and individual names appeared in the sections. It seemed to function like an electronic screen at home, there being no way of adding or moving the names by hand. It must all be controlled remotely from somewhere.

Some names were displayed with obvious affection, in a friendly script with hearts next to them. Others were displayed with numbers, suggesting it was their birthday and that was their age today. Much more numerous were the names shown in black, dripping with blood or with little bits chipped off the letters. It looked as though these names were somehow cursed or represented recent victims of religious justice. A small number of names were shown in white.

"Admiring our Curse Wall?" said a voice behind them.

Sapphire and Ferdinal jumped and turned round, switching hands as they did so to maintain contact.

"My name is Runsus," smiled the stranger. He was a good-looking man in red robes, who spoke softly and politely. "I am one of the priests of Carcus. And, yes, I can see invisible creatures. Would you like your names added to the Curse Wall?"

"Er... in a good way?" asked Sapphire.

Runsus looked shocked. "Please! Don't use that word here. This is a respectable establishment devoted to chaos and evil. But if you mean can your names be added in a non-harmful way, yes. We can show unions, name days, curses and tortures on the wall. Those names in white are the former names of today's batch of animated zombies. They'll all be voting in the election."

"Well, we were just browsing," said Ferdinal, trying to look casual. "We've not been to the temple before."

"I thought you must be new to the city," said Runsus, smiling again. "Have you considered starting with an ethos change? It's one of the earliest initiation rites into the religion of Carcus. We have another side chapel for that if you're interested?"

"What sorts of ethos do you recommend?" asked Sapphire, trying to avoid either attracting attention or accidentally signing up for immediate zombie conversion.

"Most people choose Chaotic Evil," admitted Runsus. "It's always the most popular and it's what Carcus himself adopts. The ethos to avoid is Lawful Evil, that's for *devils*," whispering the word confidentially, "but I myself am Neutral Evil. I find that law and chaos place undue restrictions on the pursuit of premeditated villainy and somehow they dilute the purity of the void of true despair."

This smiling priest was starting to make both Ferdinal and Sapphire feel uncomfortable, with his offhand but precise assessment of why he had chosen the path of evil. He was not the sort of person with whom you really wanted to be trapped in a side chapel when you wanted to be exploring in secret. Sapphire started to realise that Neutral Evil, or pure evil, must be an even more dangerous motivation than the Chaotic Evil that infused the demons.

At this moment, another man entered the side chapel and placed some gold pieces in a dish that stood on a pedestal in one corner.

"Thank you, Revlyn," said Runsus, almost automatically.

Ferdinal and Sapphire turned to look at the Head of the Destiny Guild, who in turn nodded to Runsus.

The gold pieces vanished from the dish and a new name appeared on the Curse Wall. The word "Aspreyna" appeared, written in black, with blood dripping from it.

"It is time," said Revlyn briefly. "The Arcane Cage is needed for a new occupant. Aspreyna can be executed tomorrow. You can have her soul; I have no use for it."

Runsus nodded again, still smiling. Sapphire stared at his nonchalance; he had reacted as if a passer-by had told him it would be a sunny day tomorrow. Revlyn left again without further small talk.

"We… need to finish looking round the temple. Thanks," said Sapphire, pulling Ferdinal along with her. She was feeling physically sick from listening to casual discussion of an angel being executed.

Runsus nodded, seemingly indifferent to their departure. "Browse around," he said. "No rules here."

After a couple more minutes of browsing, Sapphire felt it was time to investigate more deeply. They were getting nowhere like this.

"We've got to stop that angel being executed," she whispered to Ferdinal. "We'll just have to rescue her tonight, somehow."

There was a silence. "Oh, er, I nodded," explained Ferdinal. He had been thinking the same thing.

"We need to find some of those demons' secrets before the invisibility wears off," said Sapphire firmly, realising as she spoke the impossibility of the task. "Which way shall we head?"

"I can see some offices up there in the gallery, above the altar," said Ferdinal. "But if there's anything hidden here, it's more likely to be underground. Maybe look for a crypt?"

The crypt turned out not to be concealed. In fact, it was signposted and appeared to be a popular attraction for tourists at the temple.

Ferdinal and Sapphire followed the signs and walked down a spiral stone stairway in some trepidation. Whatever was down here was bound to be unpleasant. Sure enough, the stairs opened out into a huge rectangular hall that resembled a production line. The output that emerged closest to the stairway was completed zombies. All along the line there were clerics of Carcus and other zombies engaged in managing parts of the process. Some were chanting spells; some were bringing in crates of parts…

This time Sapphire knew she was going to be sick. There was another door at the foot of the spiral stairs. Sapphire opened it and pulled Ferdinal onto the lower staircase. It was dark here and there was nobody about. This staircase was narrower and clearly not part of the tourist trail.

After about a minute of retching, Sapphire felt a bit better. She just could not bear to think of the casual cruelty in this horrible place. Ferdinal was now pulling her hand, heading further down the stairs, deeper into the unknown. Again, Sapphire had a bad feeling, but she felt strong enough now to suppress it.

The stairs opened out into a large, dimly lit hemispherical cave. There was nobody in here. But in the middle of the floor was a sort of pool, around twenty feet in diameter. At first glance it seemed to be bubbling like a lava pit. Then, as Ferdinal and Sapphire grew used to the dim light, they could see it was some sort of swirling light, which gave the effect of constantly moving tentacles. But the surface of the pool was completely flat. Around the edge of the pool were eight very thin red candles etched with intricate arcane markings, equally spaced around the perimeter and set in holders.

Before they could investigate there came the sound of footsteps coming down the stairs. There was no way out. Terrified, Ferdinal and Sapphire raced round the edge of the pool to a dark crevice on the far side. They knew they were still invisible, but somehow that didn't make them feel safe.

Two red-robed clerics appeared at the foot of the stairs. "Daysuh, look!" cried one.

Sapphire put one hand to her mouth to avoid screaming.

"There's nothing there," replied the second figure, in a surly voice.

"I know that! Why not? There should be another fifty bodies through the Crater by now. How are we going to fulfil the order for Mercedes if the Crater doesn't send them? Did you send the message that we're ready?"

Daysuh said nothing.

"You fool!" yelled his companion. "Wait 'til I tell Babaeski. He'll throw you into the Crater!"

"You wouldn't? Please, Lacasso. I can send the message now!"

"We went to all this trouble to open the Crater. And you can't even remember how to use it!"

Lacasso was still furious. Just as well, thought Ferdinal, or they would be bound to look across to the alcove where he was cowering. And it seemed the red-robed figures could see invisible people. Lacasso seemed to be getting even more angry, stepping closer to Daysuh and grabbing the front of his robes. Unfortunately, Ferdinal and Sapphire could no longer hear what was being said apart from occasional words: Babaeski... Runsus... book of something?

The conversation ended by Daysuh running back up the stairs, pursued by Lacasso.

"We've got to get out of here," said Sapphire, trying to keep her voice steady. "We need to get Harbinger or Flaxen to tell us what all this means. What were they saying about a book? Was it Book of Deeds?"

"It sounded to me more like Book of Misdeeds. But that doesn't make sense either. Maybe they're going to do some obscure ritual in here."

"Wait by the stairs for a moment," said Sapphire urgently. "I've got an idea. There's something I have to do."

She let go of Ferdinal's hand. As she was invisible, he had no idea where she had gone in the dimly lit cave, although he could hear her footsteps. About a minute later he heard her close by and felt her hand reach for his once more.

"That's better," Sapphire giggled. "Now they can't do the ritual, whatever it is. I've got their candles!"

Ferdinal almost laughed from sheer nervous tension. Still, anything that might slow the demon clerics down was time gained.

Still holding hands and still invisible, Ferdinal and Sapphire set off back up the stairs to the production room and then up the spiral stairs into the temple. They weren't sure how long their invisibility would last and they certainly did not want to be challenged on what they had been doing in the basement by the strange pool, or Crater, as Lacasso had called it. Once they were outside the temple, they paused for a moment and noticed that it was just then they became visible again as Marvexio's spell wore off. Without another word, they both ran to Flaxen's house as fast as they could.

Another gathering took place in Flaxen's secret meeting room. Pullywuggles was absent, as Flaxen had sent him to doze in his pocket dimension. Flaxen, Harbinger, Champrice, Marid and Talisman listened in grave silence as first Pumpkin and then Ferdinal and Sapphire recounted their day's work. Montrachet had not come to the meeting, having guild business to see to, and Perancia had refused to come upon hearing that there wasn't going to be any food provided.

Talisman questioned Ferdinal and Sapphire at length about the appearance of the Crater at the temple. He seemed fascinated by it.

"So, Lamothe mentioned the Archmayor's will?" said Harbinger slowly.

Pumpkin nodded.

"And the priests, Lacasso and Daysuh, they were arguing about a book? Tell me again exactly what you heard."

"Well, I thought they said deeds," said Sapphire. "But Henry, sorry, Ferdinal thought they said Book of Misdeeds, as if they meant one unique and special book."

"What about the candles?" asked Talisman, leaning forward. "They had markings on them?"

"I'll show you," said Sapphire proudly, and emptied out her haul of eight thin red candles from the inside of her peacock-coloured robes.

Flaxen and Harbinger looked at each other. It was the first time the Heroes had seen Flaxen look worried.

"It does all make sense, at least it does to us," said Flaxen. "You see, the Crater is a gate to another plane of existence. It must have been opened specially for the election. This is how Mercedes is convinced she's going to win. She's enlisted the help of Babaeski at the temple to open a gate to bring in zombies from elsewhere by the thousand. Far more than they could make just by animating corpses. Babaeski wants Mercedes to win."

"But clearly the demon Junta is divided," added Harbinger softly. "Lamothe sounds terrified from Pumpkin's account. He's not as powerful as the other three top demons. Maybe he thinks Babaeski has gone too far."

"But what's the Book of Misdeeds?" asked Sapphire.

"It is a book, about the size of a spellbook," explained Talisman. "It exists to close gates that appear in the city. Unattended gates can be very dangerous. All sorts of monsters can just walk through. It's like an open border. The Book of Misdeeds is a powerful artifact. I've no idea where it is, though."

"I know where it used to be," said Marid. Harbinger and Talisman turned to him in astonishment. "Yes, it used to belong to the Archmayor. I've seen it sometimes at his palace. But now he's dead, I've no idea where it might be."

Pumpkin sat up suddenly. "That's what Lamothe meant!" she exclaimed. "He said to look for the Archmayor's will. I bet that says who he gave the book to! Somebody must have it for safekeeping."

Marid looked crestfallen. Evidently he had hoped he would be the one the Archmayor trusted most, having served him for centuries.

"Can't you close a gate to another plane yourselves?" asked Ferdinal in surprise. "I thought you opened a gate when you summoned us?"

"Probably not this time," said Talisman sadly. "The summoning did open a gate. But this Crater sounds much bigger and it may have been open for some time. We don't know which other plane it's connected to. All this makes it much harder to close. We must find the Book of Misdeeds."

"Well, the first thing is to search the palace to find the will," said Harbinger, in his professional way. He always seemed to enjoy organising people.

"No!" said Sapphire and Pumpkin together. There was silence.

"The first thing we have to do," said Pumpkin quietly, "is to rescue that angel in the Arcane Cage. They're going to execute her tomorrow. We've got to save her tonight or it will be too late."

Flaxen and Harbinger looked at each other again, with the same worried expression.

"It's too dangerous," said Flaxen at last. "We can't. And I can't let you do it. If you get caught, well, I don't like to think what the beldarks would do to you."

A heated argument followed. It finished with Harbinger and Talisman forcibly escorting the Heroes to Flaxen's spare room for the night.

***

The atmosphere that night was subdued. Nobody really wanted to talk. Sapphire was almost in tears at the thought of Aspreyna being executed. Much later, when the house was silent and Harbinger and Talisman had departed, Pumpkin sat up.

"We will rescue the angel," she said, with determination. "Just us. Right now."

Ferdinal and Sapphire stared at her.

"We're not locked in here," said Pumpkin. "It's easy enough to walk out of the door. All I need to do then is send a quasit to fetch Montrachet and Perancia. We might need their help and I'm not sure I know the way to the cage in Central Square from here."

"But how are you going to get the angel out of the cage?" asked Ferdinal, astonished at his sister.

Pumpkin looked at him with a guilty expression. "When we had that scuffle with Harbinger and Talisman and I was pretending to refuse to go to the room," she said, her eyes sparkling, "I reached into Harbinger's robes and got his spellbook. It's not that big. I hid it here, under the bed. We'll use it to rescue Aspreyna. I can give the book back tomorrow."

She pulled out from under the bed a book the size of a hardback bible. Inside it was a wide variety of incantations, written in a language that Ferdinal and Sapphire could not understand.

Sapphire beamed. She sat down next to Pumpkin, took her hand and squeezed it. "It's a wonderful idea, Pumpkin. Well done. I suppose we'd better send quasits now for Montrachet and Perancia."

Ferdinal nodded. "It has to be done. But it's going to be really dangerous. Always count your friends; they may not all come home again."

Chapter 12

Good Deeds Get Punished

Up to this point the Heroes had been working hand-in-hand with Flaxen and Harbinger. Now they had gone off on their own, borrowing Harbinger's spellbook in the process. What if it went wrong? Pumpkin felt a real sense of exhilaration. At home she was always a well-behaved, law-abiding girl. Now some of the chaotic aura of Carceron seemed to have rubbed off on her. There were no rules in Carceron, but she felt she was taking a big risk in a really special cause. It was a good feeling.

The Heroes reached the edge of Central Square. Although it was dark, Pumpkin could see the bright golden bars of the Arcane Cage, oscillating and arcing even at night. The square looked empty for once, apart from the forlorn figure of Aspreyna the angel, sitting in the middle of the cage. She was facing away from the Heroes, but Pumpkin wondered if some sixth sense would alert Aspreyna to their presence. Maybe she was beyond caring by now?

"I need to go up to the cage to have enough light to read by," whispered Pumpkin to Ferdinal.

"Let's go, then," hissed Ferdinal. "Perancia, you keep watch. Sapphire, get ready to help Aspreyna out of the cage once we get it open."

Montrachet was given no instructions, but he pursed his lips and followed, a look of grim determination on his face.

Pumpkin led the way up to the cage, clutching Harbinger's precious spellbook.

"Now, what we need is Destroy Matter," she muttered, more to remind herself than to tell the others what she was doing. She leafed through the pages as she spoke. "That's the only way to destroy a forcecage… Oh!"

"Whassamatter?" interjected Sapphire, looking at the book over Pumpkin's shoulder.

"Er… Destroy Matter isn't in the book," said Pumpkin nervously. "That means Harbinger doesn't know the spell. He's never needed to cast it. It's a more advanced spell than I normally use – I've never tried to learn it before."

Ferdinal felt the hairs on his neck start to rise. "You mean… we're here in the middle of the busiest part of town, probably about to be arrested, and we can't get the cage open?"

Pumpkin bit her lip and nodded silently.

"You are *so* going to get busted by the beldarks," giggled Perancia. She liked the sound of the phrase and repeated it. The other four glared at her. Ferdinal wished he had the power to dismiss Perancia to a pocket dimension the way spellcasters did with their familiars.

"Come back into the shadows," ordered Sapphire, taking charge. "Let's figure it out."

They retreated to one of the alleyways leading into

Central Square. There were still no passers-by or patrolling demons on the prowl. Ferdinal kept nervously looking around while the others conferred.

"Now, what else can destroy an Arcane Cage?" asked Sapphire, realising that she sounded just like a schoolteacher coaching a reluctant student on the difference between an isthmus and a causeway. "What's wrong with a good, old-fashioned Dispel?"

"That doesn't work on an Arcane Cage," said Pumpkin, knitting her brows and leafing through the spellbook for ideas. "Flaxen said only Destroy Matter would disintegrate it."

"But we only want to open it," insisted Montrachet.

"Well, we could try Open Portal. But the cage doesn't have a door. Wait here, I'll give it a go."

Perancia looked bored and kicked a stone into the gutter. She had no interest in the trapped angel and was trying to calculate in her head how many credits Revlyn might pay if she could steal the spellbook and bring it to him. She'd need to study the book more closely to get an idea of its contents.

Ferdinal was still looking round, trying to face all ways at once. His eyes were wide in the darkness and he felt incredibly alert, poised to smite any foes. Demon guards might come at any moment.

Pumpkin crept back to the cage and muttered some arcane words, reading from Harbinger's spellbook. Nothing happened. Pumpkin stayed by the cage and chanted a slightly longer incantation. All that happened was that Pumpkin reappeared next to the other Heroes, but the cage remained intact and Aspreyna was still huddled in the middle of it.

"I tried Open Portal and Dimensional Leap," she said, her voice shaking as she suppressed a sob. "I can't do it. That angel's going to be trapped there now. They'll kill her."

Just then, a wonderful thing happened, something Pumpkin looked back on afterwards as a special moment. Strong hands grasped the book and took it from her trembling hands. She realised then how heavy it had been. Montrachet had taken the book and opened it. The pages glowed with a faint light as he skimmed through the spells, looking at them with a keen arcane interest in his large, dark eyes.

"We can't destroy the cage," he said slowly. "And it can't be dispelled. It has no door, so it can't be opened. You can't teleport in and out of it. I suppose a Wish spell would do it, but that's way too hard for us to cast."

Pumpkin watched him, every nerve on edge. For once, Montrachet seemed calm, knowledgeable and in command of the situation. She looked at him in silence.

"We need a low-level spell, something simple to bypass its magic, without destroying it or harming Aspreyna," he went on, murmuring under his breath. Ferdinal wondered idly where Montrachet had learned all this.

Suddenly, Montrachet's face lit up. "I know what to do!"

Even Perancia was excited by his tone of voice.

"Pumpkin, go and ask Aspreyna if she needs air to breathe. Can she breathe in water?" asked Montrachet.

Too confused to ask why, Pumpkin dashed off to the cage and hissed a few words at the angel. She returned only seconds later. Aspreyna was now standing up in the cage.

"She says she doesn't need air to breathe," said Pumpkin, now full of curiosity. "What do you have in mind?"

"We can't destroy the cage as such, but maybe we can burst it," said Montrachet, his eyes dancing. "One of the spells in Harbinger's book is Floodwave. It's not a complex spell. I can cast that between the bars. If the cage had solid walls, we couldn't do it. The spell will create enough swirling water inside the cage that it will burst the bars open. It has to. Water doesn't compress and it has nowhere else to go. It can't seep through between the bars because the cage won't let anything through. We can't destroy the cage, but we can burst it!"

"Won't the cage just reform afterwards?" asked Ferdinal, still not quite believing the idea.

"Maybe. But by then Aspreyna – and the water – will be outside it. The cage can reform, but it will be empty."

"It's like making a giant washing machine," smiled Sapphire, fascinated by the idea of using obscure magic to duplicate a common domestic appliance.

Pumpkin was still gazing at Montrachet. She couldn't say anything. The shy rogue, who wasn't even a proper wizard, had come up with a plan of real genius.

Without stopping to check for guards, Montrachet strode up to the Arcane Cage, the spellbook open in his hand. The other Heroes hurried after him, only Perancia lurking in the shadows. Her instinct for self-preservation told her she would have far more options in the event of trouble if she guarded the Heroes' escape route instead of standing in the middle of the square.

Montrachet chanted confidently for about ten seconds. Pumpkin could feel her heart beating rapidly as the arcane words hung in the air, waiting to take effect. Suddenly there was a rush and the cage filled with water up to the top, engulfing Aspreyna. For a moment, the cage swayed as if the bars were straining against the force. Perhaps real water would have had no effect, but this was conjured water and the Arcane Cage could not negate the inexorable physics of its presence. The Heroes leapt back, just in time, as the bars broke open for a second, just long enough for the water and the imprisoned angel to pour out. Then the cage reformed, empty as Montrachet had prophesised.

Aspreyna got up. Already she seemed alert and in control of herself.

"Quickly," she hissed. "Which way?"

Ferdinal took the lead. "Back to Harbinger's house. We'll be safe there."

Sapphire supported the angel as they scuttled off towards the alleyway. Montrachet put the spellbook under his arm and Pumpkin followed him. Perancia stalked along at the rear. She was trying to stay close to that spellbook – Montrachet was bound to put it down some time.

———

As they walked along, Pumpkin put her hand on Montrachet's arm.

"That was amazing, what you did with that Floodwave spell," she said, looking up at him.

Perancia realised that there was going to be a boring conversation coming and she skipped ahead to walk with Sapphire.

"Oh, you know, I do pick up a few arcane things here and there," blushed Montrachet. He composed himself.

"How do you know wizard spells, anyway? I thought you were a cleric?"

"I did learn some wizard spells. Remember, I used to be a dark elf sorcerer?"

Montrachet looked puzzled. How could someone just change their race and abilities?

Pumpkin leaned up and gave him a quick kiss on the cheek. As she did so, she reflected how much she had changed already from her fourteen-year-old self at home. The two of them stopped, barely noticing their companions and the angel walking on ahead to Harbinger's house. Montrachet, still with the spellbook under his arm, took Pumpkin's hands in his own and gazed down at her affectionately.

Just briefly, it was a special moment. But it was interrupted by the sound of scampering feet. In an instant two beldarks were standing next to them. Pumpkin recognised two of them, Cremorne's henchmen whom she had seen at the Dancehall.

"What is your business here?" demanded one of the beldarks.

Pumpkin was startled. She knew that the gaze from a beldark could be fatal, but these ones seemed more interested in interrogation than execution.

"Oh, er, my... boyfriend and I were just... saying goodnight," she stammered, blushing to the roots of her hair as she spoke. Montrachet looked at her intently, but this time she couldn't meet his gaze.

"No matter. You will come with us," came the curt reply. One beldark marched ahead and behind as they marched off briskly in the opposite direction to Harbinger's house.

Pumpkin, trotting along behind Montrachet, noticed that the spellbook was no longer under his arm.

"Where's the book?" she whispered. But the beldarks did not seem to mind them talking.

"I felt small hands take it from me while the beldarks were talking, just before they led us away," gasped Montrachet, out of breath from struggling to match the beldarks' pace.

"Perancia!" exclaimed Pumpkin. "She must have come back. Little sneaking warlock!"

"At least the book is safe. And she'll know where we are."

"Those are both good points," thought Pumpkin. Montrachet might seem languid and shy, but he really seemed to come to life in a crisis.

———

Pumpkin and Montrachet sat on a bench in a stone cell. They had been there several hours, perhaps most of the night. It was cold in the cell and they were huddled together for warmth under Pumpkin's velvet cloak. There was a small, barred window high up in the wall, through which Pumpkin could hear sounds from the street. The cell must be below ground, probably under the Court of Limbo, thought Pumpkin. It was the first time she had felt cold since arriving in Carceron. Somehow snuggling up to Montrachet made her feel warmer inside. They might be here some time; they might be executed at any moment. Demons did not really seem to have any regular routine by which they worked.

"Why do demons have cells and a court anyway?" grumbled Pumpkin. "If they don't have proper rules, what's the point?"

"I suppose they like to keep people in suspense," said Montrachet thoughtfully. "You know, prolong the agony, part of the whole chaos and evil thing. The Court of Limbo is run by a really nasty creature called Hood. He's really the clerk to the court, but he looks like a real hood that an executioner wears."

He shuddered and fell silent.

Pumpkin decided to drop that part of the conversation and instead make the most of the moment.

"You know you told me you're not really a wizard," she said confidentially, trying to burrow deeper into Montrachet's side as she spoke. "You seemed to do pretty well with that spellbook. Maybe you're more of a wizard than you think."

"Well, I never really studied properly," said Montrachet shyly. "You know, I got found out."

"Perhaps you're more of a sorcerer," said Pumpkin thoughtfully. "They just know how to do magic innately; they don't need lessons and books. But the effects are just as good."

"Psst!" came a sound from outside the barred window.

Montrachet jumped. "Who's there?" he asked, standing up. The window was so high in the wall that he could only just reach the bars with his hands.

"It's Souzira," came a female voice. "From Maelstrom Potions. I was passing and I heard voices. Who's down there?"

"It's Montrachet," he said. "And Pumpkin is with me. Can you get us out?"

"Not likely," said Souzira sharply. "But I can tell Flaxen you're here. He might be able to bust the cell open. I'll go see him now."

Pumpkin felt a bit better. At least her friends would know where she was.

"You were really good with Šapka and Crayler," said Montrachet, returning to the earlier conversation and responding to Pumpkin's compliment in his own quiet way. "Negotiating with a top musical promoter and the Head of the Assassins' Guild isn't easy. And Fulcrum is really creepy. I don't want to see him again in a hurry."

Just then, the door of the cell was unlocked and flung open by a beldark. It did not enter the cell but stood deferentially to one side.

Fulcrum the crow stalked slowly into the cell. He stood in the middle of the floor and looked from Pumpkin to Montrachet with his beady dark eyes.

━━━

When Ferdinal heard the voices of the two beldarks behind him as he and Sapphire were hustling Aspreyna to safety, he had to make an instant decision. Should he dash back to help his sister? Or should he stick to getting his girlfriend and the angel out of danger and seek proper help? And where was Perancia? Maybe she had sneaked off to fetch the beldarks? Treacherous girl.

There was no good option. Ferdinal knew he could not defeat beldark guards. He decided to get Flaxen and Harbinger to help. Harbinger's house was close by. He opened the door. He was surprised again at the way people in a dangerous city like Carceron never locked their doors, but he remembered that Harbinger had glyphs to protect the house.

Ferdinal went in first, with Sapphire helping the slow-moving Aspreyna into the house. Almost at once there was a commotion in the hallway. It was Redwing, who had been dozing near the door. At once the little micro-dragon dashed off to fetch his master, Harbinger, and the hall was full of magical light from somewhere.

Ferdinal's first sense was one of relief, as if he could pass responsibility for decisions to Harbinger. This was the moment for someone more powerful to take charge. Harbinger appeared almost at once, pulling on scarlet- and gold-coloured robes as he took in the situation.

"So, you rescued her," said Harbinger grimly. Then he smiled. "Well done. That's very impressive. I tried weeks ago and I couldn't break the cage. Redwing! Take Aspreyna to the back room to rest. I will activate the nondetection ward."

"What about Pumpkin?" whispered Sapphire, as Aspreyna was being taken care of.

"Yes, what about her?" asked Harbinger, wheeling round to face Sapphire. "Where is she?"

"Er… we need your help," said Ferdinal, feeling that this was one situation in which even a paladin would need to call for backup.

"You see, she and Montrachet were arrested by the beldarks," said Sapphire meekly.

"What!" yelled Harbinger. He turned round again to start issuing orders. "Redwing, send a quasit to wake Flaxen and bring him here right now. Where's my spellbook?"

"Oh, er, we borrowed that too," said Ferdinal quietly.

"Well, give it back at once," snapped Harbinger. "How can I rescue Pumpkin from the beldarks without it?"

"I think Pumpkin and Montrachet still had it when the beldarks took them," explained Ferdinal, feeling even more stupid and embarrassed. This was like being in trouble at school, except this time it was a life-and-death matter.

Just at that moment, Flaxen appeared in the hall. He was wearing his usual golden robes and looked unperturbed. "Maybe," thought Ferdinal, "even if he's no longer a lich, perhaps he doesn't need sleep?"

Harbinger explained the situation in a few short phrases. He sounded more worried than angry. When he admitted that his spellbook was gone, Flaxen pursed his lips.

"Souzira has just been to see me. They're being held at the Court of Limbo. I don't think we should try blasting them out," he said. "Pumpkin might get hurt. We need her. I don't care about Montrachet. There's only one person who can fix this. I'll go and see him now. You all stay here. Especially our young paladin and bard!"

With those swift instructions, he began casting a spell and a few seconds later he vanished.

"Who's he gone to see?" asked Sapphire meekly.

"Only one person who can fix it," said Harbinger, thinking. "He means Fulcrum. But there's always a price."

—

Pumpkin and Montrachet stayed huddled under the velvet cloak, too frightened to move. Fulcrum the crow was tiny, but his manner was so imposing that they couldn't speak.

What was the point? They wouldn't be able to understand the crow's beaky replies.

To their immense relief, Flaxen walked into the cell a few seconds later. "It's as if he actually wanted to leave a dramatic pause," thought Pumpkin, "before making his entry." Typical Flaxen, vain creature that he was.

"I have spoken with Fulcrum," announced Flaxen, in the tone of a judge passing sentence. "He has discussed the matter with the Superiors. I think on this occasion even Cremorne was consulted. We have a solution. You will be released at once."

Pumpkin felt such a sense of relief she gave an involuntary sob and leapt up.

Montrachet continued to sit on the bench. He gulped. He knew that Fulcrum the crow was a master negotiator. There was bound to be a price to pay and it was certain to be bad news for somebody.

Flaxen ambled round the cell, as if talking to himself as he explained. Fulcrum stood on the floor in a corner and kept an eye on Pumpkin, his head tilted to one side.

"Releasing the angel is a major offence," continued Flaxen. "The angel herself is worth nothing to the Superiors. She was going to be killed today anyway and her life or death is of no matter from the Superiors' point of view. And the Arcane Cage is undamaged. It can be used again. The real issue is the defiance of the Superiors' power. Releasing someone they imprisoned is a direct challenge to the Junta that cannot be ignored. You can walk free. But there is a price."

Pumpkin tried to look brave. "W-what price?" she stammered.

Fulcrum continued to watch her closely. Pumpkin realised that the little crow was in complete control of the situation.

"Montrachet. You cast the spell that burst the cage open. Where is the spellbook you used?" Flaxen's tone was stern and the words shot out like arrows.

"It's in a safe place," said Montrachet, meeting Flaxen's gaze. "I can get it."

"Very well," said Flaxen. "Do so and return it to Harbinger. In that case you have nothing to worry about. Pumpkin!"

"Yes, Flaxen," said Pumpkin meekly.

"You were the prime mover in this," scolded Flaxen. "I told you not to get involved. The Superiors consider you the main threat to them by inducing Montrachet to cast the spells. You will go with Fulcrum and Montrachet this morning to see Revlyn. You will join the Destiny Guild, of thieves. You won't work for Revlyn all the time, as Montrachet does, but you have to obey his orders and carry out tasks for him."

"Yes, Flaxen," said Pumpkin again. She didn't like the sound of this, although it might mean she could work with Montrachet sometimes. "Can I see the others this afternoon, once I've seen Revlyn?"

Flaxen smiled for the first time that morning. Montrachet said nothing but was looking horrified. "Of course," he said, grinning. "Nobody in the city will be working this afternoon and evening. It's a special day. Had you forgotten? Today is the Festival of Pandemonium."

Chapter 13
Festival of Pandemonium

Once Pumpkin had agreed to join the Thieves' Guild, Flaxen was only too anxious to get her and Montrachet released from prison and to hustle Pumpkin back to Harbinger's house. Montrachet and Fulcrum headed off to the Southwest District, towards the guild.

"Flaxen, I've been meaning to ask you," said Pumpkin, as they hurried past the Interplanar Bank. "Why is it called the Book of Misdeeds?"

"The book is an artifact," replied Flaxen. "It has the power to open and close gates to other planes. But really what it's doing is making connections to people and places described in its pages. The book contains tales of villains and their chaotic adventures, of places they visited and evil they caused. It's like an anthology of evil fairy tales. The gates it can open are links to those villains. Any gate the book opened can be closed again by the book."

"Thank you for rescuing me, by the way," said Pumpkin, smiling at the old sorcerer. "I was a bit worried."

Flaxen looked at her briefly as they walked. "So you

should be," he said. "This is a dangerous city. There's a shadow demon following us right now, in case you hadn't noticed, to make sure you go to see Revlyn and join his guild. But you need to come to Harbinger's to see your brother first. He's been worried."

Pumpkin hadn't noticed, but she could not help glancing over her shoulder now. There was indeed a shadow demon, following every twist and turn of their route, only a few paces behind. It dawned on her just what a risk she had taken to rescue the angel and also how much Flaxen had changed. The De-Liching had stripped away his undead senses and given him back feelings of compassion and friendship that he must have had centuries ago. Already Pumpkin felt that she and her companions were making a difference in this strange city.

"It looks like business as usual in the street today," she said. "How come there are no preparations going on for this famous festival?"

"You must realise," said Flaxen impatiently, "we do everything in Carceron spontaneously. Things don't get planned. There are no schedules or timescales. We don't even have an idea of how often the festival should take place. This is a city of chaos. We just leave it up to the whims of whoever in town is the most powerful. That's how chaos works."

Back at Harbinger's house, Pumpkin realised how hungry she was. She had managed to sleep briefly in the cell, but the beldarks had not brought any food for her or Montrachet. She had not really expected that they would. While one of Harbinger's quasits rather reluctantly prepared a hasty snack, she chatted with Ferdinal and Sapphire, who were most relieved to see her back.

"Out of everyone in the family, you're the last person I'd have thought would be arrested," laughed Ferdinal.

Pumpkin gave a cheeky grin. She had half expected such a comment.

"It's not every day you get to save an angel from execution. How is Aspreyna, anyway?"

"She's still asleep. She's recovering from her time in that cage. But I think she'll be all right."

"Oh, by the way," interrupted Harbinger, entering the room carrying a big bowl of soup for Pumpkin, "where's my spellbook?"

"Ah, yes," said Pumpkin, dipping a spoon into the steaming brew. "I can get it for you later today. It's somewhere safe. Don't send a quasit, one of us will bring it here."

"Be sure you do," said Harbinger, rather gruffly. "It's valuable and contains some rare spells. I don't want thieves getting their hands on it."

"If it had been really valuable," thought Pumpkin, "it would have contained the spell Destroy Matter and saved everyone a lot of trouble." But she didn't say that out loud.

Pumpkin and Montrachet sat at a table together in the Acid House bar. It was the same table at which they had had a drink together before. So much had happened since then. Pumpkin had gone first to the Destiny Guild, escorted by Redwing, who still sat on her shoulder. Her initiation from Revlyn had been perfunctory in the extreme. He seemed to have something else on his mind. He had given her some basic instruction about not taking orders from anyone but himself and in particular about how to avoid divulging any information she acquired. Then he had ordered Montrachet to instruct her on the guild's procedures, ordering them to discuss it at Acid House, on the basis that the majority of the guild's business took place in the bars and restaurants of Carceron.

"Maybe he'll be more forthcoming later?" pondered Pumpkin. She was sipping a new light blue-coloured drink called Cyan, which the bar had just begun serving, to mark the start of the Festival of Pandemonium.

"Never gives away much, does Revlyn," said Montrachet, shaking his head. He wasn't keen on the taste of Cyan; he could feel it burning his throat.

"Teach me something about thieving, then," said Pumpkin demurely, leaning forward across the table in a conspiratorial fashion. "Do I have to turn evil?"

Montrachet frowned. "No. Anyone can be a thief. But there are a lot of tricks. It relies on information and contacts. Revlyn's right, there's no better place to work than a bar. He hasn't taught you lock-picking or burglary. So, he doesn't expect you to be that kind of thief. And we don't normally kill people, that's for Šapka and the Assassins' Guild."

Just then, they spotted Perancia coming into Acid House. She had not noticed them and seemed to be looking for someone else. As she went up to the bar, Pumpkin noticed that she was carrying a sack.

In a moment Pumpkin was at the bar with her, Redwing clinging to her shoulder as she ran. Montrachet was close behind. This involved shoving their way past numerous other customers, but such casual rudeness seemed to be expected in this bar. Pumpkin and Montrachet stood on either side of Perancia.

"Can't play with you today," said Perancia, dismissively. "Got to find someone. Ooh, they've got Cyan here today! That stuff's great. Really stomach-churning."

"We want to talk to you," said Pumpkin sternly. "Where's Harbinger's spellbook? You had it last."

"Of course," said Perancia crossly, paying for her Cyan and still looking around the bar. "If I hadn't then the beldarks would have got it and you'd have been in even deeper trouble. How come you got out so soon?"

"Fulcrum fixed it," said Montrachet briefly.

"Makes sense," nodded Perancia, sipping her Cyan and wincing as it hissed in her throat. "Actually, the spellbook is why I'm here. I've found a buyer for it already. I told CT I had it and he said it was too valuable to burn so I might as well sell it. Ah!"

She had spotted Lamar and Fredinal, who had slunk up behind Pumpkin and were standing uncomfortably close. Perancia did not know that Fredinal was really Pumpkin's brother Oliver. Had she known, she would not have cared.

"That it?" asked Lamar, pointing to the sack.

Pumpkin turned to face the two of them. Redwing's eyes began to widen.

"You're not having it," she said simply. "It's Harbinger's spellbook. We're going to return it. And as for *you*, Oliver, wait 'til we get you home!"

Fredinal laughed in a cocky, sneering way and put a hand to the hilt of his shortsword.

Lamar ignored her. "Here's the gold," he said gruffly,

tossing a small leather pouch to Perancia, who caught it deftly and pocketed it with a single flick of her wrist.

Just then, two things happened at once. Montrachet put out his arm to stop Perancia handing over the bag that contained the precious spellbook. As the two of them fought for supremacy, Redwing spread his tiny wings, swooped down off Pumpkin's shoulder and grabbed the spellbook bag by its neck, ripping it from Perancia's grasp. An instant later, the little dragon flew into the air and vanished, turning invisible and, Pumpkin supposed, zooming off towards the door to dash back to Harbinger's house.

Lamar turned to Pumpkin, who was closest, and grasped her roughly by the shoulders.

"This is your fault!" he yelled. "Give my book back."

He had grabbed the wrong person. Perancia, ever quick to spot an opportunity, had slipped away from the bar and was weaving her way with great speed past the other customers in the bar, towards the door. She was no longer interested in the book, nor in Redwing. She had Lamar's pouch of gold and had upheld her side of the bargain. "CT will be pleased with this little bit of skulduggery," she thought, as she dashed to freedom. "Unless Lamar filled the bag with iron drabs, that is."

Fredinal dashed towards the door in pursuit of Perancia, but he was no match for the dextrous little urchin. Trying to jostle the other customers aside, he was soon held fast by a couple of tough-looking henchmen.

Pumpkin was too shocked to move, caught in Lamar's grasp. But Montrachet did not hesitate to come to her rescue. He chanted a few quick words and pointed at Lamar, who was immediately hurled backwards against the bar, letting go of Pumpkin as he slipped. The other customers, who had ignored the rest of the conversation, turned with interest at the prospect of a fight. But the barkeeper had other ideas.

"No more of that," he said, putting an arm across the bar between Montrachet and Lamar. "Three-drink minimum for fights. And don't spill Cyan on the bar. That stuff eats straight through wood."

Lamar, breathing heavily, straightened himself up. The money was gone and the book was gone. Without another word he turned and walked out of the bar.

Pumpkin turned to Montrachet. "Will I get in trouble with Revlyn? That was my first chance to help with a theft and I handed the goods back to their rightful owner."

"Not at all," laughed Montrachet. "Lamar's from the Assassins' Guild, The Velvet Glove. If anyone's lost money today, it's Šapka not Revlyn. Lamar will be very upset, though."

"Maybe my brother is working with Lamar now," said Pumpkin, depressed at the idea. "We've got to get him back to his senses and rescue him, too."

The barkeeper leaned across the bar again, under the pretence of mopping up some spilled Cyan.

"Message from the boss," he muttered to Montrachet. "He says Pumpkin is to try and infiltrate the Enigma Club. Some dangerous elements meet there and the Superiors want it watched." He turned away to serve a customer.

Pumpkin looked at Montrachet. "What does that mean?" she asked.

"Don't know," said Montrachet, frowning. "When he says boss, he means Revlyn. I've heard of the Enigma Club, but it's very secretive and I've no idea who's in it. Perhaps we should ask Harbinger."

———

Pumpkin and Montrachet went to Harbinger's house but found nobody there except the quasit who had prepared Pumpkin's soup. It told them that Harbinger and the others had gone to the Dancehall for the start of the festival, then slammed the front door in their faces.

There was a queue of people outside The Irresistible Dancehall, but Mr Ottoman spotted Pumpkin and waved the two of them in past the waiting line of tourists. Soon Pumpkin and Montrachet were sitting at a table on the dancefloor with Flaxen, Harbinger, Ferdinal and Sapphire. Pumpkin immediately ordered a glass of Cerise, to wash away the horrible corrosive aftertaste of Cyan that lingered in her mouth.

"Heard the latest tune?" asked Ferdinal, grinning at his sister.

Pumpkin turned towards the raised dais at which the four zombies from The Horde were performing. The tune was lively and people were dancing to it with great vigour. It was a sort of rock song, with the Magic Mouth behind the band yelling out the words.

"It's Marvexio's latest song," explained Flaxen. "He wrote it for my campaign. It's called 'Lich on the Loose'. I think it's really catchy."

"It's a good tune," agreed Pumpkin. "But don't you see what's really important? It's being sung by The Horde. That's one of the bands promoted by Apollonius Crayler, isn't it? That means he's really backing the campaign and he wants people to know it."

"A toast to Crayler," said Harbinger. Everyone stayed

seated, thanks to the crowd in the bar, but they raised their glasses and drank. This was the first tangible sign that Flaxen's campaign had influential backing. And it was a good song.

"Can he write one that includes our campaign slogan?" asked Sapphire, who had been listening intently to the lyrics. "The one I made up – 'Vote for chaos, not evil.'"

"I'll make a point of asking him," said Flaxen indulgently. "Maybe Tinsel would sing it for us."

"Harbinger, what's the Enigma Club?" asked Montrachet, quietly. He had to repeat the question, not wanting to yell it openly but struggling to compete with the din from the countless revellers in The Irresistible Dancehall.

"Where did you hear that name?" snapped Harbinger sharply.

Montrachet explained the strange orders from Revlyn. Flaxen and Harbinger looked at each other in some concern.

"It began as an apocalypse cult," said Flaxen slowly. "You know, the leader foretells the end of the world and everyone's going to die. But then the end of the world never came, so the cult had to find a new purpose. It's a combination now of secret society, network of contacts and social group. I think the Archmayor was a member."

"Marid might know more," admitted Harbinger. "But the Superiors always suppress other sects. They see them as a threat. Anything they don't control is potentially a threat."

Flaxen called out to the Late Mr Melville, who was serving at the next table.

"Melville! If Marid comes in, will you point him over to our table, please?"

The ghost nodded disdainfully and corrected him. "The *Late* Mr Melville, please!"

It did not take long for the ghost to find Marid. "Ghosts clearly have a big advantage in a crowded bar," thought Sapphire, "just being able to glide through the crowd." Marid sat down at the table.

"We need your advice on a sensitive matter," said Flaxen. "Pumpkin had to join the Thieves' Guild this morning. It was a deal with Fulcrum. Revlyn has asked her to infiltrate the Enigma Club. We don't know why, but I bet it's something to do with the Superiors. The Archmayor was a member. Do you know who else is involved?"

"I've never been in it myself," said Marid. "The Archmayor never invited me. But I think Talisman might be. He mentioned that the Club was heavily involved with the harvesting of corpses for the election. He must know something."

The conversation was interrupted by Mr Ottoman approaching the table. "Flaxen! Did you know that Pullywuggles is here, in the bar?"

"No. Where is he? What's he doing?"

"He's up on the stage, next to The Horde. Can you please remove him before he gets hurt? His signature move turns out to be breakdancing. Tortoises seem to be very good at it."

━━

Flaxen dismissed Pullywuggles back to his pocket dimension. He then proposed that they make the most of the Festival of Pandemonium by going round some of the other restaurants and bars, to meet as many people as possible. Pumpkin would privately have preferred to look for Talisman and ask him about the Enigma Club, but she was eager to do some more campaigning too.

As they emerged into Central Square it was late afternoon. Flaxen, Harbinger and the Heroes were joined by Marid and Souzira. The crowds were building up at all the bars and the casinos were busy too, with crowds trying to get into Electrum, The Deck of Delusions and The Fates.

Suddenly they heard the sound of trumpets. It turned out to be a magic mouth spell, cast on the side of a wagon, which was being hauled into the square by two beautiful chestnut horses. The wagon was also bedecked with "Vote Vampire" banners.

Standing on the back of the wagon was Mercedes, waving and yelling to the crowds. At her side were Jagglespur and his assistant, scattering sweets to the crowd ("Just what Amber would do!" thought Sapphire crossly). The wagon was surrounded by guards. Ferdinal recognised Captain Manacle the slave-dealer, Zarek, Gortol and another ogre who might be his brother Kuthol. At least there was no sign of Oliver this time.

Mercedes was heading slowly round the square with her wagon. She began pointing upwards at intervals of ten seconds or so, sending fiery spheres into the sky each time. Many in the crowd were impressed and began cheering.

Flaxen stood watching the scene with his arms folded, as if he thought it a pathetic spectacle. The sight of him passively watching his opponent grabbing the attention during the Festival of Pandemonium enraged Sapphire.

"We've got to interrupt them," she whispered to Ferdinal and Pumpkin. "See if you can distract the guards. I'm going to take out the horses."

"You're not going to hurt them?" asked Pumpkin in real alarm. "They're so lovely."

"No, I'm going to use a simple Animal Friendship charm on them to make them steer where I tell them."

"Sapphire, if you have to use a charm spell, it isn't really your friend," mocked Ferdinal. As usual, he was making a joke to take his mind off what was bound to be a nasty fight. He had played a paladin in a roleplaying game, but he had never actually used a real sword to try and hurt someone. Would it come naturally? Would the sword be too heavy? And those two ogres were each twice his size and looked tough.

"I can use Radiant Flame at a distance," added Pumpkin. The wagon was still about thirty feet away.

"Make sure you don't hit me," put in Ferdinal, drawing his sword in readiness.

"Radiant damage only hurts the sinful," said Pumpkin the Cleric, with an elaborate show of piety.

There was no time to lose. Sapphire the Bard began casting her charm on the horses. Ferdinal raced up to attack Zarek, who was closest to him in size. Pumpkin cast Radiant Flame on Gortol, who looked as though he would be too slow and stupid to dodge it. As she was casting, she became aware of another figure next to her. It was Perancia, also casting a spell. She was looking at Kuthol, smiling and beckoning to him as she chanted.

The first visible sign of battle was that a flash of light, like a tiny lightning strike, appeared above Gortol's head and struck him. The ogre bellowed in pain and smashed the side of the wagon as he struck out at random. He happened to hit the panel where the magic mouth had been cast and the trumpet sound stopped at once.

Ferdinal ran up to Zarek and immediately engaged him in combat. He realised at once that Zarek, an experienced swashbuckler, was much more skilled than he was. Soon the two were fencing together, steel clanging against steel as blows were exchanged and parried. Ferdinal began to enjoy himself, slashing and smiting as if he'd been doing so for years.

The horses started to move away, under Sapphire's control. The wagon began moving towards the centre of the square.

Perancia's spell seemed to be affecting Kuthol. She had made a hypnotic suggestion to charm him, making him believe that Gortol had been betraying him all along and was even now plotting his demise. With a cry of fury, Kuthol tore off a plank from the wagon and, using it as an improvised club, smote his brother round the head with it.

The crowd scattered to the sides of Central Square. Even the beldarks and shadow demons paused their patrols. This was the Festival of Pandemonium and here, in the centre of the town, was a free display of brawling, duelling and magic.

Flaxen, Harbinger and Marid were not slow to respond either. Pumpkin was unsure who cast which spell, but there was an explosion under the wagon, throwing Jagglespur off, while a bolt of lightning struck the squabbling ogres.

Mercedes was slower to react, being more intent on showing off and charming the crowds. But soon she began a barrage of spells and counterspells with Flaxen and Marid, making that part of the square a deadly battle zone of arcane missiles.

"My spell lasts for six hours," confided Perancia gleefully to Pumpkin, as she egged on Kuthol to further acts of devastation. "Think what I can do with a tame ogre in six hours! He's the bursar of the Temple of Carcus, for a start. I can get the keys to their strong room!"

Once again, Pumpkin thought that Perancia's love of pure anarchy was leading her into real trouble. She began to sidle closer to Harbinger.

Soon Gortol was lying on the ground, unconscious. Kuthol was walking away in the direction of the temple, followed by Perancia, who seemed to be giving him detailed instructions. Ferdinal and Zarek were still locked in combat, but Captain Manacle had fled.

Seeing her triumph turning to defeat, Mercedes gave one loud yell and her body disappeared, turning into mist. The misty form quickly moved away eastwards towards the demons' mansions in Delirium Drive. Jagglespur ran after her. The battle was over. It had lasted for barely a minute.

With fighting now stopping, Zarek deftly leapt backwards out of Ferdinal's reach.

"You fight well, young paladin! Happy Pandemonium to you," cried Zarek. He sheathed his sword and calmly turned his back, walking off towards Hightower Square as if he hadn't a care in the world.

"Happy Pandemonium," said Ferdinal, watching with wry satisfaction as his foe slunk away.

Chapter 14

The Campaign Trail

"Is Gortol dead?" asked Sapphire, running over to the inert body of the ogre.

"He looks it," said Harbinger. "Are any of you hurt? You didn't tell me you were going to start an arcane street brawl!"

The Heroes looked at each other. Nobody was bleeding.

"Where's Montrachet?" asked Pumpkin suddenly. "He was with us when we came out of the Dancehall. But he's not here now."

"Haven't seen him," said Flaxen, unconcernedly.

"There!" cried Sapphire.

Montrachet was walking back from the road Mercedes had taken. He approached Pumpkin and smiled. "I've put a Portable Eye in Mercedes' pocket," he said. "I ran along beside her as she was passing the Trident Hotel. I don't think she saw. Now we'll know where she goes. We can track her."

For once, Flaxen was impressed. "We'll know which demons she meets and who's on her side," he said approvingly.

"What about Gortol?" asked Sapphire. "I didn't want anyone to get killed."

Harbinger and Marid dragged the body of the ogre to one side of the square.

"Let me look, I'm a cleric," said Pumpkin bossily, pushing Harbinger aside.

Harbinger looked as though he was going to say something in reply but stayed silent.

"He's dead all right," concluded Pumpkin. "I have a spell that might help."

Ferdinal was not at all convinced that resuscitating a lifeless ogre would be beneficial, but he let Pumpkin finish her spell. When her chanting finished, the ogre remained lifeless.

"Didn't it work?" asked Sapphire anxiously.

"I'm not trying to bring him to life," said Pumpkin crossly. "It's a Speak with the Slain spell. I want to ask him what Mercedes was doing. Now let me think. It's telepathic."

There was silence around the body as they all watched Pumpkin. They heard no words from Pumpkin or the ogre, but they could see Pumpkin mouthing words and changing her facial expression, as if having a silent conversation. Ferdinal noticed Perancia coming back into the square to watch. At last Pumpkin spoke.

"He says that Mercedes' campaign is based at Captain Manacle's shop," she said. "That's where he goes for orders. And Mercedes has probably run off to see Cremorne. The rest of what he said was about what he's going to do to Kuthol in the afterlife."

"I'd better get some quasits to take the body away," said Harbinger, going off to give the order.

"That wasn't very helpful," said Ferdinal scornfully.

"We could resurrect him, kill him and cast the spell again?" suggested Perancia helpfully.

They all looked at her.

"Well, that's what CT recommends!" explained the young warlock defensively. If in doubt, blame the patron.

Back at Harbinger's house the Heroes ate a big dinner and planned out their next move. Harbinger had to reassure Sapphire once again that the food was vegan. The Heroes still had to find Talisman to get details of the Enigma Club, assuming he was willing to discuss it. They had to find the Book of Misdeeds in order to close the Crater at the temple, to stop Mercedes bringing thousands of undead in to vote in the election. And to do that, they first needed to find the Archmayor's will, as Lamothe had insisted, to find out to whom the Archmayor would have bequeathed the Book of Misdeeds.

Montrachet and Perancia were there too. Harbinger seemed to have forgiven Perancia for trying to steal and sell his precious spellbook. "Perhaps," thought Pumpkin, "such behaviour is not so unusual in Carceron." Montrachet was disappointed to find that the Portable Eye he had planted on Mercedes had failed to report anything back. Evidently the wily vampire had been expecting some such ploy.

"I think we should stick together from now on," said Ferdinal. "When we split up to go to the Botanical Gardens and the temple, we could have got into real trouble. We've been lucky. That fight earlier with Mercedes shows how dangerous it is here."

Pumpkin and Sapphire looked at each other. Much as they hated to admit it, Ferdinal was right. Although Pumpkin had once insisted that being born on Halloween meant that she was used to putting up with vampires, it was very different coming face to face with one like Mercedes – a villain, who was at once intelligent, beguiling, powerful, ruthless and determined.

"Oh, and we need to find Oliver and rescue him, too," added Pumpkin. After all, Oliver was still their brother, even if he was calling himself Fredinal the Assassin right now.

"And in the middle of all that, win the election for Flaxen," finished Sapphire.

"Stick together if you like," said Perancia indifferently. "I'll tag along sometimes. Other times, I've got my own things to do. I get given errands by CT, you know."

"Don't tell me you actually obey him sometimes?" asked Sapphire indignantly. Crixus Telmarine must have limitless patience.

"Well, I have to every now and then. Otherwise, he'll stop training me. But I think he rather likes me being independent."

"I am very interested in the divisions that are starting to show within the demon Junta," said Flaxen thoughtfully. "Their power lies in their unity and in everyone being afraid of them. If we can isolate Babaeski as a heretic for backing Mercedes and force Lamothe to back us, that would be very useful. I wonder where Cremorne stands in all of this. He's always hard to read."

"Perhaps Champrice could find out?" asked Harbinger. He said it with a straight face, but a twinkle in his eye implied mischief in his suggestion.

Flaxen nodded abstractly, too deep in thought to reply.

"Well, where to first?" demanded Perancia.

"We simply have to do some more campaigning today," announced Sapphire firmly. "We may be able to find Talisman while we're out meeting people. Then tonight we go to the Mayor's Palace. Flaxen, I assume you can give us some scrolls of spells that will get us in and help us search?"

"Certainly, certainly," said Flaxen. He still did not seem to be concentrating.

"I don't think there are any valuables there," said Harbinger. "They would have been looted years ago by half the rogues in Carceron. But there may be ordinary things, like the Archmayor's will, that may have been overlooked."

"As well as campaigning in the streets, we need to buy up votes wholesale where we can," added Sapphire, in the manner of an underworld boss, for all her demure manner. "Harbinger, can you cut a deal with Rent-a-Zombie? I bet they're dealing with Mercedes as well, but we need all the bodies they can supply."

Ferdinal smiled to himself at Sapphire's ruthlessness. She had adapted very quickly to the role of giving orders to strangers and she made an excellent Campaign Manager.

"Then let's get our campaign gear," said Pumpkin, efficient as ever. "It's time our candidate met more of the public!"

"Where to first?" asked Flaxen, as they left the house.

"We've been to The Irresistible Dancehall plenty of times," declared Sapphire. "And Pumpkin says Acid House is no good for meeting the public. It's too crowded and too full of rogues. Šapka and Revlyn will be telling them how to vote."

"Let's go to some of the demon bars!" cried Perancia. "And the casinos. There'll be lots of tourists there. They'll be easy to persuade."

Pumpkin looked at her. Perancia's suggestions were actually good ones, from the campaign's point of view. The tourists would be more open to persuasion or bribery than many of the Carceron residents. And so far the campaign had mostly avoided the demons. No doubt Perancia actually intended to pickpocket the demons and swindle the tourists, but that was her problem. "When Perancia ends up in prison under the Court of Limbo," thought Pumpkin, "I'll personally send Fulcrum to offer some hideous deal in return for freedom."

"All right," nodded Pumpkin. "What are the casinos like?"

"The bars and restaurant in Carceron are enjoyed by locals and tourists alike," explained Harbinger. "But the casinos are really for tourists only. Electrum is a small, traditional establishment with cards and games of pure chance. The Deck of Delusions attracts people who play for higher stakes and it has a huge deck of cards in one room which, when dealt, bring forth creatures to fight or occasionally piles of treasure as a reward."

"What about The Fates?" asked Ferdinal.

"We won't go there," said Flaxen. "It's really not that safe."

"They have a Deck of Infinite Outcomes," said Perancia confidentially, as if worried that the hazards would overhear her description. "I know three people who were killed by that. And they have a Wheel of Fortune. You get tied to a vertical disk that spins on the spot while people throw daggers at it. The longer you survive before getting hit by one, the more money you win. People bet on it. There's some card game that you play really quickly with cards dealt by a lady demon with seven arms. Then in the Shuriken Room, they—"

"Have you actually been there?" challenged Sapphire.

"I used to go every day," replied Perancia, surprised. "I got bored of going when I was about twelve, after a couple of my friends died. It was one of the few places I didn't have to pay for drinks."

"Did you get barred in the end?" asked Ferdinal, smiling. "Didn't they want you coming back?"

"Barred!" cackled Perancia. "Nobody gets barred in Carceron. I just got into other things. It's really dull throwing daggers at strangers tied to a disk for hours at a time."

"We'll try the Deck of Delusions," said Pumpkin. "Is that all right, Flaxen? Then maybe some demon bars."

"I never thought I'd find myself choosing casinos and seeking out demons," she thought to herself. "And it's not even for fun."

"I'm coming too," said a voice.

Everyone turned towards the doorway. Aspreyna the angel was standing there. Drawn up to her full height she was nearly eight feet tall, with a statuesque figure. Her voice conveyed passion and resolve, and the fire in her eyes proved that she meant business. She seemed to have completely recovered her powers since being rescued. Now she meant to show her gratitude by joining Flaxen's team. Her face and arms gave off a faint shimmering light. "It's actually possible," thought Ferdinal, as he gazed in wonder at the angel, "for someone to be radiantly beautiful."

"Bravo!" cried Flaxen, standing up and applauding. Even Perancia seemed impressed.

"Henry!" snapped Sapphire to her boyfriend, as she followed his gaze. "Stop gaping and get ready!"

———

The Heroes marched confidently into Central Square. There was no sign of Mercedes or her campaign wagon. Sapphire wondered for a moment what had happened to the chestnut horses and hoped they were being well looked after.

Mercedes had not left the square unattended, however. A wooden market stall had been set up in the middle of the square. It was bedecked with Mercedes' campaign banners, while two people were handing out pictures of Mercedes to passers-by. Ferdinal recognised Zarek as one of the two. The other was a strange-looking woman, clearly a demon to judge by her horns, tail and fangs, but strangely beautiful in appearance. Again, Ferdinal found himself gazing in bewilderment at the creature, even though he knew she was a demon.

A strong hand clutched his jaw, wrenching his head round to the side and tilting his chin upwards. It was Aspreyna.

"Think she's more beautiful than me, do you?" snarled Aspreyna. Ferdinal at once realised that he didn't and said so.

Sapphire watched this with ever-increasing fury and even stamped her foot. But she said nothing. Just wait until she got her boyfriend on his own. Then she would have something to say to him about falling for strange angels and demons!

Flaxen went up to the market stall, as if he were a casual tourist. He took one of the pictures from the demon and looked at the image.

"Why, she's hardly changed in five hundred years," he reminisced fondly.

The demon scowled at him. "These are campaign pictures. You voting for her?"

"Shouldn't you be at your restaurant, Mylar?" asked Harbinger idly. "How does The Inferno run itself without you?"

The demon turned a deeper shade of red and snarled at him. Flaxen continued to look affectionately at the picture of Mercedes.

"She looks just the same," he said. "Does she still have those hairy moles on her arms? I can see why she chose loose-fitting clothes, to fit her scaly backbone in more easily."

He was talking loudly and a large crowd was forming to listen to him with great interest. On the other side of the stall, Zarek was listening with interest but continuing to hand out pictures and ignoring him.

"Did you have to alter the picture at all?" asked Flaxen, speaking to Mylar the demon. "Didn't she have one green eye and one yellow one? But I recognise that diamond jewellery. It's the necklace of flame that I stole for her name day one year. That must be six hundred years ago if it's a day."

Mylar lunged at him as he spoke, but Harbinger grabbed her scaly arm and threw her off balance. At the same moment Pumpkin noticed smoke coming from the wooden stall. Perancia had set fire to the unused stock of printed pictures, which were catching alight rapidly. The wooden stall itself would burn any moment. Mylar turned. As a demon she was not afraid of fire, but she had no way of extinguishing the flames. Zarek, seeing disaster unfold, dropped his handful of pictures and ran off towards the Interplanar Bank. Ferdinal watched him flee and thought, "That's two fights he's run away from in two days. Not much of a swashbuckler!"

Mylar saw that she was on her own facing Flaxen and a posse of opponents. A devoted follower of Mercedes might have stood their ground and fought. But Mylar was first and foremost a restaurant owner. Being injured in a fight in front of hundreds of tourists could only be bad for business. And Flaxen had that tall angel on his side now, too. Mylar unfurled wings from her side, which the Heroes had not noticed before, and soared into the air above their heads. It was little more than a leap really, as she glided down at the edge of the square. She was signalling that she had no desire to argue further.

The Heroes watched her go in some relief. Montrachet pointed to the smouldering market stall and rapped out some words that put out the flames and stopped them spreading. He seemed relieved when the spell worked as intended.

"Can we *please* go to a casino?" begged Perancia. "I'm bored now."

The Deck of Delusions lived up to its name. It stood next to the Trident Hotel and its frontage was a colourful array of swirling patterns that moved as you watched until it was painful to the eyes.

There was nobody on duty at the door, so any customer could walk in. Pumpkin started to understand how Perancia had got into The Fates so easily. It was not as if proof of age was needed in a city like Carceron.

Inside the casino was quite dark. There were endless card tables and large numbers of tourists spending money freely on games that Pumpkin didn't want to try to understand. Some seemed to be games of pure chance, people betting on whether a card would be odd or even, or whether it would be a face card.

One of the first things she noticed was that the decks themselves were different from those she had seen at home. Rather than having an ace, King, Queen and Jack as face cards, these were labelled with different types of demon. The card for Queen looked very much like Mylar the succubus. And there were more of them, species of major and minor demons. Even the cards below ten in value displayed some demon type, all the way down to a quasit as the "three" in each suit and a demon larva as the lowest-ranking "two". The suits were also different. In place of Clubs, Diamonds, Hearts and Spades, there were Coins, Daggers, Limbs and Souls, only the hierarchical alphabetic order being the same. There was also some sort of no-trump suit labelled "Voids".

"What's special about the Voids suit?" she asked Perancia, who was watching one of the games.

"Those can be tricky," whispered Perancia. "If you get too many of the Void suit in your hand, some casinos teleport the player into the plane of Limbo. Some gamblers get trapped there for years. CT warned me about that."

"Does this casino do that to the customers?" stammered Pumpkin anxiously.

"How should I know?" said Perancia carelessly. "They're not likely to tell you in advance that they're going to do it, are they? The uncertainty's part of the fun. It's what gamblers like."

Sapphire and Ferdinal were being more practical. With Aspreyna leading the way and attracting attention, they were walking round the casino's tables handing out gold-coloured campaign hats and badges. Montrachet went with them, his arms full of further inventory.

"Don't forget to wear these, gold brings good luck to gamblers," called out Ferdinal, trying to keep a straight face.

"We give you gold; Mercedes only offers iron drabs," added Sapphire more cheekily.

Flaxen followed behind them, escorted by Harbinger, shaking hands with the tourists and explaining about the election. "This at least looks more like a proper campaign," thought Ferdinal.

They had difficulty coaxing Perancia away from the gaming tables, but in the end they moved on to the next venue.

"We'll skip going to The Inferno," said Harbinger. "I don't think Mylar would welcome us there and the demons might attack us. Let's try YouChoose."

The restaurant YouChoose was certainly a favourite of the demons. The idea of picking out one's food while it was still alive and having the chef slaughter and prepare it while you watched clearly appealed to them. The place was noisy, with most of the talking being in a guttural hissing language which Pumpkin supposed was Demonic. Flaxen moved freely amongst the tables, greeting many of the demons by name but rarely staying to chat. Aspreyna waited outside. She wasn't so keen on the demon diners.

"Demons often have a short attention span and a short temper," explained Harbinger, as the Heroes watched. "They don't want to be disturbed when they're eating. Most people wouldn't get away with what Flaxen's doing. But they seem to tolerate him."

Ferdinal thought Flaxen's progress round the restaurant looked a bit like a zookeeper walking round the wolverines' enclosure at feeding time and probably equally risky. The Heroes didn't hand out gold-coloured merchandise this time but stayed a safe distance away. Perancia considered whether to pop into the kitchen to see if she could steal from the chefs but thought better of it.

Flaxen seemed to be doing well. To Pumpkin's surprise the demons seemed to accept him. They had a respect for his arcane power, for demons only really respect strength. "And," thought Pumpkin, "the fact that Flaxen has been undead for several centuries stops him coming across as too wholesome for demon tastes." She had thought it unlikely that many demons would vote for Flaxen if they voted at all. The campaign had not kept any records of who exactly might vote for its candidate. Somehow, the technique of canvassing support in Carceron seemed impossible. You couldn't trust what anybody told you. But the demons weren't entirely a lost cause. Some of them might well vote for Flaxen.

At one table sat Talisman, talking to a plump man whom the Heroes didn't recognise.

"We need to talk to him," whispered Sapphire. "Who's that he's eating with?"

"It's Blatherwick, the ambassador from the City of Spires," said Harbinger. "I'll introduce you."

They went up to the table and Harbinger introduced the Heroes to Blatherwick as Flaxen's campaign managers. Harbinger engaged Blatherwick in conversation, which did not seem difficult as the ambassador never seemed to stop talking. This helped the Heroes to talk to Talisman briefly.

"Later on, we need to see you," hissed Sapphire. "It's about a certain Club."

Talisman gasped and dropped a piece of food off his fork onto the floor. There was a squeak and the food scuttled off towards the kitchen. Pumpkin jumped back.

"Eww!" she cried. "It's still alive! How horrid!"

"Not here," said Talisman in an urgent whisper. "How did you…? Never mind. Come and see me at my shop tomorrow. I've been discussing with Blatherwick about opening another branch in the City of Spires."

Flaxen returned from working the room. "All done here?" he asked. "Let's go on to the next one! Seeds next, then Eye to Eye if there's time."

"What about The Abyss?" asked Montrachet.

"Too many levels," said Harbinger. "I hate all those stairs."

"That's not the spirit," admonished Flaxen in a tone of mock reproach. "Energy and enthusiasm's what we need now!"

Sapphire was impressed. At last Flaxen seemed to be really getting into the swing of the campaign. It seemed to be giving him a zest for life that he must have lost centuries ago.

"At this rate you might even win," she said admiringly.

Chapter 15

In the Mayor's Palace

Flaxen's campaigning zeal had tired out his young team, but they were determined to go out again after dark, as planned. There was time for a short rest at Flaxen's house first. They couldn't see Talisman until tomorrow to ask about the Enigma Club, but in the meantime there was the Mayor's Palace to be searched. The palace was on the other side of the city, but the Heroes were excited.

Ferdinal had insisted earlier that everyone stick together. The idea of sneaking into a palace at night was itself enough to win Perancia's attention. Montrachet was pleased to be asked, although he realised that it was his thieving skills as much as his magical prowess that was in demand. He would be the one called upon to open locks or scale walls. Aspreyna surprised them by insisting on coming too and the Heroes felt reassured by her enthusiasm.

"Is the palace empty at the moment then?" asked Pumpkin.

"Yes," said Flaxen. "The Archmayor lived there on his own. Well, I say lived, he was undead really. But for 150 years that was his home. I expect there are other creatures living there, though."

"All the formal rooms are on a single level above ground," explained Harbinger. "But there's a lot more below ground. That's where the Archmayor's quarters were. I've never been down there. I don't think even Marid has."

"So, I expect if he did leave a will, it will be down there too?" asked Sapphire.

"Probably. I don't think he was very good with paperwork, though. Could be anywhere."

Flaxen had been talking to Pullywuggles in a corner of the room. He brought over a bundle of scrolls and put them on the table.

"Pullywuggles says you might need these," he said. "They're all wizard and sorcerer spells. Montrachet, you'd better take them; you know how to use them. Each spell has its own scroll: Open Portal, Climb, Charm, Arcane Spy, Speakall, Dispel. Quite a selection. One of the scrolls isn't labelled; not sure what that one does. I bought them as a set at a market stall once."

It was late in the evening, but not yet night. Aspreyna led the way to the palace, reasoning that her aura would deter any but the most powerful demons from attacking the group. Ferdinal and Sapphire strode behind her, Ferdinal with his sword always at the ready, Sapphire keeping an eye on her boyfriend to make sure he didn't go all soppy over the tall, imposing angel yet again. Pumpkin and Montrachet walked behind them, Montrachet having borrowed a backpack to put the spell scrolls in. Instinctively Pumpkin sought out and held Montrachet's hand. She was feeling just a little bit homesick, despite all the excitement, and needed reassurance. Perancia stalked along at the back, ever alert to danger and looking always for an escape route if things got tough.

Even in the late evening the streets were still crowded. Carceron was a city that never really seemed to sleep. "Then again," thought Pumpkin, "there isn't a real night and day here." The daytime light was too weak and grey to count as sunshine, while at night things were so noisy and the lights from restaurants and bars so garish that night and day seemed to merge.

As they passed through Central Square, one group of revellers approached them as they walked. They pointed at Aspreyna admiringly. Rather than barge through the crowd, Aspreyna paused. The others stopped behind her.

"Ooh, look at you," shrieked a well-dressed elven lady, who seemed to have drunk as much Vermillion as she could hold.

"Where d'you get that stuff?" asked another.

"Is it from Dark Celestial? Can we get it at Nameless?" cooed a third lady.

Aspreyna ignored them. She stood still, looking straight ahead. "It isn't worth the effort of sonic booming them aside," she thought. "They'll soon get bored and move on." The Heroes waited anxiously behind.

After a minute of fingering Aspreyna's clothes and stroking her wings, the elves did move along and the group continued on its way. They reached the eastern side of the city without further trouble. Beldark patrols ignored them and shadow demons moved aside when they saw the tall celestial figure of Aspreyna approaching. Sapphire grudgingly admitted to herself that Aspreyna was quite an asset to Flaxen's team.

As they passed the doorway to The Abyss restaurant and bar, they could see the palace straight ahead. The Hades Gate into the city was next to it, while to the left was Delirium Drive, the road that contained the private mansions of all the Superiors and some of the middle-ranking demons. It was the only street in the city to which entry seemed to be prohibited, as there was a metal gate guarded by beldarks that blocked the way in.

———

The mayor's palace was unguarded and unattended. There were metal gates leading in, but these stood open. There was a low wall all the way round, with metal railings above. The palace itself was built of the same drab stone or concrete material that was used for most of the structures in Carceron. Where other palaces might have some formal gardens or lawns, this palace had an endless sea of small marble chips, bigger than gravel, which crunched underfoot. Square ornamental pillars stood either side of the gateway, forming two lines up to the doors. There was no path up to the door, so the only way to reach the building from the gate was across the marble chips. They reminded Pumpkin of the decorations used to mark certain designs of flat gravestones.

The palace itself was of an irregular pattern. Concrete gables protruded at odd angles. There were no windows, so it was impossible to tell how many storeys the building might have internally. There was one pair of iron double doors, strongly reinforced, facing towards the gateway. Each door had an ornamental handle, also made of iron, set into its centre. Overall, the place had the feel of an abandoned mausoleum. In a bustling city like Carceron it felt especially creepy for one of the largest buildings to stand alone and silent. The whole site seemed well maintained; there were no weeds growing through the marble chips and all the masonry was in good condition. It was not neglected. This heightened the sense that there might be something inside, still using it. Only Aspreyna seemed oblivious of the unsettling nature of the place as the group crept up to the tall iron doors.

Aspreyna pushed against them. "They're not opening."

She pushed harder. The doors did not move at all. There was no lock. Aspreyna turned to Montrachet.

"Is there a back way in?"

"Not that I know," said Montrachet nervously. He was a bit afraid of the angel. Ferdinal and Sapphire were looking round quickly to see that there was nobody else about. Pumpkin looked up, in case there was some sign on the doors, or ornamental gargoyles who might answer questions. But there were none.

"Does anyone have the spell Searing Heat?" asked Sapphire. "We might be able to melt the doors or buckle them, so they no longer fit the frame."

"Leave it to me," said Perancia, in a bored tone of voice. She pushed her way to the front. Sapphire was surprised to see her taking a leading role at a difficult time. That wasn't Perancia's style at all.

Perancia stood in front of the doors for a moment, her head on one side. Aspreyna looked on haughtily. If she, a powerful celestial, hadn't been strong enough to open the doors, how was this tiny urchin going to succeed?

Perancia reached up and took hold of the handle of the left door. Suddenly she put her whole weight on it, dragging the handle forwards. The door opened a few inches. The young warlock stepped back.

"CT says the doors open outwards," she said simply. "No good pushing. You should listen to CT. He knows things."

Aspreyna snorted. She put her hand on the edge of the door that Perancia had shifted. With a flick of her sinewy wrist, she flung the door wide open. The huge door did not even creak on its hinges. Perancia sauntered in first, revelling in her brief moment of supremacy.

"What's the matter?" she taunted the others, glancing back over her shoulder. "Scared of a doorway? Have you all got portalphobia? Aaah!"

From outside the door, the others saw Perancia fall forward into the darkness inside the building. She had stumbled over something. Was it a trap, a creature? They dashed forward into the gloom, Aspreyna's celestial aura casting a dim light.

They were in a grand hallway. There were no stairs, only tall doorways leading off to other rooms. Around the edge of the room were pedestals, each displaying a bronze bust of a former mayor of the city. The walls and floor were made of the same drab, unadorned concrete material, taking minimalism to a new extreme.

Sprawled on the floor were two figures. Perancia was already picking herself up, yelling and kicking at the other. In the dim light Montrachet recognised the stranger as Zirca the pedlar. He seemed just as annoyed as Perancia and was calling her all sorts of vicious names, until his language grew so coarse that Aspreyna struck him on the side of the head to shut him up.

The Heroes gathered round Zirca in a circle.

"What are you doing in the palace?" asked Ferdinal sternly. "Stealing the Archmayor's valuables?"

"How can ya steal from a dead man?" yelled Zirca. "I've got every right to be here. Nobody stops me. And what about you?"

Pumpkin was looking at Zirca's possessions. He had a bedroll laid out on the floor and a backpack for a pillow.

"You've been sleeping here!" she challenged.

"Nothing wrong with that," growled the pedlar defiantly. "Hotels are full of tourists and people here for the election. These days if you sleep in the street, someone comes along and whisks you away thinking you're a spare corpse that can be animated for voting. Not safe these days."

"He has a point," thought Pumpkin.

"We're wasting time," said Aspreyna. "This fool clearly doesn't have it."

She marched ahead through one of the doorways beyond. As she was the only source of light, the others rushed after her, leaving the pedlar to continue his interrupted slumber.

Montrachet hurriedly cast a simple cantrip and the end of his wand lit up like a torch.

The room into which Aspreyna had strode was some sort of audience chamber. The only furnishing was an ornate high-backed chair, which looked as though it was carved from ebony. It had intricate patterns on the arms and curious arcane sigils on the backrest. Behind the chair, in an alcove below one of the concrete gables, was a large stone sarcophagus. Murals on the other three sides of the room looked as though they were made of the same material as everything else here, depicting scenes of the construction of some of the Carceron buildings which the Heroes recognised. There were four free-standing candelabra on the floor, but the candles in them were unlit. Altogether it was the most plain and depressing audience chamber imaginable. It was difficult to imagine how the Archmayor could have presided over countless meetings here, sitting in that ebony chair, day after day for 150 years. "Maybe it was a relief in the end to be murdered," thought Sapphire.

There were archways off to various side chambers. Perancia stuck her head into each one in turn and called out what she found: "Guardroom… Waiting room… What's this… eww, toilet."

Aspreyna examined the ebony chair. She motioned to the others not to come close, frowning as she looked at the carvings and sigils. Montrachet stood behind her, trying to decipher the writing. In the end, he reached for the scroll of Speakall and cast the spell, so that he could then understand all the languages.

Ferdinal, Sapphire and Pumpkin went up to the sarcophagus. It was almost as tall as they were, the sort of structure that might, in a cathedral, be the last resting place of a monarch.

"These sigils contain powerful magic," said Aspreyna slowly. "There is a power source here somewhere. Perhaps below, like Harbinger said. But how do we get down?"

Montrachet tapped parts of the floor with his foot. It was solid. Perancia continued searching the side chambers, but she found no stairs going up or down.

"Never open a sarcophagus," said Ferdinal warily. He was used to roleplaying games in which they always contained unpleasant undead things that clawed their way out if disturbed.

"I bet it's easy to open," said Sapphire, giving the stone lid a playful poke with her finger. "Oh!"

The lid *was* easy to open. At the lightest touch from Sapphire's finger, the lid swung horizontally round away from her. Pumpkin, who was standing on that side, had to leap out of the way of the spinning stone slab.

For once, Ferdinal was disappointed. The sarcophagus did not contain undead mummies and wraiths. Inside were stone steps descending steeply into a murky darkness below. As if to offset the gloom, as soon as the lid was open, all four candelabra lit up by themselves.

"See, strong magic," said Aspreyna, still frowning. "I'll go first. Montrachet, you've got the other light. You go at the back."

So saying, she climbed into the sarcophagus and started to descend the stairs. Everybody else fell silent as they followed. Perancia and Pumpkin needed help getting over the top of the stone sides. Montrachet, going last, had a final look around the audience chamber before going down the stairs. The ebony chair was now glowing with a faint red light.

"I hope that's a good sign," he thought, as he took up his position at the rear and followed the others down into the depths.

The stairs descended a long way in a straight line, with neither landings nor side passages. Aspreyna reached the foot of the stairs and looked around. The others were still walking slowly down, being careful not to miss their footing on the steep steps. The angel's aura spread a faint light around the open area at the bottom. At once there was a cry from a frightened voice.

"D-don't come any closer! I can see you clearly."

Sapphire, who was closest behind Aspreyna, almost fainted in shock at the sudden sound so nearby.

The angel showed no fear or surprise but turned to face the speaker, who was out of sight of everyone on the stairs.

But Perancia burst out laughing. "Champrice, is that you? Are you living in the Archmayor's basement? Maybe you rented it from Zirca, eh?"

"Her merciless joking is pretty rude," thought Ferdinal, "but it certainly dispelled the fear and tension in a moment." It wasn't some enemy or trap at the bottom. The whole group followed Aspreyna to the foot of the steps and looked around them. Once Montrachet's light was there, they could see much more clearly. They seemed to be in a small hallway, which might have doubled as a guardroom. Champrice was sitting on a chair to one side. She was on her own.

"I'm really glad you're here," she said shakily. "I thought I might get trapped."

"What are you doing here?" challenged Aspreyna roughly.

Champrice looked at her in wonder. She was clearly not aware that the angel had been freed. "Looking for the Book of Misdeeds," she said quietly.

"Don't trust her," said Montrachet suddenly. Pumpkin looked at him in surprise. "She used to be Cremorne's girlfriend. She's working with the demons, the Superiors."

"I'm not," said Champrice, pursing her lips. "I'm… working alone."

But Pumpkin was already guessing the truth. Only someone very powerful or very foolish would break into the Archmayor's basement on their own.

"You're in the Enigma Club!" she gasped. "That's why you're here. You're looking for the book!"

Champrice drew in her breath. Ferdinal's eyes widened. Sapphire glared at her suspiciously. Only Aspreyna seemed uninterested in the news.

"Come with us," said the angel shortly. "We're here to look for the Archmayor's will. We can talk as we search."

"What else is down here?" asked Ferdinal, looking down one of the dark passages that led away from the guardroom.

"There are lots of empty rooms," said Champrice, more confident now that she knew she could get out. "And I heard something tunnelling, somewhere deep. There's something heavy moving as well. I heard stone wheels."

Just at that moment there was a loud rumbling, as if something with stone wheels was being propelled across a stone floor. But which direction did it come from? How far away? Was it coming closer?

Pumpkin began to see how scary it must have been down here for Champrice. Worse, really, for she would have been alone and in the dark.

"Only one thing to do with danger," said Aspreyna firmly, listening for the source of the noise. "Move towards it. Face it. This way."

She marched off down one of the passages. Montrachet, at the rear once more with his light, made a quick note of the look of the passage, to make sure they wouldn't get lost.

The rumbling noise had stopped. Now and then Aspreyna would stop to listen for it, but it did not return. The passageway seemed to be a central corridor, with many rooms leading off on each side. Perancia had great fun exploring each one. She appeared to be able to see clearly even in the dark, which was unnerving at first, but it soon became useful.

The rooms were much better furnished than those upstairs. These seemed to be the main living quarters of the Archmayor. There was a sitting room with comfortable chairs, a meeting room and a small library. There was no kitchen or eating area – Sapphire pointed out that an undead mayor wouldn't eat much – but everything was pleasantly furnished and tasteful. It was bitterly cold, but that too would not worry an undead inhabitant.

The group spent some time searching the library for important papers. There were books about the history of Carceron and the religious doctrines of Carcus, god of the undead. On the desk was a Gleam Globe, slightly bigger than a tennis ball, which shone a perpetual light, stronger than the beam from Montrachet's wand. Pumpkin took it. After all, the Archmayor wouldn't be needing it. But there was no sign of the Archmayor's will, nor of anything about demons or vampires.

Pumpkin found a locked metal strong box on a shelf. "Might be something in here?" she called out.

"Give!" cried Perancia, snatching the box and shaking it up and down. She scowled and handed it back. "Doesn't rattle. No money in it."

Montrachet examined the lock. There was no key. "I can't open this," he said. "Wait. I'll use my scroll."

He rummaged in the backpack for the scroll of Open Portal. The others stood back. Aspreyna kept watch on the corridor in case the rumbling sound returned.

Montrachet cast the spell and there was a loud echoing bang as if an invisible hand had pounded the lid. The box opened.

The Heroes looked through the papers. Only Montrachet, with the Speakall spell still working on him, was able to decipher many of the obscure languages. There was a paper about dragons, lots about commercial plans for Carceron, and there was a map. Everyone crowded round, trying to work out which way up it should go.

At last, Champrice exclaimed, "It's here! A map of this part of the palace. Look, there's the guardroom and the passage. This is the library we're in now. It even shows the bookshelves around the walls."

It was true. "At least we won't get lost now," thought Montrachet.

"Where to next?" asked Aspreyna, looking at the map.

"It seems to have been drawn while these tunnels were still under construction," said Montrachet, tracing the lines with his finger. "Some of them end abruptly and the walls are roughly cut. Oh, what's this?"

He was pointing at a symbol in an alcove at the corner

of one of the corridors. "It looks like the silhouette of a large beast, a bit like an elephant," thought Pumpkin.

"Look here, below it!" cried Sapphire. "It's a bedroom. We should search there next!"

This seemed like the best plan. This time Montrachet went first with the map, while Aspreyna guarded the rear. Pumpkin went in the middle with her new Gleam Globe.

The route to the bedroom took them past some of the unfinished passages. These were not lined with stone but were cut through rock. Suddenly came the tunnelling sound Champrice had mentioned. An instant later, a huge evil-looking worm burst through the rock floor into the group's midst. Montrachet and Ferdinal were ahead of it, Champrice, Sapphire and Aspreyna behind. It appeared next to Pumpkin and Perancia.

It was deep red in colour, about ten feet long and a couple of feet in diameter. It had no face, but one end was a gaping maw, like the face of a python about to swallow its hapless prey. It was a burrower, the sort of creature Flaxen had mentioned briefly as one of the few that communicates in Deep Dialect.

The worm snapped at Pumpkin's and Perancia's feet. They leapt clear just in time and the worm turned in an instant to face them.

Ferdinal wheeled round, drawing his longsword and driving it into the worm's face. Pumpkin cast Radiant Flame at it and the worm writhed in pain as the radiant damage seared into its hide. Perancia also cast a spell, some bolt of energy, it seemed to Pumpkin. This also hit the worm and it snapped at Perancia again.

Before the worm could coil itself for another attack,

Aspreyna set to work. She remained motionless at the back, pointing her palm at the worm and lowering her head as if concentrating hard. A moment later the worm froze as if paralysed for a second and then exploded with a muffled bang, showering everyone with fragments.

The fight was over.

Chapter 16
The Elephant in the Room

"Radiant Burst," shrugged Aspreyna, looking at the remains of the worm. "Powerful spell, but very effective on voracious creatures. Whatever they last devoured just explodes inside them."

"Look what you've done!" yelled Perancia. "I'm covered in worm breakfast!"

She and Pumpkin had been closest to the worm at the critical moment and the Radiant Burst had drenched both of them. They were now dripping with a sticky greenish goo from the worm's insides, which was clinging to their clothes. Montrachet pushed past Ferdinal to assist.

"I can fix it," he said, casting a quick incantation on Pumpkin. Tiny magical hands appeared and began to brush the goo off. When they finished, he cast the same cantrip on Perancia. Afterwards, their clothes seemed fresher than ever and even a couple of minor rips had been invisibly mended.

"I learnt that one from Revlyn," he said. "It's a simple cantrip called Velvet Valet. Don't get to use it much."

Sapphire was looking anxiously around for signs of more burrowers, but there was no sound of any. Pumpkin tried to reassure her.

"I know there's no sound," said Sapphire crossly. "But it's the same with all pests. There's never just one mouse, is there?"

The group crept along the tunnel more cautiously, in the direction of the Archmayor's bedroom marked on the map. They reached an iron door at the side of the passage. It was locked.

Montrachet handed his wand to Pumpkin and got down on his knees. He brought out a set of lockpicks from his robes and began expertly to explore the mechanism with his professional tools. Pumpkin watched him in admiration. Perancia watched him to learn how to do the same thing herself, if CT would give her the right gear. The others gathered around Sapphire, who was now holding the map, examining it in the light from Pumpkin's Gleam Globe.

"We're not far from the passage with the elephant thing in it," she said. "Once we've searched this room, I think we should investigate that too."

Champrice wasn't keen. She just wanted to find the will – or better still, the Book of Misdeeds – and then get out. Ferdinal, being a paladin, felt that a spirit of adventure was called for. Just then, the lock clicked open and Montrachet opened the bedroom door.

The bedroom was more simply furnished than the other rooms. There was a bed, although Pumpkin could not imagine why, as the Archmayor surely didn't need to sleep. Perhaps this was just his innermost sanctum, a lair where he would be free from all interruption?

There was a chest containing spare robes ("Nothing magic," called Perancia after a perfunctory search) and a desk. The Heroes searched the desk and once again Aspreyna kept watch in the corridor. The papers in the desk were a haphazard jumble of meeting notes, bills, receipts and messages from various demons. There was a bundle of letters, tied up with a purple ribbon.

"That's Hijinx's writing!" said Champrice, laughing as she picked up the bundle. "I bet she and the Archmayor… well, I'm taking these."

"You can't take other people's love letters!" said Sapphire, aghast. "They belong to the Archmayor."

Montrachet, Perancia and Champrice, all Carceron residents, looked at her blankly.

"They're not his!" said Perancia scornfully. "We're here, we're taking them. They're ours now."

"Nothing belongs to anyone," said Champrice, pocketing the letters. "And Hijinx would probably pay me a lot to give them to her. She's after Cremorne now."

"The Archmayor's dead anyway," said Montrachet. "He doesn't have anything anymore."

Ferdinal, Sapphire and Pumpkin looked at each other uneasily. The total lack of any kind of morality in Carceron should not really still surprise them, but the truth was that it did still make them very uncomfortable.

"Here, this looks like it!" said Ferdinal. He was looking at the next document in the desk. It was a rolled-up scroll, sealed in red wax. There were some draconic symbols next to the seal.

Montrachet took the scroll and examined it in the light of his wand. "It's protected by a glyph," he said slowly.

"You need the right response word, or some trap will be triggered. Wait a bit."

He reached into the backpack again, pulled out Flaxen's scroll of Dispel and cast it at the draconic markings. They disappeared. The seal broke at the same time and the scroll unfurled itself.

It was indeed the Archmayor's will. It was a long document and the Heroes did not try to read it all. Some paragraphs seemed to be written in Draconic, which only Montrachet and Perancia could understand. They were all looking for any mention of the Book of Misdeeds.

"There," cried Champrice, highly excited, pointing to the text. "I do hereby… blah blah… he left it to Blatherwick!"

They stared at each other in amazement. Blatherwick, the plump, garrulous ambassador. He didn't look as though he would put up any kind of fight if threatened. Why give a powerful artifact to him?

"I think I get it," said Pumpkin, thinking aloud. "Imagine you're the Archmayor. There are some people you trust like Marid, or Ethema. But you want to make sure the book is put away safely, in the hands of someone that nobody would think of. Someone with powerful connections that can't just be eliminated by the demons. But someone who has no idea what the Book of Misdeeds can do. They might not even think of it as valuable. Blatherwick is the most unlikely choice. So, he's the one you pick!"

Sapphire beamed at her. "Pumpkin, I know I said it before. Beneath that angelic face lurks the mind of an evil genius!"

Champrice looked disappointed. Pumpkin drew her aside from the others. "Did the Archmayor promise the

Enigma Club that they could guard the book?" she asked gently.

"Yes," admitted Champrice. "I know he trusted us. But you're right. The demons would have hunted us down to get control of such an artifact. None of us would have been safe."

"I need to go to see Talisman tomorrow," whispered Pumpkin confidentially. "Let's talk about it then. If the book is that powerful, I may need the whole Enigma Club just to be able to use it."

The group had a short rest in the bedroom. Aspreyna seemed not to need any rest and stood silently guarding the corridor outside. The mood was very upbeat and confident now that they had found the will.

"Before we go, I do want to find that elephant," said Sapphire.

Champrice was reluctant, having spent long enough in the basement of the palace, but in the end she gave in to the majority view.

Montrachet led the way again, with Aspreyna at the rear. The passages were lined with smooth stone in this section of the basement, but there were very few side rooms here.

"Look at the water," said Perancia suddenly. She pointed to seepage through a crack in the stone wall. It formed a small puddle on the ground and a narrow rivulet was flowing in the direction they were heading. Without realising it they had been heading slightly downhill.

The tiny stream of water continued to flow along the passage, which turned sharply to the right at one point.

Montrachet followed it. This led into a long straight section, a couple of hundred feet in length. About halfway along there were two very small alcoves carved into opposite sides of the passage. Montrachet walked just beyond the alcoves and then stopped to consult the map.

"That's odd," he said. "The alcoves are marked on the map. We should be able to see the elephant from here."

Montrachet, Pumpkin and Ferdinal followed the trickle of water to the far end of the corridor. There was a small puddle there and the water seemed to soak into the floor. Ferdinal bent down to see where the water went, but it seemed to be just a tiny crack in the floor.

"There's a slight glow from this alcove," said the sharp-eyed Perancia. She began to search the walls and floor of the alcove, looking for the source of the illumination while Montrachet and Pumpkin puzzled over the map. Aspreyna remained at the back of the group. Just then, they heard a sudden click. A flagstone in the floor Perancia had stepped upon in the alcove had triggered some sort of mechanical device.

Everybody whirled round, trying to look in all directions at once. Then Aspreyna looked behind her, at the sharp right turn in the passage that they had passed a minute earlier. A stone panel in the wall had moved to one side. Facing them down the corridor was the elephant. It was sitting in a secret compartment into which it would only just fit, for the elephant was as wide as the corridor itself and almost as tall.

"Well done, Perancia!" exclaimed Sapphire. "You found the elephant. Isn't it pretty?"

The elephant seemed to be made of stone and was

painted with elaborate red war paint. The paint was a similar shade to the glow in Perancia's alcove. But its expression was hostile. Suddenly it started moving slowly towards them, advancing a few feet every second. Everyone realised that the elephant's feet were mounted on stone rollers. It was coming at them, steadily, inexorably, unavoidably.

Panic immediately followed, everyone yelling at once. The elephant was already ten feet along the corridor. There wasn't time to dash behind it the way they had come, past the sharp turn in the corridor. The elephant was at least ten feet tall and as wide as the corridor. Its sheer stone front could not be climbed. In less than a minute, unless it chose to stop, it would have rumbled all the way to the far end of the corridor, where Montrachet, Pumpkin and Ferdinal were standing.

Just then Montrachet cried out, "It's a dead end. There's no way out here."

Champrice and Sapphire flung themselves into the alcoves. Nobody else could squeeze in with them, as the spaces were so tiny. Perancia pulled up the flagstone in Sapphire's alcove and cowered in the small depression underneath, next to the mechanism she had triggered.

Aspreyna was in the corridor, closest to the elephant. Montrachet, Pumpkin and Ferdinal were at the far end, desperately searching for a secret exit, pulling at the walls and frantically examining the map.

While the three at the end made their frenzied search, Aspreyna faced the advancing elephant. She cast several spells at it, designed to slow it down, shatter it or force it backwards. Nothing seemed to have any effect. Aspreyna had to back away from the advancing form, moving past the alcoves as she did and towards the dead end where the secret door search continued. In the alcoves, Sapphire, Perancia and Champrice cowered in utter terror as the huge stone construct moved magically past on its stone rollers.

Soon there was only fifty feet between the elephant and the end of the corridor. Aspreyna, Montrachet, Pumpkin and Ferdinal were all in this space. Unless they could get out, they would all be crushed against the wall. Pumpkin realised that the red decoration on the elephant wasn't war paint. It was the dried blood of others who had been crushed against the wall over the years. The stone rollers were the deep rumbling that Champrice had heard before.

Forty feet left. The elephant would reach the far wall of the corridor in fifteen or twenty seconds. Its slow progress was more terrifying than speed would have been.

"There, on top of it," Aspreyna cried out. She unfurled her wings, just having space to do so in the corridor and flew up onto the elephant's head. Once there she reached down to help the others up. Ferdinal was the tallest, but he could not reach the angel's outstretched hand.

"Use magic!" yelled Pumpkin to Montrachet. There was no time for further explanation. Pumpkin cast a spell, concentrating hard on its composition. She and Ferdinal vanished and reappeared a hundred feet behind the elephant, in the safe half of the corridor. Only Montrachet remained in deadly peril, less than ten seconds from certain death.

Montrachet ripped the backpack off and threw the remaining scrolls on the floor. He picked up one and read the incantation, struggling in his terror to chant the words correctly. Then suddenly he put his hands to the wall and gripped the smooth stones with his fingernails, climbing up to the roof in a second or two. He had cast Climb from Flaxen's scroll. A simple, low-level spell had once again been the difference between life and death. He squeezed on top of the elephant, next to Aspreyna, just as the huge construct ground against the far end of the corridor and stopped. The elephant stayed where it was. The rolling noise stopped. Everyone had survived.

Aspreyna and Montrachet climbed down off the back of the elephant. Sapphire, Champrice and Perancia came out of the alcoves. Ferdinal and Pumpkin ran to join them.

"Montrachet, I'm sorry, I'm sorry," wailed Pumpkin in tears, throwing her arms around his neck. "I cast Dimensional Leap to get Ferdinal and me to safety. I had to leave you. The spell only teleports two people."

Montrachet looked into her eyes. He found it difficult to speak. "How did you learn that spell?" he asked. "I don't know how to cast it. Is it one you remember from your sorcerer days?"

"No," said Pumpkin, her tears subsiding. "It was in Harbinger's spellbook. I cast it to try to get Aspreyna out of the Arcane Cage, but it didn't work. Somehow I remembered the spell from having used it then."

Perancia broke the mood. "Let's get out of here," she said abruptly. "The last thing I want is to have to watch you two kiss."

———

Having retrieved the Archmayor's will, everyone was only too pleased to get out of the palace. Pumpkin was not sure what time of the night it was, but after the encounter with the elephant she suddenly felt very fatigued.

Aspreyna took the lead in escorting the group back to the stairs that led to the sarcophagus. She did not seem to need Montrachet's map. Back on the ground floor of the building, there was no sign of Zirca the pedlar. Perhaps he had already gone off for his day's work. "It's unlikely that he's ever found the steps down to the basement level," thought Ferdinal. He probably wouldn't have come out alive. Champrice parted from them at the palace gates, thanking them again for rescuing her. She promised to meet Pumpkin at Talisman's shop later that day, once everyone had had a good rest.

It was very early morning as Aspreyna led the exhausted group back to Harbinger's house. They did not meet anyone on the way. Dawn, if it could be called that in Carceron, was the quietest time of day, with only a few quasit messengers to be seen running errands. The only beldarks they saw were the ones at the end of Delirium Drive, guarding the demons' mansions.

Montrachet had his own home, but after the night's adventure he was more than glad to collapse into sleep in one of Harbinger's spare beds. Pumpkin found it fascinating that anyone with a large house, such as Harbinger and Flaxen, seemed to take it for granted that friends and casual acquaintances would arrive unannounced at all times of day requiring food and accommodation. It seemed to be a natural part of the chaotic, bohemian nature of the city – one of its more agreeable features.

It was nearly the middle of the day by the time the Heroes were having a quick breakfast, prepared by

Harbinger's quasits. Pumpkin felt suddenly guilty for fear that Champrice might be waiting impatiently for her at Talisman's shop Looks Could Kill but realised that Champrice must be equally exhausted.

There was no sign of Aspreyna that morning. Evidently angels didn't bother with breakfast. Perancia did stay for breakfast, being both lazy and greedy, but she showed no inclination to stay and help.

"I've got some things to get at Nameless," she said vaguely. "I'll be there if you need me for anything."

Ferdinal, Sapphire, Pumpkin and Montrachet went to Talisman's shop together. There was no sign of Mercedes' campaign team that day. Clearly the misfortunes that befell the market stall and the wagon had led them to switch to less visible tactics. Pumpkin felt a sense of conflicted loyalties.

"What are we going to say to Talisman?" she whispered to Montrachet as they walked. "The Destiny Guild says I'm to infiltrate the Enigma Club, but we want to use it to help us with the Book of Misdeeds."

Montrachet was more indifferent towards such ethical dilemmas. "They said to infiltrate the Club," he said. "Nothing yet about reporting back to Revlyn, stealing the Club's secrets, betraying its members and so on. If Revlyn asks, we'll just say it's in progress."

They found Champrice at Talisman's shop in Hightower Square. She had only just arrived and was chatting with Talisman about the election. Talisman was listening to her as he fed raw meat to the cage of Creeping Omnivores.

"Er, do we need to wear a mask or something?" asked Sapphire nervously as they went in. "I don't want to get petrified today as well as nearly killed."

She paused in the shop's doorway and eyed Talisman's collection of stone statues.

"No, no," said Talisman, ushering them in and closing the shop door behind them. "I've got the basilisk sleeping in a kennel in the basement. The medusa is in the back room and she doesn't have any snakes at the moment."

"What happened to the snakes?" asked Ferdinal, then wished he hadn't.

"I sold them," said Talisman brightly. "Tentacle were almost out of supplies one day. So, I sold them the medusa's hair to serve to the diners. They had to come over and cut it off themselves; I wasn't going to do that for them. I also sold them a corrosive cube that I happened to have in stock. They cut it up into individual dessert portions. Really saved their reputation. They were very grateful."

"Really? They didn't get hurt?"

"Oh, one of the Tentacle people was petrified by the medusa. His statue is over there in the corner. Should be all right tomorrow. And the medusa's very cross, of course. So, I thought I'd keep her away from the customers for a bit."

Sapphire decided that for their own safety they probably shouldn't browse too long in the shop. She nudged Champrice.

"They rescued me from the palace last night," said Champrice to Talisman. "And they found the will. We know who has the book."

Talisman's eyes widened. "Wow. And do you trust them all?"

It was a strange question to ask someone in Carceron, but Champrice did not seem surprised. "They rescued me. They're all working for Flaxen, it's okay."

"And I'm interested in joining the Enigma Club," added Pumpkin quietly.

Talisman was silent for a moment, studying their faces. His hand strayed to one of the medallions he was wearing and he stroked it as he thought. After a full minute of pondering, he spoke. "You know who has the book?"

"Yes."

"Don't tell me. Just get the book and bring it to me in the library at midnight. Then we'll talk about the Club."

"Just you four come," said Champrice. "Don't bring Perancia."

Pumpkin nodded and the four Heroes left the shop. Outside they stopped to confer.

"Why bring the book there? Why not hide it here?" wondered Ferdinal.

"I don't think the demons use the library much," said Sapphire. "It's probably a good place for a secret meeting, especially at that hour. And if you're trying to hide a book, it's a really good place."

"Is it really open at midnight?" Pumpkin asked Montrachet.

"They never bother to close it," said Montrachet. "No rules, remember? But I expect it's pretty quiet there at midnight."

"First, we have to get the book," said Ferdinal. "We have to find Blatherwick. Where does he hang out? We've hardly seen him."

"I suppose we could use magic to trace him," pondered Pumpkin. "We could use a tracking spell. Or maybe Perancia could get us an Invisible Servant? They're said to be great for finding objects and people. She could ask CT to lend us one."

"Too hard to control," said Ferdinal. "Wouldn't work. That's powerful magic."

"Blatherwick might be at one of the hotels or at the Demon Consulate," said Montrachet doubtfully. "But he's an ambassador. Most likely he'll be in one of the most expensive restaurants or bars."

"True," smiled Pumpkin. "As the saying goes, a diplomat is someone who lays down their liver for their country."

Chapter 17

The Enigma Club

The four Heroes went from one restaurant to another as a group. At YouChoose and Eye to Eye, they found plenty of tourists and a few demons, but no sign of the plump ambassador. Rather anxiously they opened the door to The Abyss. This was the bar most favoured by demons. The Heroes had not been into it before.

The door opened into an ordinary foyer, such as might be found in any restaurant. There was a small desk by the door, on which sat a reservation book. Several dozen staircases led down from the foyer. None of the staircases was marked to indicate where they led, but Pumpkin realised they must be to some of the many different levels in the bar.

To their relief, the reservation desk was being run by Tinsel. She smiled as they came in.

"So that's what you do during the day!" said Montrachet. He should have realised that Tinsel couldn't spend all her time singing ear-shattering songs at The Irresistible Dancehall.

"I'm looking forward to singing Marvexio's new one, 'Vote for Chaos, Not Evil,'" she smiled. "Do you have a reservation?"

"You mean there are rules? People make bookings?" Ferdinal was astonished.

"Oh, no," said Tinsel. "But we always ask. It makes the demon princes feel more special. I ask; they say they haven't booked; I let them in anyway. Avoids a lot of argument. And we never run out of tables here. That's the beauty of having so many levels."

"Do you have Blatherwick the ambassador here today?" asked Pumpkin. She felt they were getting distracted from their task.

"Certainly," said Tinsel, smiling again. "He's having a drink with Apollonius Crayler, the musical promoter. I think they're on level 193. You need the seventh staircase for that section."

The Heroes looked at each other. That meant a lot of stairs.

"What are we going to do if he won't give us the book?" asked Ferdinal as they walked down.

"I could try a Suggestion spell on him," said Montrachet. "But it might not work. Could make him angry."

"We'll just have to be persuasive," said Sapphire. "Let me try."

It took about ten minutes to reach level 193. Ferdinal wondered if this was just an elaborate way of dissuading customers from bothering to leave once they were happily ensconced at a table. This level was very dark, with only dimly lit red trails on the floor showing the way between tables. There were thirty or forty tables in the room, with a bar at the far end of the room. Most of the customers were demons of various sorts, although Ferdinal thought he could see Carcus priests Lacasso and Runsus in their red robes at one of the tables by the bar.

Crayler and Blatherwick were at a table near the stairs by which the Heroes entered. Crayler greeted them enthusiastically and invited them to sit down. He hailed a passing quasit.

"Four mugs of Darkbrew for my young friends!" he ordered cheerily.

Pumpkin wasn't sure what that was but hoped it wouldn't have anything alive in it.

"What brings you to this desperate place?" asked Crayler, in the same welcoming tone.

"Well, it's always a pleasure to see you, Crayler," said Montrachet politely. "But really we need to ask Blatherwick something."

"By all means, certainly," said Crayler, smirking still. But he followed the conversation with a keen interest, like a cat keeping one eye on a nearby mouse.

Sapphire leaned forward across the table and looked into the eyes of the ambassador. "Look, Mr Blatherwick, we know you were asked to look after something by the Archmayor," she said shyly. "Something really important. A book. Because he trusted you. And we really need to use it."

Blatherwick, who had been slumped drunkenly in his chair, suddenly sat up. "I don't even know you," he said petulantly. "Such impertinence. You come here, disturbing us—"

"Easy, friend," interrupted Crayler. He leant forward

towards Sapphire and lowered his voice. "A book, you say? Now, which one would that be?"

"It's called the Book of Misdeeds," said Sapphire. "We need it… for the campaign."

"You promised to help," reminded Pumpkin.

"I did indeed," grinned Crayler. "Blatherwick! Do you have this book?"

"Eh? Oh, yes. It's in my box at the Interplanar Bank."

"Well," said Crayler, in a tone that implied the matter was settled. "You have it. You don't need it. They want it. It's for the campaign. Give them your token so they can get it."

Pumpkin hadn't really believed Crayler when he and Šapka had promised to help, back in the Botanical Gardens. But he was serious. Blatherwick was stammering in dissent, but Crayler raised a hand, almost as if he were momentarily in control of Blatherwick's thoughts and actions. Blatherwick reached into his robes and drew out a green disk, the size of a small coin. He handed it to Sapphire without a word.

Sapphire pocketed the disk. She stared hard at Crayler. He had made everything look so easy. She had come prepared to coax, cajole or even threaten in order to get the Book of Misdeeds. Crayler's backing and his straightforward confidence had turned the situation around. A useful ally to have, she decided.

The quasit returned with four mugs and set them down heavily on the table. The mugs contained a dark steaming liquid that smelt as though its ingredients had come from a swamp.

"Thanks," said Sapphire quickly, rising from the table before Blatherwick could change his mind. "And thanks for the drinks."

The four Heroes rushed to the stairs, leaving their Darkbrew untouched on the table.

Business at the Interplanar Bank that afternoon could not have been easier.

The bank was laid out like a very old-fashioned establishment which was used to handling large amounts of currency in coin form. The double doors led into a large room dominated by cashier's windows on three sides. The windows were set at different heights, to enable all species of creature to stand eye to eye facing the cashier. Quasits were busy in the background hauling large chests around on wheeled trolleys. The chests were of a standard design, which Pumpkin presumed was unique to the bank. Perhaps these were the chests Perancia had talked about.

Sapphire led the way in, marching up to a vacant cashier's window. She felt that the only way to behave if you were nervous was to strut around as if you owned the place and give short, staccato orders to everyone. She nodded to the cashier and handed over Blatherwick's green token.

The cashier examined it in his hand, then held it up to the light. Then he weighed it on a small scale beside the counter and made an entry with a quill pen in a large ledger. "Name on the box?" he asked, in a bored tone.

"Blatherwick, City of Spires."

"Contents?"

"Large book."

"Please wait here," said the cashier. He turned and handed the counter to a quasit, who dashed off with a trolley.

About a minute later the creature came back, wheeling one of the bank's chests behind. The cashier glanced at the name on the chest, opened it and pulled out a large tome, bound in leather, with gilded corners. He handed it across the counter to Sapphire without a word.

"Next," he called.

Sapphire handed the book to Montrachet, whose robes were better suited to concealing it. They could hardly walk around the streets clasping a priceless artifact.

Outside the bank they met Perancia, who was carrying several large bags.

"Been to Nameless," she announced proudly.

"Buy anything nice?" asked Pumpkin, pretending she cared. They didn't really want Perancia tagging along while they had the precious book in their possession.

"I wasn't able to buy anything," said Perancia, puzzled. "I stole as much as I could carry, so didn't have enough bags for purchases. CT told me what to get. He needs some robes in my size and various components for rituals. See you later." She hurried off towards the Southwest District.

Ferdinal laughed. "Just as well, or she'd have tried to join us," he said.

"Doubt it," said Montrachet. "Not if we told her we're going to the library."

"I thought we'd have a lot more trouble at the bank," said Sapphire, as they walked along.

"It's normally pretty simple," said Montrachet. "If you have the token and don't cast any spells in there, the system works well. If you lose the token, you're in real trouble."

They reached the library early in the evening. It was empty apart from Carina, who was putting away some scrolls. She smiled at them.

"Come to browse around?" she asked. "Please, enjoy yourselves."

"Can we browse anywhere?" asked Pumpkin. "There isn't a restricted section, or special books you look after?"

Carina looked puzzled, then laughed. "Oh, yes, you're used to libraries that have *rules*," she grinned, stressing the last word as if it were an unusual technical term that might require definition. "No rules here. Obviously, there's magic that prevents anyone starting fires in here and some of the spellbooks are glyphed. Probably best to leave those."

Now Pumpkin smiled. There were no rules. But as usual in Carceron, there was a hierarchy of power, coupled with guards or deadly traps, so that the effect was much the same. No wonder the library was always left open, without the need for Carina to oversee its use. At night there was magical lighting that turned itself on automatically. It didn't need any supervision.

After Carina had left for the evening and the Heroes were alone, they sat down at a table and examined the Book of Misdeeds for the first time. Montrachet opened the cover.

The book contained thick vellum pages. It seemed to be very old, judging by its cover and design, but it showed no signs of wear and tear. However, the vellum pages were all blank.

"Is it the wrong book?" asked Sapphire, her rising voice betraying the sense of panic that had gripped her.

"No," said Montrachet, frowning. "It's the right book. But it's a powerful artifact. You need to be attuned to it, to use its powers. We may think we're examining the book, but I can sense the book examining me. It's trying to work out if we're worthy. If we're powerful enough. It's a possession that chooses its owner."

All four Heroes took turns sitting at the table with the book in front of them, open or closed. Only Montrachet sensed the book's telepathic power, but none of the four were able to make anything appear on its pages. In the end Montrachet shut the book and put it on the library shelves, next to a history of the Interplanar Bank.

"Should be safe there for a few hours," he said. "I don't think that section gets used much."

"Before the others get here," said Pumpkin eagerly. "We should research as much as we can about demons. There must be heaps of books here about them."

She was right. Many of the works on demons turned out to be cookery books, explaining what they ate and how best to prepare the ingredients. ("Don't look at those," confided Sapphire to Pumpkin, after opening one and promptly closing it. "They're disgusting.") Some were about other planes of existence and how to reach them. One of them even contained a diagram purporting to be a map of where the demon princes lived in the Abyss. ("Some tourists will believe anything," said Montrachet.) Ferdinal found a book on the history of demons in Carceron. He flicked idly through it.

"It has a bit about the demons and the mayor," he said. He carried on reading, skipping ahead a few pages. "The mayor has always been a sort of figurehead. A ceremonial thing. The demons run the place."

"But why do they bother?" asked Pumpkin. "Don't they have more important things to do?"

"It says here that Carcus sends them," said Ferdinal, still examining the book. "Cremorne isn't in charge because he chose to be. Someone more powerful sent him here. He had to come. And he has to stay until Carcus sends him somewhere else. And Cremorne then picks the rest of the Junta and bosses them around."

It was a useful reminder that there were forces more important than Cremorne at work. The Heroes were still debating this point when the door of the library opened. They hadn't realised it was midnight already. Talisman entered, followed by Champrice, Marvexio and Thorkell, who closed the door behind them.

"Jagglespur is also a member," said Talisman, as they sat down at the table with the Heroes. "But I felt it best not to invite him this evening. He is rather too close to Mercedes. He's under her charm, at least for now."

"Where's the book?" asked Champrice.

"First, you have to make me a member of your Club," said Pumpkin firmly. "Then you can see the book."

Sapphire giggled. They hadn't discussed how to treat the members of the Enigma Club. Pumpkin was driving a hard bargain.

"No," said Talisman, equally firmly.

"Then you don't get the book," said Pumpkin, in a relaxed tone. "Of course, you could search the library for it. But it might take a while. Even with a Detect Arcana spell. I expect half the tomes in here are either magical or protected with magical traps."

Champrice and Talisman looked at each other. Marvexio nodded.

"All right," said Talisman, suppressing his anger. "You,

Pumpkin, are now a member of the Enigma Club. You others aren't. Where's the book?"

Montrachet went over to the financial section and retrieved the precious artifact from its ignominious position next to the history of the Interplanar Bank. He put it on the table in front of Talisman.

"This is a special moment," gloated Talisman, opening the book. "Now to attune."

He sat there, his hands lightly touching the vellum pages, his eyes closed.

Nothing happened.

"It isn't for you," said Thorkell, speaking for the first time. "You are not the one."

Champrice took Talisman's place at the table and sat in the same position. Almost at once there was a faint humming and then a sigh from the book. Strange text and beautiful illustrations in rare ink began to appear on its pages. Champrice lowered her head and opened her eyes to look at it. She turned several pages in silence. The others watched for several minutes. At last, she looked up at Pumpkin.

"Where is the Crater?" she asked.

Pumpkin looked at Ferdinal and Sapphire.

Thorkell interjected. "In the lower basement of the Temple of Carcus," he said. "It is open."

"But aren't you one of the priests looking after the Crater?" challenged Pumpkin. "Surely you want the Crater to be open? Why would you help us to close it?"

"I am a priest of Carcus," said Thorkell, without emotion. "My only purpose is to serve the god of the undead. But Babaeski, the top demon at the temple, has been diverted from the true path. He is more interested in demon affairs and conspiring about the election. Carcus will not be pleased. My duty is clear: to close the Crater. If Carcus wanted it open, he would say so."

"I must admit, I never thought they'd let her into the Enigma Club so easily," whispered Sapphire to Ferdinal.

Marvexio overheard her. He had been quietly composing more campaign songs and ignoring the more important parts of the conversation. "We already knew Pumpkin would join us," he remarked absently.

"You knew? All of you knew?"

"Yes, you see, almost everyone in the Enigma Club has psionic powers. I don't know if Pumpkin has. It's not essential. Some of us have telepathy, or ESP. Some can use arcane powers, like spells, just by mental concentration. Some have a limited power to foretell the future."

Sapphire and Ferdinal looked at him sceptically. Marvexio repeated the last assertion hotly.

"It's true," he insisted. "At the end of each meeting, we read and agree the minutes. You know, a record of the meeting's events, discussions and decisions."

"Lots of committees do that," pointed out Ferdinal.

"But we're psychic. We agree the minutes of the *next* meeting. At our last meeting, we could foresee that Pumpkin would attend and be elected to the Club. So, at this meeting it was bound to happen."

Marvexio went back to scribbling notes for future songs. "At least," thought Sapphire, "he would be able to know in advance exactly what tunes his audiences would like."

Pumpkin, Talisman and Champrice were still debating what should be done with the Crater.

"Flaxen really needs this," pleaded Pumpkin. "The Crater is bringing in huge numbers of undead. Babaeski is saving them for Mercedes' campaign so they can vote in the election."

"We have not been able to tell who will win the election," said Talisman doubtfully. "It could be very close. The future is cloudy."

"But you're on Flaxen's side," persisted Pumpkin, refusing to let the matter drop.

"She's right," said Champrice, intervening. "She rescued me from the basement of the palace. She found the book. We need to help by closing the Crater."

"I suppose only you can do it?" asked Pumpkin.

"Only I am attuned to the Book of Misdeeds, so only I can use it," said Champrice proudly. She said it with the confidence of one who had a hunch that this would happen. "I will need to study it to see how to use it to close the Crater. But it can be done."

"I can let you in to the temple and escort you through," said Thorkell. He said it with the fatalistic certainty that Carcus would expect it.

"I will keep the Book of Misdeeds," said Champrice. "I am now its custodian. I will bring it there at midnight. Pumpkin, you'll need to bring the others, too."

Pumpkin felt a sense of relief. She now possessed an inner confidence that the Crater would be closed in time. More importantly, some of the burden of the campaign at last seemed to be shared by the people of Carceron.

"So, what else does the Enigma Club do?" she asked in a more relaxed tone. "What will we be doing at our next meeting?"

"The next meeting will be after the election of the new mayor," said Talisman. "We are already putting together a network of contacts and information that is a rival to Revlyn's Destiny Guild. The new mayor is bound to bring changes, especially if Mercedes wins. We must focus on how to profit from that."

"As always in Carceron there's a commercial angle," thought Pumpkin. Still, these psychics were clearly good at thinking ahead.

—

"So, it means another late night," said Sapphire, as she walked slowly back to Harbinger's house with Ferdinal and Pumpkin. Montrachet was walking with them but was planning to go on to his own home, which he shared with Lamar, after saying goodnight to them.

"I think we're going to need the whole team tomorrow," said Ferdinal. "It's going to be dangerous."

"Except Aspreyna," said Pumpkin. "She's an angel, a celestial. She might explode if she goes into an evil temple. I'm not madly keen on it myself."

As they passed the Demon Consulate they could hear an argument in progress. The talking was all in Demonic, so the Heroes could not make out any words. Montrachet's spell of Speakall had long since worn off, so he could not understand the argument either.

They stopped outside the Demon Consulate, but the windows were too high up in the wall to see through. There were no guards outside, but none of them felt very safe loitering in this part of the city.

"Wait," said Montrachet, searching the inside pockets of his robes. He brought out one of the scrolls Flaxen had given them, opened it and began to cast the incantation. When he finished, nothing seemed to have happened, but Montrachet was concentrating hard on something.

"It's the Arcane Spy spell," he said, his brows knit as if thinking hard. "I can see as if I'm in the room."

"Come round the corner of the building out of sight," hissed Sapphire, tugging at the sleeve of his robe. All four Heroes retreated into an alleyway beside the Consulate.

"I can see inside the room," said Montrachet, describing the scene like a sports commentator. "I still can't understand the language, though. All four members of the Junta are there. Babaeski from the temple is yelling at Lamothe. That's why they're here at the Consulate. Luleburgaz is looking on. Cremorne is staying silent. He likes to see who's winning before he picks a side."

"What are they arguing about?" whispered Ferdinal, forgetting that the words would make no sense.

"They're angry with Lamothe about something. I heard Mercedes' name mentioned. They must be arguing about the election, which side to support."

A snarling sound from the end of the alley stopped the conversation suddenly. The alley was a dead end, but it seemed that there was something at the far end of the passageway. It must have been either asleep or on guard there. A creature got up from the ground and stood on two legs. Even in the dark it was obvious that this was a demon. Taller than human size, with horns and a tail, it did not seem pleased to see them. It spoke in the Common language.

"That cloak," it rasped, pointing at Pumpkin's velvet cape. "Pretty cloak. Furry. I want it. Give it to me."

The creature had no concept of property rights or politeness. It had seen something it liked, worn by someone it considered weaker than itself. The request was just a way of requiring the item to be handed over without going to the trouble of fighting for it.

Montrachet was still concentrating on his spell and hardly seemed aware of the intrusion. Ferdinal drew his sword and stepped towards the creature, although as he said afterwards, he couldn't have hoped to defeat a towering demon on his own. Maybe he could hold it off while the others ran towards the open end of the alleyway and away to freedom?

"Run!" yelled Sapphire, turning to face the demon and holding her outstretched palm towards it. She chanted some words and flicked her head downwards.

The demon yelled out in rage and frustration. Slimy red bonds were emerging magically from the ground where it stood. They grasped its ankles and held it in place. The demon couldn't move and began struggling and yelling.

Ferdinal and Sapphire ran together back the way they had come, into the open square. It was time to head back to Harbinger's house, as fast as possible. Pumpkin reached for Montrachet's hand and pulled him along as she fled too.

After a minute of running the Heroes stopped outside the Trident Hotel to get their breath back.

"Sorry I wasn't much help," panted Montrachet. "I was thinking too hard, trying to see everything going on in that room."

"Don't worry, I had it covered," said Sapphire smugly.

"What was that spell you cast?" asked Pumpkin, impressed. Sapphire hadn't made much use of her bardic abilities so far.

"I think it's called Tentacles," grinned Sapphire. "Bards use it if they have a difficult audience. You cast it on them in a performance to hold them in their seats and stop them walking out. I'm not sure if there are side effects when it's cast on a single creature. It's not designed for that."

"Well, if the demon is still transfixed on the spot in the morning," said Pumpkin, "we'll know the spell is for use on crowds only."

Chapter 18

Closing the Crater

In the largest suite at the Pilgrim Hotel, Mercedes was relaxing on the morning before election day. Gathered around her were some of her most faithful followers, receiving their instructions.

While Mercedes stretched out on the huge four-poster bed, Revlyn and Zarek sat in armchairs. Kuthol stood guarding the door. Jagglespur, Captain Manacle and Lamar sat in upright chairs around a small table. All were watching Mercedes, eager to learn her next moves.

Mercedes was immaculately dressed as always in her black gown and fine jewellery. She looked around the room at her team. All were loyal. Some in the city had backed her because they believed in her, but mostly her key supporters were those who hoped to gain from her ascendancy or whose devotion she had ensured by charming them. While she remained in the city the charm would be unbreakable, she was sure of that. And there were others, not core to the campaign, who would do their best to help – Fredinal or Hijinx, perhaps. Babaeski of the demon Junta was one of her key backers, but he had more urgent business than campaign meetings. As for Cremorne and Luleburgaz… you could never rely on demon princes, but Mercedes knew that they were not hostile to her. Still, it was Babaeski who would be the most important on election day.

Mercedes got up from the bed and began to issue instructions to her team, covering every aspect of the work required over the next two days.

A similar meeting was taking place at Flaxen's house. The Heroes wanted to check what Flaxen and Harbinger had been doing and to make sure everything was in place for victory. Marid was there too, with Talisman and Marvexio. Souzira sat in a corner, watching Flaxen closely. Montrachet and Perancia sat listening.

"We've had some preparations to make," said Harbinger stiffly, when questioned about his plans. "Flaxen and I have some ideas of our own for election day. That doesn't affect what you need to be doing."

Sapphire went through the list of tasks, checking with each in turn. Talisman had been busy amongst the traders of the city. A small number were known supporters of Mercedes, but most were keen for Flaxen to win. The question was: would those traders exert themselves fully and spend all day fully committed to the cause? Talisman was keeping an eye on them.

"If any of them cause any trouble, I can threaten to medusa them," he said casually. "I've got the creature pretty much trained now. It would be good to have the chance to test her out on a few people."

"What about Šapka and Crayler?" asked Pumpkin. "They're supposed to help, but I don't trust either of them."

"You can't trust them to be friendly, or even to keep their promises," agreed Harbinger. "That's not what happens in Carceron. They will be active because it's in their interests. I'll deal with Šapka if necessary."

"I've been busy amongst the tourists," boasted Marvexio. "I've charmed some of the tour guides. Carina has been helping. We're going to have them voting continuously during the day."

"How are the demons?" asked Ferdinal. "Are you winning them round?"

"Flaxen and I have been busy there," said Marid. "They're not especially pro-Mercedes, nor pro-Flaxen. If one candidate takes a clear lead, they will all back the winner. It's not really a bandwagon effect of popularity, they just want to inflict the most humiliating defeat possible on the loser. So, they probably won't start voting until later in the day."

"The undead are still a problem," admitted Harbinger. "I've hired as many as I could from Rent-a-Zombie. But I know the campaign team have plans."

He smiled and looked at the Heroes. They hadn't told Harbinger what they planned to do, except that it involved going to the Temple of Carcus that night. They did not have much time: the election would be starting at midnight.

"Have you got everything you need?" asked Flaxen, ever casual in his tone. He might have been enquiring if the group had the necessary ingredients for a picnic, rather than checking they had all the spells and weapons needed for an assault on an undead temple.

"I think we'll be all right," said Montrachet, speaking up boldly. "I've got a number of spells prepared."

"And if they get into any trouble," said Perancia fiercely, "I'll be there to save them."

There was a peal of laughter from everyone else in the room. Perancia was indignant at their lack of faith in her powers. Then she realised that they were laughing at the idea that she would stand by her friends in time of need, rather than being the first to escape. Even Perancia had to smile at the truth.

The Heroes had spent the day resting and preparing. Election day was tomorrow and there was a vital task to be carried out first: creeping into the Temple of Carcus with Champrice, to use the Book of Misdeeds to close the Crater. If they failed, Mercedes could use the gate to bring countless undead into the city from other planes of existence, to build an unassailable majority.

After an early dinner at Flaxen's house, the Heroes set off. Ferdinal led the way, feeling confident in his sturdy armour, his longsword at his side. Aspreyna walked with him, her wings furled. She would accompany the group as far as the temple, but as a celestial she would not go into the building. Champrice marched behind Aspreyna, carrying the Book of Misdeeds in a backpack, while Pumpkin walked beside her. Montrachet and Sapphire followed, with Perancia in her usual place at the rear.

Pumpkin was glad to be in a large group. She felt confident that between them they would have enough strength and arcane knowledge to get through. Aspreyna was undoubtedly very powerful and would be a real asset on election day. Champrice seemed to know all about how to use the Book of Misdeeds. And Montrachet had shown several times that he could be really resourceful in a crisis. Then there was Thorkell, who had promised to meet them at the doors to the Temple. What could go wrong?

The first thing to go wrong happened even before they could get inside the temple. As they walked across Carcus Square, they saw that the huge doors of the temple were shut. Normally the temple was open night and day. There was no sign of Thorkell.

"We could wait for him?" suggested Sapphire doubtfully.

"Not safe to wait here," said Aspreyna, already looking jumpy so close to the undead headquarters.

"If the doors are shut, there's something big happening or about to happen," said Montrachet firmly.

"Is there a back way in?" asked Pumpkin.

"There's a secret door that leads into the Chief Priest's quarters," said Perancia, to everyone's surprise. "That's how we sneak in sometimes to rob the gold that Kuthol collects." She realised that everyone was scowling at her. "What's the matter?" she asked. "We never take enough for anyone to notice. This way."

Surprised to find Perancia leading once more, the group followed her around the side of the temple. There were signs of recent activity in the adjacent cemetery. Many of the graves had been opened up and there were piles of grey sand and earth next to the tombstones. Picks and shovels lay on the ground. There was nobody about. Evidently the graves had been rifled by eager campaigners trying to animate corpses for Mercedes' campaign. "Some of them might have been taken for Flaxen's campaign," thought Ferdinal grimly as he picked his way through the debris. Almost anything was possible in this mad city.

The back of the temple was bland and windowless. It had no path or back door, but there was a thin border of stone paving slabs around the base of the building. Perancia approached a spot near the north-west corner of the temple and began tapping with her hands, dextrously exploring the wall with her probing fingers. After about a minute, Perancia heard a quiet metallic clunk, as if a hidden lever had fallen into place. A small hatch, not much bigger than a cat would use, had sprung open.

"Some chief priest years ago had it put in so that his familiar could go out hunting at night," she whispered. "This way."

Perancia crawled through the hatch. Everyone else followed apart from Aspreyna, who would have been too big to fit through the gap anyway. The angel remained on guard outside, anxiously watching the cemetery.

The hatch led into some sort of study or private office. The furniture looked expensive, but with the same hostile minimalism that was typical of Carceron decor. A desk and bookshelves were all moulded into the room and built of the same concrete or stone material as the building itself. The red marble surface of the desk reflected a sinister and evil dim light. The only concession to comfort was a well-padded chaise longue.

Being first into the room Perancia naturally began to

rifle through it for valuables, opening each desk drawer in turn and examining its contents. She picked up and peered with roguish expertise at a paperweight, before replacing it on the desk as worthless. As Pumpkin squeezed through the hatch, Perancia and Montrachet were looking and tapping at some sort of safe or strong box sealed into the wall. Its stone front was almost entirely flush with the wall and it had no lock, dial or handle.

"I know it's not why we came, but this could be important," said Montrachet apologetically, as Pumpkin came forward to remonstrate. "Just give us a minute."

Montrachet and Perancia conferred in whispers, while the others stood well back. Perancia picked up the paperweight again and held it against the stone door. Then she nodded to Montrachet and each began to cast a spell at once. Seconds later, the door of the safe clicked open. Perancia replaced the paperweight.

"It's an arcane key," explained Perancia, as if she had been opening safes all her life, which possibly she had. "Holding the paperweight against the door and casting Open Portal and Dispel together is enough to suppress the magical lock for a time."

The safe contained a leather bag, which Perancia pocketed before anyone else could. Montrachet pulled out a scroll, which he put on the desk while he closed the door of the safe.

"The book is a sort of ledger of all the temple's work," said Sapphire, leafing through its giant pages. "But some of it is in Demonic."

"The scroll is interesting," said Pumpkin. "I can understand it… it's a spell scroll. What does Truename do?"

"Don't read it!" cried Champrice in an urgent tone.

"It's very rare," said Montrachet excitedly. "You cast it on a major demon and you can find out their real Demonic name, not just the name they use day to day. With the true name you can command them. That could be very useful!"

Pumpkin could not help chuckling. It would be rather like defeating a demon by the equivalent of stealing its passwords and identity, then holding it to ransom. Maybe the demon would be mildly upset by such treatment, but the scroll must be bound to come in handy.

"Leave the book. Let's take the scroll and get on," said Ferdinal. The delay was making him feel edgy and all the spellcasting was beyond what he as a paladin could understand. "We need to find Thorkell."

The group crept out into the main area of the temple. This time there were no tourists and demon worshippers. It was instantly clear why. Three quarters of the huge temple was filled with people, all standing up and all silent. There were rows upon rows of skeletons and zombies, all animated from the cemetery or brought in through the Crater from another dimension. Here and there were narrow aisles through which people could walk to access the other rooms of the temple. Soon it would be packed to capacity with undead. None of these undead had been summoned as part of Flaxen's campaign. This huge necromantic crowd represented an obedient horde that would be voting for Mercedes in a few hours' time.

Sapphire and Pumpkin gazed in horror. Ferdinal was still looking for Thorkell and spied him at last, near the entrance to the basement level. Without a word, Ferdinal began to walk along the aisles between the undead voters, suppressing his nausea as he went, beckoning for the others to follow. Even Perancia seemed to find the sight of so many zombies abhorrent. She was more into chaos than evil – exactly the sort of person who belonged in the Flaxen camp.

Thorkell was on duty guarding the entrance to the basement.

"Sorry, I couldn't get away to tell you what was happening," he hissed in a desperate tone to Ferdinal. "I got some spare robes for you as a disguise."

"Good work!" replied Ferdinal in an upbeat tone, trying to imbue Thorkell with confidence.

He pointed to a pile on the floor near the door. There was a spare pair of his own red robes and half a dozen suits of ordinary white ones. Ferdinal nodded.

Everyone quickly chose a set of robes and pulled them on over their clothes and armour. Pumpkin, as the group's cleric, took the red robes, although they were slightly too big for her. Perancia put on some robes, but then cast an invisibility spell on herself, to be doubly sure of her disguise.

Dressed as temple acolytes, the group headed down the stairs. Thorkell led the way, with Champrice behind him. Nobody was sure where the invisible Perancia was, but Pumpkin could hear her breathing sometimes.

Thorkell strode confidently past the undead factory. It too was filled with lines of undead and looked more like a sinister warehouse now. White-robed acolytes were checking and adjusting some of the zombies, overseen by Daysuh.

The group crept quietly down the lower steps that led to the Crater. Thorkell brought them out into the cave, then stopped abruptly. The others followed him into the cave. Ferdinal and Sapphire knew what to expect from their previous visit to the temple. As expected, more zombies were emerging slowly through the huge dimensional portal, with Runsus and Lacasso helping some of them out. Pumpkin's heart sank. They hadn't really discussed what to do if the Crater was guarded. It had been unattended when Ferdinal and Sapphire came here before.

Just then they heard an angry shout. A large demon was running round the perimeter of the Crater towards Thorkell. It was Babaeski, the chief priest.

"Why are you not on guard?" he yelled, in a towering rage. "And you have brought... *infidels* into the temple! For this you will pay the ultimate price."

Everyone acted at once, according to their instincts and abilities. Babaeski was already raising his hand to cast a spell. Montrachet was simultaneously casting one to block it, as Thorkell cried out in terror and hid his face.

Runsus and Lacasso dropped the zombies that they had been helping and began running round the edge of the Crater to Babaeski's aid. Ferdinal drew his longsword and rushed round to meet them, blocking them from attacking the others. Pumpkin and Sapphire fired spells at Babaeski. Champrice brought out the Book of Misdeeds and opened it. Nobody knew where Perancia had gone.

Babaeski's spell was cast. Montrachet's attempt to block it had failed; evidently the demon's incantation was of too high a potency. There was a flash of light, almost like a bolt of lightning, which flashed from the demon's finger. Thorkell screamed and doubled up in pain. Then he dropped lifeless to the ground. He would never live again but would have an indefinite existence thereafter once he rose as a zombie under Babaeski's command.

Pumpkin's and Sapphire's spells went off, but the demon had sensed their casting and put out a claw in their direction. This seemed to deflect their spells harmlessly away. Pumpkin began to realise just what powerful creatures these demons were.

Champrice began chanting. The Crater began to contract in size, its circumference diminishing and the hard rocky floor of the cave reappearing where the Crater had been. Babaeski screamed.

Runsus and Lacasso reached Ferdinal, and a desperate melee began as the priests attacked him with maces, while Ferdinal struck out with his sword. Sapphire wished she'd gone to help him, although Babaeski was clearly the main threat. But what could she do?

Pumpkin and Sapphire moved slightly apart, so that the demon's outstretched claw could only deflect one of their spells, not both.

Babaeski advanced round the perimeter of the Crater towards them, grinning.

"Nothing can stop us now," he said, beginning a fresh incantation.

Just then sounded a loud booming noise next to Babaeski. Perancia, who had been standing there, became visible. She had cast the spell that had caused the noise. The demon had been looking at Sapphire and Pumpkin, and had either ignored or not spotted the invisible warlock.

Babaeski tottered on the spot as he was hit broadside by Perancia's Sonic Boom. He had not been expecting it. His scaly feet slipped on the uneven floor of the cave. For an instant he lingered at a strange angle, clawing at the air to regain his balance. Then he fell sideways into the Crater, vanishing from sight with a hideous yell.

Instantly upon seeing his leader fall, Runsus dropped his mace and gave Lacasso an almighty shove. Lacasso, his attention diverted by the same sight, was caught completely off guard. He screamed and toppled into the Crater on the opposite side to Babaeski.

Seconds later Champrice stopped chanting from the Book of Misdeeds. The Crater contracted until there was nothing left. As the last of it vanished there was an almighty clunk, as if an invisible hand had sealed the stone door to an enormous vault. Sapphire stared in wonder at the transformation. It seemed to be permanent. No trace of the Crater remained on the floor. The cave was just an empty hemispherical chamber again.

Runsus smiled and stretched his empty hands towards Ferdinal in a gesture of surrender. "I can see when it's time to change sides," he said simply.

Pumpkin gaped at him in astonishment. In the space of a few seconds this priest had gone from being a major demon's lackey to being a supporter of a rival campaign. Religion, devotion and loyalty meant nothing to him: only survival and success at any price.

"Er, welcome aboard," said Ferdinal hoarsely. "Always good to have more supporters."

Champrice closed the Book of Misdeeds with a smile. She had not shown any sense of fright during the brief battle, confident that the special tome would use her to fulfil its purpose.

Pumpkin and Sapphire felt a huge sense of relief and

hugged each other. The Crater was closed. And Babaeski couldn't now turn them into zombies. They didn't know if he was still alive after being sucked through that huge gateway to another dimension, but it was clear he wasn't coming back any time soon. They had had the narrowest of escapes.

Only Perancia seemed disappointed. "I bet he had some really good stuff on him," she pouted. "I was going to take his wands first, then scarabs and medallions. Now it's all gone."

"Oh, get real," snorted Ferdinal crossly. "You've destroyed a major demon and robbed him of all the money in his safe. Isn't that enough for one night?"

—

The group did not linger in the cave. They hurriedly ascended the stairs to the ground floor of the temple, Runsus joining them in place of the fallen Thorkell. They hurried back to Babaeski's ransacked study. Runsus was impressed.

"I see you've made a thorough job of it," he said. "Oh, I'll take this." He grabbed the temple's ledger from Babaeski's desk.

"So, are you joining us now?" asked Ferdinal. "We could use you on election day."

"I'll be on your side," smiled Runsus. "But right now, I'm going to hide. When Carcus realises what's happened tonight he will be *really* peeved, as only a demon god can be. Perhaps even irked. It'll spoil his day. I'm not waiting around for that. I think I'll go and hang out with Lamar for a bit and lie low. See you at the election."

There was no need for further discussion. Aspreyna was still waiting outside the hatch and was greatly relieved at the Heroes' return. She was surprised to see Runsus with them instead of Thorkell but was more than happy for Runsus to head off on his own.

"It's a shame about Thorkell," said Champrice sadly as they headed back to Flaxen's house. "He was a loyal member of the Enigma Club. But he could never have stood up to Babaeski."

Sapphire felt suddenly tired, as the stress of the encounter caught up with her. "I'm glad that's over," she whispered, walking arm in arm with Pumpkin for mutual support.

"Over? It's just beginning," replied Pumpkin calmly. "Voting in the election begins at midnight, remember? There's probably time for a short nap and then the really tough bit begins."

Chapter 19

Election Day

Voting had started. At first Pumpkin was impressed by how orderly everything seemed. For a city without rules, Carceron did seem to be showing some signs of logical organisation.

All the voting would be taking place on a single day, from midnight to midnight. A running tally of the candidates' votes was on constant display, to avoid counting the votes at the end of the poll. There was only one place to cast a ballot, which was in the auditorium at the Playhouse, into which even the largest creatures could squeeze. Ethema was overseeing the process as Returning Officer of the election, although she never seemed to make any intervention in it. The running total of the votes was kept by Gavri, who posted updates according to Ethema's instructions. Champrice, as proprietor of the Playhouse, seemed to be doing a roaring trade by providing food and drink to the creatures voting – except for the demons and undead, who showed no interest.

Gradually it dawned on Pumpkin that these systems, which she recognised as rules that must be kept, were obeyed in Carceron purely for convenience. Both Flaxen's team and Mercedes' team followed the system up to that point because the alternative – tampering with the underlying logic – was simply too risky. One's opponent might prove to be better at such deviant tactics, in which case all effort would be in vain.

Flaxen had explained that attempts had been made in the past to wreck the whole system. One mayoral candidate centuries ago had tried to charm the druids who ran the election or who kept the tally. The druids retaliated by immediately declaring that candidate's opponent to be the winner. And it was no good trying to bribe druids. They just did not care about money or possessions.

Another enterprising would-be politician in the city had tried using a chain of Temporal Pause spells to increase the length of time for which the polls were open, thereby giving him more time to hustle hordes of supporters through to vote. He had also lost, as the citizens of Carceron rebelled and declared his rival the winner. Elections weren't really popular in Carceron. People put up with them, no more than that. They certainly did not want candidates prolonging the agony.

"I wonder how much havoc we caused in Mercedes' camp?" Pumpkin asked Montrachet. "Closing the Crater and dealing with Babaeski must have started a panic."

But Montrachet was looking at the orderly lines of undead who were voting in large numbers.

"Mercedes has this pretty well organised," he said seriously. "Vampires are good at that. She won't just have been relying on Babaeski. At most I think we've disrupted the early voting for her and stopped her bringing in more zombies."

"We should have chopped up all the ones Babaeski had stored at the temple," said Pumpkin mournfully.

"There wasn't time," said Montrachet. "The other acolytes at the temple – Daysuh and the minor priests – would have attacked us and maybe summoned help from the beldarks. I don't think we'd have got out alive."

"I'm going to stay and watch the voting for a bit," said Pumpkin. "We need to see how it's going."

It was now mid-morning. Columns of skeletons and zombies had been voting from midnight onwards, although it looked as though Pumpkin was right that Mercedes' plans for the temple hordes to vote often had been disrupted early on. Marvexio had been busy, too. Helped by Carina and Ferdinal, he had been shepherding large groups of tourists to vote at the Playhouse. Once there, they were led back through the auditorium to vote again and again. There was no restriction on this. The main limitation seemed to be how long each person could stay on their feet to keep plodding through, before collapsing of hunger or fatigue. In the space of a few hours, each tourist seemed able to vote several hundred times. "Marvexio's charm spells are impressive," thought Pumpkin.

Runsus and Lamar sauntered into the Playhouse to vote.

"What's the mood in the Southwest District?" asked Montrachet. He didn't trust Runsus because he hardly knew him. He didn't trust Lamar because he *did* know him.

"Šapka's certainly putting the word out for Flaxen," said Runsus. "He's doing well. But most rogues won't be awake to vote yet."

"Revlyn is getting everyone out for Mercedes," grinned

Lamar. "All the main apartment blocks, he's got teams of people there. It's all arranged."

"And who are you voting for?" asked Montrachet. He didn't like Lamar's tone.

"I'm for Mercedes, of course," sneered Lamar truculently. "You don't have a chance."

"I'm for both of them," remarked Runsus blandly. "I can see I shall have to vote several times."

Sapphire dashed into the auditorium. "Quick, come outside," she shouted excitedly. "Mercedes is in the street outside the Playhouse. She's giving a speech, making all sorts of promises."

All three dashed outside. Mercedes was there, standing on a box and addressing the crowd. She wasn't haranguing them or yelling. She was speaking in soft, gentle tones that wafted over you like a lullaby, forcing you to believe her.

"Don't listen to the words, it's a charm," yelled Montrachet, trying to raise his voice above the melody.

In a moment, both Mercedes and Montrachet were drowned out by another noise, an ear-splitting trilling and warbling that grated upon the ears so much it made you want to cover them to shut out the cacophony. Perancia and Tinsel had appeared on the edge of the crowd. It was Tinsel's singing that was causing the racket.

"Mercedes has been crooning to crowds all morning," shouted Perancia into Pumpkin's ear. "Harbinger told me to run interference. So, I went and found Tinsel to help. We've been disrupting each of Mercedes' attempts at Mass Charm and fled each time before Jagglespur and his mob could find us."

"Better go now, then," yelled Pumpkin in reply, as a group of tough warriors appeared nearby.

———

By the middle of the day, Pumpkin was feeling a lot less confident. Up to this point, she had felt certain that Flaxen was the better candidate, that he had a team bound to him by loyalty, not by charms or tricks, and that he was manifestly better suited to being mayor. She had assumed that voters would find this equally apparent.

It was dawning on her that elections were not really won or lost in such a way. A perception of the candidates that seemed obvious to her was evidently not clear to the voters at large. The early voting had been a perfunctory trickle, given the delay in turnout of the zombies. But now large numbers of traders, undead and tourists were voting, and each voted many times. The constant tally of votes that Gavri displayed was showing Mercedes ahead and her lead was increasing by the hour. Pumpkin realised that, as things stood, Mercedes was on course to win. Not only would that mean the end of all their efforts in Carceron, but the city might also not be safe for the Heroes. Mercedes would have no love for a defeated rival's campaign team.

Only the demons and the rogues from the Southwest District had not yet begun to vote in force. Pumpkin looked around the auditorium. She spotted Lamothe just entering. Seizing Montrachet by the hand, she pulled him over to greet the head of the Demon Consulate.

Lamothe might not be an imposing figure by the standards of the other members of the Junta, but he was still one of the most powerful creatures in the city. The crowds of voters shrank aside to let him through. Lamothe paused as Pumpkin and Montrachet hurried up to him.

"You heard what happened to Babaeski!" he exclaimed. "No trace left of him. Gone. And several of the temple priests, too. That's something for the new mayor to deal with."

"Yes, yes, we know," snapped Pumpkin impatiently. "We did that. The important thing is: which candidate are you backing? You can't hide anymore. People need to know."

Lamothe was not often addressed this way by humans, especially in public. But he ignored the slight. Pumpkin was right.

"I am backing Flaxen," he said. "Everyone at the Demon Consulate will do likewise – beldarks, shadow demons and quasits. I can't speak for the ones under Luleburgaz's command, of course. She may have a different view. Demons always like to back the winner."

There was a hushed chatter around the auditorium. Many traders and residents of the city had heard Lamothe's statement. True, he carried less authority than Cremorne or Luleburgaz. But he was the first of the Superiors to state openly a preference in the campaign. His confidence would clearly sway more neutral voters in the same direction, on the assumption that the demons were strong enough to affect the outcome.

Lamothe approached Ethema to cast his vote. Having done so, he voted about a dozen times, showing confidence in his decision. Flaxen's tally started to catch up with Mercedes'.

"Where is Flaxen, anyway?" asked Pumpkin. She suddenly had a bad feeling. "We need to find him."

"I'll send some quasits," agreed Montrachet. "You're right, we should be with him."

———

They found Flaxen and Harbinger in Hightower Square. They were shaking hands with the crowds, urging them to go to the auditorium and cast their votes. Aspreyna was standing guard, protecting the candidate from hostile voters.

"Why should we vote for you?" demanded one angry man, dressed in platemail armour. "Mercedes has said what she'll do if she wins. You haven't promised anything. Your winning wouldn't be worth a handful of iron drabs to us!"

A murmur went round the crowd. Pumpkin could see that this was an issue for some of them. Flaxen had defined himself entirely in terms of how he was different from Mercedes and in tune with the ethos of the city. He had offered no positive reason to back him.

"Can't you get him to promise something?" she whispered to Harbinger.

"No. That's not his style. Just watch."

Flaxen smiled back at the angry man. He seemed unperturbed.

"Promises, you say? We're a city of chaos. Nobody believes in promises. They imply organisation, delivery, precision. Carceron as a city rejects all those things. I tell you this: any candidate who makes promises isn't fit to be mayor of Carceron. I stand for chaos. Mercedes stands for evil. That is the choice."

This reply sparked off a loud debate amongst people in the crowd. Flaxen and Harbinger joined in. They did not notice a new figure approach them until she was only a few feet away.

"Mercedes!" shouted Aspreyna, moving to stand between the newcomer and her rival.

Flaxen and Harbinger wheeled round to face the vampire. Pumpkin and Montrachet started in horror. Jagglespur stood behind Mercedes, but she was otherwise unguarded.

"So," said the vampire softly. "It's a simple matter of evil versus chaos, is it? Which is more powerful? I think we should have a practical demonstration."

"It won't work, Mercedes," said Flaxen, shaking his head gravely. "I'll tell you that now."

There was silence as everybody watched in awe. Nobody could work out what Flaxen and Mercedes meant. It was as if they had a private joke.

"I will show you, then," whispered Mercedes. She stood facing Flaxen, her arms held out in his direction, with the palms outstretched. Flaxen seemed to know what was about to happen and stood motionless.

Mercedes chanted a quick incantation, raising her voice to a high-pitched scream. It was as if she had yelled a terrible curse or expressed a horrific portent. Flaxen quivered on the spot as if struck by an invisible force. Then his body collapsed to the ground and turned to dust.

There was total silence for a couple of seconds. Then Aspreyna screamed. Harbinger at once shepherded both Pumpkin and Montrachet away from the area, as if they might be Mercedes' next victims.

"Come to my shop at once," he ordered. Pumpkin and Montrachet were too terror-stricken to do otherwise. They dashed with Harbinger to Quasicom. Aspreyna followed them and shut the door behind them. While Harbinger led Pumpkin and Montrachet to the back of the shop, Aspreyna kept watch out of the window.

"She's moved off," said Aspreyna, a moment later.

Pumpkin gasped. Aspreyna's tone was normal. There was none of the terror she felt herself. It was as if Aspreyna had already understood, assimilated and moved on from the sudden assassination of the candidate. There was only one explanation. She had known it was going to happen.

"You knew!" she cried. "You both knew. You've killed Flaxen. It's election day and now Mercedes will win and you planned it!"

"Nice idea, but no," said Harbinger soothingly. He turned behind him and called towards one of the back rooms. "I think you'd better come out. They're not going to believe me."

They heard slow footsteps from a storeroom at the rear of the shop. Then, to their astonishment, Flaxen emerged. He was grinning.

"Neat, isn't it?" he asked, as if boasting of a successful conjuring trick. "How many people do you know who've survived a Power Surge spell?"

"But... we saw you crumble to dust," stammered Pumpkin. "You didn't survive it."

Montrachet had more arcane knowledge and was closer to the truth. "You're Flaxen's simulacrum, SimuFlaxen," he cried. "An exact copy of the original, with the same powers!"

"Almost," said Flaxen. "Actually, it was the simulacrum you saw crumble to dust just now. It was an exact replica of me. Both Harbinger and I thought it might not be too safe in this election, so we've been using the simulacrum for all high-profile events. Like a body double."

"It's been really useful, actually," added Harbinger, practical as always. "You see, with two Flaxens, we've been able to do twice as much campaigning!"

"Now that Mercedes has moved off," said Flaxen, "we ought to be back out in the square. It wouldn't do for the voters to think I've really turned to dust. But the news may take longer to reach Mercedes. I don't think anyone will want to tell her."

Pumpkin and Montrachet headed back to the auditorium. It was mid-afternoon. The rogues were now voting in large numbers. Lamar was right: Revlyn's thieves were backing Mercedes, while Šapka's assassins and their contacts were voting for Flaxen. The assassins seemed to have more power to persuade others. "They can probably be quite threatening when they choose," thought Pumpkin with a shudder.

The demons were starting to gather. They were watching Gavri's tally with great interest. Mercedes was still ahead on votes, but her margin was less than it had been in the morning. News of the showdown in Hightower Square seemed to have got around quickly to Flaxen's advantage. But it might not be enough. He still hadn't overtaken the vampire.

The closeness of the tally was causing confusion. The demons had set aside more agreeable pursuits – eating huge meals at YouChoose, or yelling at each other in the Pandemonium, for example – to come and see who was ahead. They would then back the winner. But no clear winner had as yet emerged. The demons began to squabble. The mood in the auditorium turned ugly. No fights broke out, but the noise from the arguments was rapidly rising.

Pumpkin spotted Cremorne and Hijinx standing together, watching the tally as it was updated by Gavri. Nobody else dared to stand close to the leader of the demon Junta, apart from the sinister-looking beldarks. Plucking up her courage, Pumpkin walked purposefully up to Cremorne, dragging Montrachet with her.

"We're catching up," she said, trying to sound nonchalant.

Cremorne gazed down at her with displeasure. He wasn't used to mortals engaging him in small talk.

"Go away. Shoo!" said Hijinx haughtily, trying to hustle them aside. But Pumpkin was determined.

"We want you to back Flaxen," she said. "Here and now. You don't have to say why. Just that it's your decision. Tell the other demons to do the same. They'll follow you."

"Why would I do that?" asked Cremorne. Despite his annoyance, he was intrigued by the mortal's audacity. He could always devour her or wrack her soul in torment when he got bored of chatting.

Pumpkin nudged Montrachet hard in the ribs. "Get your scroll ready," she whispered.

Montrachet finally understood what was happening. He summoned the courage to speak. "I've got the scroll of Truename," he said, trying not to stammer as he eyed the demon lord. "We took it from Babaeski's study. If you don't do what she says, I'll read the scroll. I'll know your true name and I'll use it here in front of thousands of people. No demon has ever had such a humiliation."

Cremorne was silent. Hijinx watched him nervously, waiting for him to smite these insignificant mortals aside. But Cremorne knew Montrachet wasn't joking. How else would they know that Babaeski had such a scroll? And someone had clearly broken into the temple last night, according to the beldarks. Cremorne could see a scroll poking out of Montrachet's robes. He stared hard into Montrachet's eyes, as if reading his thoughts. A quick glance was all he needed. If a mortal knew his true name, or cast magic to find it out, he would be ruined for all eternity. No demon would respect him again and the god Carcus would conjure up special punishments for one who was stripped so suddenly of power. Even a powerful demon like Cremorne knew when to compromise. He had been careful not to back either candidate in the election so far. He still had the option, even at this late stage, to pick a side.

"It shall be so," said Cremorne, betraying no emotion. He raised his arms. Silence fell in the auditorium, apart from the druids conferring over the votes. Cremorne knew there was only one option. What did the election matter, anyway?

"I now declare," boomed Cremorne, "my decision in this election. I am voting for Flaxen. You will too. That is all."

He marched up to Ethema and cast his vote, just once, for Flaxen. Hijinx did the same. Then the two of them marched towards the exit from the auditorium.

Pumpkin stopped him on his way out. "Please, there's something I've been meaning to ask," she said politely. "Why do your minions call you 'The Master'?"

"Because they want to!" bellowed Cremorne confidently. He strode out into the street and away towards Delirium Drive.

A stampede of demons followed his lead and cast their votes. A number of Harbinger's quasits did likewise, afraid to follow their master's orders until the leading demons had shown how they would vote. Some of the biggest demons voted only a few times, but the quasits proved as dedicated as the undead, voting as often as possible.

"It's sweet that the quasits show such enthusiasm," said Pumpkin affectionately. "I can see why Harbinger likes them, even if Flaxen doesn't."

As the evening drew on, fewer and fewer humans voted. The activity was dominated by quasits and undead, both voting in large numbers. The quasits were mostly for Flaxen, marshalled effectively by Harbinger. The undead were more numerous and were mainly for Mercedes. The numbers displayed on the voting tally were rising rapidly, so that the ever-changing figures became a blur.

"It won't be possible to show numbers now until the end," explained Ethema, when Pumpkin timidly asked. "They're changing too quickly. It's as much as Gavri can do to keep track at all. For the final couple of hours, you'll just have to guess who's ahead."

"Or ask one of the Enigma Club," said Montrachet sarcastically. "They reckon they always know."

It was nearly midnight when Ferdinal, Sapphire and Perancia joined them. Ferdinal had been helping Marvexio and Carina corralling tourists most of the day and was exhausted. Sapphire had been at the centre of operations at Harbinger's house, sending quasits to run messages and keeping the leading figures in touch with each other. Perancia had spent her time wrecking things, taking Tinsel to interrupt Mercedes' speeches, warping the wheels on Jagglespur's wagon and directing undead hordes out of the city to get lost in the arid wastelands. She had had a good day and still looked perky.

Nobody else had much energy left for further chat. The voting would cease in a few minutes and the result would come almost at once.

Flaxen, Harbinger, Marid and Talisman joined them just before midnight. The campaign team stood as a group and smiled to give each other confidence. The voting numbers were still a blur, so nobody knew who was winning. It could be very close.

By midnight the auditorium was packed with traders, residents and demons waiting for the result. On the other side of the hall stood Mercedes, together with her loyal servants Jagglespur, Zarek and Revlyn. Mercedes glared at Harbinger but otherwise kept her eyes on Ethema, realising that the result was imminent.

Ethema finished conferring with Gavri. The two of them stood at the front of the stage. Ethema unfurled her scroll and began to read aloud. Her voice was somehow magnified by magic built into the stage, so that her words boomed across the hall.

"I, being the Archdruid of the City of Carceron and the Demon Wastes, declare the total number of votes cast for each candidate in the election of Mayor of Carceron to be as follows:

"Flaxen the Golden, Sorcerer, Four million, six hundred and twenty-two thousand, eight hundred and forty-two.

"Mercedes the Ever-living, Vampire, Four million, six hundred and nine thousand, one hundred and eight.

"I therefore declare Flaxen the Golden elected as Mayor of the City of Carceron."

There was a roar of cheering, yelling and shouting.

Flaxen began to move through the crowd to the stage. Luleburgaz was in the auditorium and nudged him as he went past, a sign of respect, Pumpkin thought. The demon bent down to speak to Flaxen, who paused for a moment.

"Bear in mind," warned Luleburgaz sternly, "you're only mayor for life."

Chapter 20
The New Regime

"Harbinger, I thought you said only about fifty thousand people lived in this city?" said Pumpkin in astonishment. The reality of Flaxen's victory had not yet sunk in.

"True. But remember I said it's not unusual to have millions of people voting? We don't have elections here very often. People like to make the most of it."

As Flaxen ascended to the stage, a silence fell in the auditorium. Even the demons present seemed to want to listen. Ethema retreated to the wings. Flaxen stood on his own in the middle of the stage, looking around the crowd for a few seconds as he drank in the scene.

"I have made no promises in this campaign," he declared. His voice boomed out, just as Ethema's had. "If I have not promised anything, nor do I owe anything. I am grateful to my loyal team of Pumpkin, Sapphire and Ferdinal, and to Harbinger and Talisman for finding them. Now that the election is over, this is the time to make my pledges.

"Firstly, slavery will be abolished. The creation and animation of undead will continue, but Captain Manacle's emporium will be closed immediately. This change will benefit traders, tourists, demons and city residents alike. As one demon pointed out, if you need to chain someone up, how can you be sure you're superior to them?

"Secondly, trade with the City of Spires will be developed. Ambassador Blatherwick will help me to formulate detailed plans that he will take back to King Perihelion. Carceron will continue to boom.

"Thirdly, our music scene will be developed. Apollonius Crayler will arrange the refurbishment and reopening of the Decahedron as the biggest entertainment venue in this dimension. We shall hold a grand reopening and you're all invited.

"Finally, there will be changes in the Junta and the way the city is run. I will announce more detail in the days ahead. Thank you."

Flaxen stepped down from the stage. Ethema called out for Mercedes to speak if she wished to do so.

There was no response. Everyone in the auditorium looked around. The silence lasted for twenty seconds or so. Sapphire realised that Mercedes was no longer in the hall. Sensing defeat, she had slipped away.

"She's gone!" yelled Sapphire wildly.

A great cheer went up. Several things had become clear at once. If Mercedes wasn't there, she wouldn't be trying to contest the result. Flaxen had won and she knew it. And if she fled the city, the effects of her vampiric charm would fade. People like Zarek who had been beguiled by her would return to their normal selves. "So will Oliver," thought Ferdinal, excitedly. His brother would cease to be the assassin Fredinal and would return to being brother

Oliver once more. Above all there would be certainty in the city. Flaxen had plans for economic growth and exciting new projects. All the plans of Harbinger and Talisman had worked out.

"I wasn't expecting the slavery announcement," said Pumpkin, still trying to take it all in.

"I think he's had it in mind for a while," said Harbinger, who had been grinning widely while Flaxen was speaking. "He's had centuries to think about these things. As Flaxen said, slavery isn't really important to demons. They need to show that they are stronger, cleverer or more powerful than others. Chaining up their minions doesn't help them do that."

"I'd hoped he was thinking about the slaves!" said Sapphire hotly.

"Maybe he was," said Harbinger. "But he wouldn't say so in front of all the demons. Anyway, the effect is much the same."

"Time to get out of this place," said Montrachet. "I feel as if I've spent all day in this auditorium."

"Celebration at The Irresistible Dancehall," yelled Harbinger.

The Irresistible Dancehall was soon packed. Flaxen admitted that if he had foreseen the impact of the victory and just how many people would turn up to a midnight celebration, he would have hired a few hundred floors of The Abyss instead. The Horde were not singing that night. In their place a band called the Deathshadows was playing.

The masked singers were all thieves and assassins and had sparked a lot of speculation about their identities.

"You could always hire the Decahedron," said Apollonius Crayler smoothly. Crayler had hardly been seen on election day, although from what the Heroes could tell he had been active quietly on Flaxen's behalf. Now he was losing no time in cultivating the winning candidate's friendship.

"I didn't think it would be this close," admitted Flaxen. He was at a table surrounded by the Heroes and about thirty other key figures from the city. Even Mr Ottoman was there drinking with the customers. "But Mercedes had the undead very well organised. I doubt that I got more than about twenty per cent of the zombie vote."

"Renouncing your undead status and becoming a proper sorcerer again won't have helped," said Marvexio.

"Nonsense," said Harbinger. "Minor undead like skeletons and zombies don't have minds. They don't think. They just obey their orders. That's great at election time."

"Closing the Crater made all the difference," said Aspreyna. "If Babaeski and Lacasso had been summoning more undead all night and directing them during the day, Mercedes would certainly have won."

"Can we toast the Returning Officer?" asked Tinsel. She was slurring her words and seemed to have drunk a lot of Vermillion.

"Ethema's not here," said Harbinger. "The druids are neutral. I expect she and Gavri have gone back to Seeds for a quiet drink."

"How soon do you take office? Will you be moving into the Mayor's Palace?" asked Sapphire excitedly.

"I think I already am in office," said Flaxen. "I'm mayor as soon as Ethema declares the result. Carceron is a bit too chaotic for such nuances."

"I think you'll have to move there, Flaxen. It's expected," said Marid.

"I'm sure Pullywuggles will like it," said Pumpkin, trying to sound encouraging. "Might be worth redecorating it a bit first, though."

Ferdinal, sitting next to Pumpkin, was suddenly aware of another figure standing behind him. He turned round instantly. It was his brother.

"Look, I'm really sorry about all this," said the leather-clad figure of Fredinal the Assassin. His expression was serious and apologetic. "Don't know what came over me. Forgiven?"

Pumpkin and Ferdinal leapt up and hugged their brother. Despite their adventuring clothes, for a moment they were Henry, Katherine and Oliver again. There was very little to be said. Oliver, like the others, had been caught up in an unexpected Summoning and had then been charmed by a powerful vampire. He could hardly be blamed for how he had behaved in that state.

"It's fine," said Ferdinal, trying not to be too emotional. "Our fault for dragging you here. But I'm glad we're all together. We've got Charisma safely tucked away too. Come and sit down and have some Vermillion."

"How long have we been away?" asked his brother, still trying to take it all in.

"Oh, it's quite all right," said Pumpkin. "Talisman says that however long we spend in Carceron, we'll return to our world exactly when and where we left. I wonder how he knows?"

They were not the only ones having an emotional night. The little auburn-haired elf Souzira squeezed through the crowds, stretched up and kissed Flaxen on the cheek.

"Well done," she said simply, squeezing his hand. "I knew you would do it."

"You didn't really know," scoffed Talisman. "You're not in the Enigma Club. *We* knew Flaxen would win."

"I thought you'd said the future was cloudy and you couldn't see?" asked Pumpkin. Talisman went silent. Perancia sniggered. She was curled up under the table so that nobody could see how much Vermillion she was drinking.

"I wonder what Mercedes will do next?" pondered Sapphire.

"My guess is that she'll focus on something new," said Harbinger. "She talks about expanding her business, the Transfusion franchise. Maybe she'll open an outlet here in Carceron, as she promised during the campaign. It could be quite popular. I don't think she'll stand for election again soon."

"It's been a special night," said Flaxen. "But I'm glad we don't have elections too often. Once every 153 years is quite enough for me."

The next day Flaxen called a meeting in Hightower Square. It was not an official meeting – nobody would have bothered to come if it had been – but such was the novelty of the situation that a large crowd gathered. The disappearances of Babaeski and Mercedes on election day had led to a lot of speculation. Most people were glad to see the back of Mercedes, but Babaeski's death had created a vacancy in the demon Junta.

Flaxen stood next to the Arcane Cage, which was still empty following Aspreyna's escape. The angel herself was standing next to Flaxen, her role as his bodyguard seemingly now permanent. Harbinger and Marid stood behind Aspreyna. They had worked and planned hard for this. Now Flaxen had won. It was the supreme moment of victory when the candidate would set out his plans in detail. Flaxen had carefully waited until the election was over before announcing his intentions. The crowd was listening expectantly. The Heroes were there too, equally curious as to what the new mayor would say.

The new mayor rose off the ground, levitating ten feet so that the whole crowd could see and hear him.

"Carceron is a great city," said Flaxen, his voice booming out across Hightower Square. "Its chaos will endure because all other systems eventually collapse upon themselves. As your new mayor, I am the custodian of that chaos. My role is to help the city flourish and to ensure that demons, traders, residents and tourists can all go about their lives. And let's not forget the rogues!"

Flaxen pointed at Šapka, who was standing on the edge of the crowd. There was a ripple of laughter. The crowd knew that assassins normally don't like to be laughed at.

"As my first action, I have to announce some appointments," continued Flaxen. "As you know, the ruling Junta of this city is determined by the great Carcus. In his infinite and immortal wisdom, Carcus has chosen to recall Cremorne, who has left the city with immediate effect.

Babaeski has gone to another plane of existence, so two new appointments to the Junta are needed."

There was an immediate babble of excitement in the crowd. Babaeski's disappearance was now common knowledge, but Cremorne was another matter. The leader of the demons in Carceron suddenly recalled by his deity! That was news.

"Why was he recalled?" Pumpkin asked Harbinger.

"Actually, it was your doing," grinned Harbinger. "You and Montrachet. During the election you told Cremorne that you would use the Truename scroll. You forced him to co-operate. You subjugated him. For a major demon, that's a massive humiliation, even without casting the spell. Carcus knew that Cremorne's authority was dead as soon as you did that in front of such a crowd. He simply had to be replaced. He'll probably be rehabilitated in a few centuries' time."

Pumpkin fell silent. She was suddenly wondering whether the undead god would seek retribution against her for humiliating his top representative in the city.

"Don't worry," whispered Montrachet, who had been listening. "Demons respect strength. I expect Carcus is just the same. You caused Cremorne to be stripped of his power. You're now a big name in the city, as far as demons are concerned!"

Flaxen raised his hands for silence and continued his address.

"Carcus has therefore decided to promote Runsus to be the new chief priest of the temple and member of the Junta in Babaeski's place. The fourth member of the Junta will be Champrice. Neither of them is a demon. Carcus does not care about that, so long as chaos is preserved. There will be no leader of the Junta for now. Carcus will determine that later. Luleburgaz and Lamothe will continue as before.

"Also, I shall soon be moving into the Mayor's Palace. Marid will be my Chief of Staff, as he was to the Archmayor years ago. That is all."

With that, he slowly lowered himself to the ground again. The crowd broke into a renewed cacophony, eager to discuss the exciting news. Many of them moved off to bars and restaurants to continue their intrigue.

Sapphire saw Runsus in the crowd and went up to congratulate him. "You've come out of this well," she said.

"I backed both campaigns," said Runsus calmly. "I was bound to win, whichever candidate was victorious."

There was something about his laid-back and amoral arrogance that was infuriating to Sapphire.

"Do Flaxen and Carcus know you're Neutral Evil, not Chaotic?" she demanded.

Runsus's grin disappeared and his expression took on a concentrated malevolence. "Not yet. But they soon will," he said.

Lamar had been standing nearby and now intervened. "All right, that's enough," he said, hustling Runsus away as he addressed Sapphire. "Stop hassling the chief priest. We have curses for people like you."

"I suppose you're going to be one of the new priests at the temple?" asked Sapphire, clenching her fists. "You've got all the right qualifications."

Lamar gave a wintry smile, disdainful and chilling. "Yeah, thanks for getting those other priests killed," he said as he walked off with Runsus. "You've really helped my career. Cheers. I'll kill someone for you some time."

As they strode away in the direction of the temple, Sapphire noticed that Hijinx, who had been lurking nearby, followed them at a distance. Of course! Now that Cremorne was gone, the ever-scheming Hijinx would be looking for a powerful successor who was on the rise. No doubt she would soon be at Runsus's side. Maybe they deserved each other, Sapphire decided.

Champrice, Marvexio, Montrachet and Pumpkin were in one of the snugs at Acid House. The crowded bar was a good place to have a secret chat. Fortunately, the supplies of the undrinkable Cyan had now been exhausted.

"So, I suppose you're one of the most important figures in the city now?" asked Pumpkin.

"Oh, I'm just the same old me," smiled Champrice. "I'm still in the Enigma Club. I think the fact that I now have a powerful artifact – that Book of Misdeeds that you gave me – was a factor in Carcus's choice. In a city like this, power is always more important than competence or loyalty."

"Did Cremorne put in a good word for you with Carcus?" asked Montrachet boldly.

Champrice looked coy. "Possibly. I was his girlfriend for a time. You know how it is. Despotism begets nepotism!"

"Will you still be involved in the Enigma Club?" asked Marvexio anxiously. With Thorkell dead, the club's membership was shrinking.

"Naturally," replied Champrice. "In fact, we need a new member to replace Thorkell."

She and Marvexio looked at each other. Pumpkin realised that both of them knew this topic would arise.

"You mean me, don't you?" stammered Montrachet.

Champrice beamed at him. "See? Already you have a limited power of foresight. You'll fit in perfectly."

"I need to be a bit careful," said Montrachet. "Revlyn isn't very happy at the moment. He knows I backed Flaxen, while his candidate lost. And he's my boss."

"He's still my boss too, I suppose?" asked Pumpkin. "Thanks to Fulcrum I'm a member of the Destiny Guild, so maybe he'll give me missions and things."

"I think the election will have weakened Revlyn's position," pondered Marvexio. "He won't hurt you. He's not in a position to right now."

Champrice and Marvexio finished their drinks and left. Pumpkin and Montrachet were left alone in the snug.

"Well done," said Pumpkin, squeezing Montrachet's hand across the table. "You made a huge difference in the election. You cast a lot of spells. I think you're a real wizard now. And you're in the Enigma Club too!"

Montrachet did not seem enthusiastic. "It's what I wanted," he said slowly. "And the election was really important. But I dread what's going to happen."

Pumpkin came over to Montrachet's side of the table and sat next to him. "You mean… Sapphire and my brothers and I are going to go back to our own existence. We… I will come and see you again here." She looked into his big dark eyes.

For once, Montrachet returned her look. "You will

come back. I know it. I can feel that it will happen. But I'll really miss you."

With that, Montrachet put his arm around Pumpkin's waist and kissed her on the lips, and time stood still.

———

"You really are sure you know how to do this?" asked Harbinger.

He was standing with Talisman in the audience chamber of the Mayor's Palace. They were waiting for Flaxen and others to join them for a Sending ritual, to reverse the Summoning Talisman had performed. Ferdinal, Sapphire and Pumpkin, together with Fredinal and Charisma the cat, were due to be returned to their own world, as promised. Flaxen had asked to be present at the ceremony, which would be performed at the palace.

Talisman had marked out the floor in the manner required. He seemed confident that he could reverse the Summoning.

There was a sudden fanfare of trumpets. The noise came from a magic mouth Talisman had cast on the wall of the audience chamber for this purpose.

Flaxen entered the room, followed by Aspreyna and Marid. He sat in the carved chair, with his companions on either side. Marid had often stood in the same position when the Archmayor was in charge. He felt delighted and relieved to be back again.

"I want those trumpets quieter next time," said Flaxen peevishly. "See to it, Talisman. And bring in our guests."

Harbinger suppressed a smile, nodded and left the

room, while Talisman hissed some arcane words at the magic mouth. Flaxen was rapidly becoming the archetypal ruler, whimsical and capricious about little things. Harbinger returned, leading Ferdinal, Sapphire, Pumpkin and Fredinal. Pumpkin was carrying Charisma in her arms. Perancia and Montrachet followed them.

The trumpet sound blared out again, but more softly this time.

"It's flat," said Flaxen, wincing at the off-key noise. He turned towards the Heroes. "You have been magnificent," he beamed. "You have made an invaluable contribution to the city of Carceron. Your time here is now coming to an end, but I don't need Champrice and the Enigma Club to tell me that you will be back again some time. The city will have need of you again, I know it."

Pumpkin turned to Talisman, who nodded agreement.

"You two, Montrachet and Perancia," said Flaxen. "You have been vital in this achievement. I don't know what reward I can offer, but I promise you this. I will grant each of you one major favour or boon. Not now, but at some point in the future. It will not be forgotten."

Perancia had opened her mouth at the word "reward" and looked as though she had some ideas in mind. But she seemed content at the idea of an open-ended wish. She decided to speak to CT later about a more immediate and material reward for her work.

Montrachet bowed his head in thanks and said nothing.

A slight movement underneath Flaxen's carved chair caught Sapphire's eye. Pullywuggles had found the perfect place to lurk, close to Flaxen but safe from the risk of being trodden on. Sapphire wondered whether the huge tortoise would bother to emerge at all.

Suddenly the trumpets blared out again. This time they struck the right note and Flaxen did not object. He was too preoccupied with the newcomer who had stepped softly into the audience chamber.

It was Souzira. She had remained shyly on the fringes of Flaxen's campaign but had steadfastly stood by him, rallied the traders to his cause and even used some of her more potent potions to incapacitate Mercedes' supporters on election day. Centuries ago, she and Flaxen had been very close. Now she was here to congratulate him.

"I've come, Flaxen," she said softly. "You are the only person who could have beaten her. I'm so glad for you."

Flaxen stood up and stretched out his hand. "Come to me, Souzira," he said affectionately but with a serious expression. "It shall be your victory too."

No further words were spoken, but Pumpkin felt deep down that this simple exchange had healed a centuries-old breach. Things were going to be all right for Souzira. Flaxen himself, following the De-Liching ceremony, seemed to be getting slightly younger and more energetic each day. He was steadily returning to the prime of his life, a thrilling transformation.

"Please, are Cremorne and Babaeski likely to come back?" asked Sapphire. She was still nervous about the Superiors whom they had vanquished.

"I don't think so," said Talisman. "Once a demon lord is beaten or humiliated, they don't return in a hurry. Perhaps in a few centuries' time, as Mercedes did. No sooner."

"Everything seems very friendly right now," added

Harbinger. "Lamothe will work with anyone. Luleburgaz is a true secret police officer; she will automatically support the new regime."

"You said you thought we would come back to the city?" asked Ferdinal. "Now that the election's over, why would you need us?"

"The future is unclear," frowned Talisman. "We detect strange events, but as yet they are cloudy and incomplete. You are now powerful adventurers. You helped win the election. We may decide to summon you once more."

"It is time," announced Flaxen, before the Heroes could speak. "Say your farewells. Talisman, have the ritual ready."

As Talisman bustled about with candles, giving instructions to Harbinger's quasits on how to help, Harbinger hugged each hero in turn. Fredinal, or Oliver, as he would soon be again, felt embarrassed. He knew he had not helped Flaxen's victory and felt out of place. But he did not want to spoil the moment.

Ferdinal felt an overwhelming sense of relief. As a paladin he had upheld his oath to protect the weak. Not that his brother had seemed especially weak as the Assassin Fredinal, while Pumpkin and Sapphire had been more than able to take care of themselves. There was more to being a paladin than standing guard with a sword over helpless people. He had helped them to prove their own strength and arcane prowess, and it had all worked out well. He was just thankful that everyone had come through the ordeal intact.

Sapphire was pondering whether any of the sneaky tricks she had seen in the last week would work back home. She shuddered. No, that sort of behaviour would never be tolerated in the real world. Would it?

Pumpkin was wracked with emotional turmoil. She had no feeling of attachment to Carceron as a city. But the people she had met there – Flaxen, Harbinger, Champrice and the others – she felt she had forged a bond with them by fighting the election alongside them. Now it was over she felt suddenly drained. And then there was Montrachet. She wanted to go home, but she knew she would miss him dreadfully. She had to make certain to return to Carceron to see him again.

"Goodbye," said Harbinger simply. To Ferdinal he added, "Talisman and the mayor are right. I think we will be needing you again in the city before long. But I expect you will be wanting to get back to your own existence?"

"Yes, we need to be getting back," said Ferdinal, keen to get everyone out of Carceron now that his tasks as a paladin were complete.

"We certainly do," agreed Sapphire, perking up at the thought of her school contest against Amber. "If I'm not mistaken, we've got another election to win!"

About the Author

Roger Bird has been hooked on roleplaying games since his father bought a boxed set one Christmas. Roger has worked as a Chief Financial Officer in the technology and education sectors and has previously been an auditor, a university lecturer and Company Secretary of a healthcare business. His first paid work involved singing on the West End stage in London. He has been involved in politics locally as an elected councillor, nationally as General Secretary of a political party and overseas at the European Parliament.

The author would like to thank: Julie, Oliver, Nelson, the Dorking, Epsom, Tiffin and Genie House RPG groups, Anjuli and Mythic Marketing, Matador, The Master, Black Kitten, and especially Runsus.

This book is printed on paper from sustainable sources managed under the Forest Stewardship Council (FSC) scheme.

It has been printed in the UK to reduce transportation miles and their impact upon the environment.

For every new title that Matador publishes, we plant a tree to offset CO_2, partnering with the More Trees scheme.

For more about how Matador offsets its environmental impact, see www.troubador.co.uk/about/